THE
TOMB OF
ALEXANDER

Seán Hemingway is an archaeologist and a curator at the Metropolitan Museum of Art in New York. He has a Ph.D. in classical art and archaeology from Bryn Mawr College and was a Fulbright Scholar to Greece. The author of numerous writings about ancient Greek art, he has also edited several books by his grandfather, Ernest Hemingway. This is his first novel.

SEÁN
HEMINGWAY

THE
TOMB OF
ALEXANDER

arrow books

Published by Arrow Books 2013

2 4 6 8 10 9 7 5 3 1

First published in Great Britain in 2012 by
Hutchinson

Arrow Books
Random House, 20 Vauxhall Bridge Road,
London SW1V 2SA

www.randomhouse.co.uk

Addresses for companies within The Random House Group Limited can be found at:
www.randomhouse.co.uk/offices.htm

The Random House Group Limited Reg. No. 954009

A CIP catalogue record for this book
is available from the British Library

ISBN 9780099556855

Typeset in Sabon LT Std by
Palimpsest Book Production Limited, Falkirk, Stirlingshire

Penguin Random House is committed to a sustainable future for
our business, our readers and our planet. This book is made from
Forest Stewardship Council® certified paper.

Printed and bound in Great Britain by Clays Ltd, Elcograf S.p.A.

To Colette

'When a man's life has left him, not by brute force or clever bartering can he get it back once his last breath is gone.'
Homer, *The Iliad* 9.48

Introduction

What is the measure of all things? Time. Time waits for no one. Time is often not kind. In fact, it can be cruel. But in the fullness of time can come new discoveries, and anonymous works of art displayed in the corners of museum galleries can yield new revelations. This is the story of one such revelation and the quest to solve one of the greatest archaeological mysteries of all time – the location of the final resting place of Alexander the Great, legendary conqueror of the East and king of the world.

THE
TOMB OF
ALEXANDER

1

SUNSHINE STREAMED INTO the court of New York City's greatest museum, illuminating the ancient marble sculptures, which seemed to radiate a happy glow in their new home. Like Pygmalion's statue of his lover, the figures warmed by the bright rays of the sun appeared on the brink of transforming into flesh and blood if only the right conjuror should come along. The gallery itself was breathtaking. A soaring peristyle colonnade of limestone-clad Doric columns rose to support a second storey in the Ionic style and sat between the black and white tessera mosaic floor of the arcade and the richly coloured marble floor of the atrium.

The space evoked the splendour of ancient Rome at the height of the Roman Empire and it was a worthy tribute to the masterpieces that it was built to showcase. New Yorkers and people from around the world poured in from the bustle of Fifth Avenue on this blustery autumn day to see the city's newest sensation and glimpse the Metropolitan Museum of Art's ancient Hellenistic, Etruscan and Roman treasures that had not been on display for so many years.

Standing in front of a row of portrait heads, a man

looked at the museum label for one and read it aloud: 'Portrait of a man. Greek, second century BC. Thought to be a king.' He shook his head as he admired the marble bust, with its proud strong face; then he turned to his girlfriend and said, 'Thought to be a king? My God, his entire life's story is lost. His contribution to this world has been obliterated from all records.'

The young woman replied, 'You know, Julius Caesar lamented when he was thirty-three that Alexander the Great had accomplished so much by that age while he himself had not done anything of consequence. Caesar went on to do great things. You've still got time.'

'That's not what I meant. Although you are right, I should do something with my life.' The man paused. 'Whoever this guy was, I'm sure he had a great story; it just got lost in the sands of time. History can be capricious. It's a hell of a portrait, though.'

The couple moved towards a small crowd of milling people who had begun to gather at the appointed place by the massive truncated Ionic column from the temple of Artemis at Sardis, one of the largest temples ever built in antiquity, for the tour of the museum's new galleries.

Leading the tour that day was a handsome, cheerful man in his late thirties with black hair and piercing greyish-blue eyes. He addressed the group. 'Good morning, ladies and gentlemen, and welcome to the Metropolitan Museum of Art. My name is Tom Carr, and I am a curator of Greek and Roman Art here at the museum. I'll be your guide this morning through the new Hellenistic and Roman galleries.'

Trailing at the end of the group was a tall, thin, beautiful woman. She was wearing a white peasant blouse and a full-length shimmering silk skirt that rustled slightly as she walked and revealed the line of her elegant shapely legs. Her strappy sandals clicked against the polished marble floor. Big black and gold Chanel sunglasses were propped in her fair hair.

As the group moved into the Fifth Avenue side galleries, she paused in the Roman Court. Born and raised a good Catholic in the Midwest, Victoria Price was surprised at how strong and instinctive her reaction to the statues was. Yes, she was an aspiring artist, but she'd always loved Impressionist paintings and Italian Baroque art – she'd never given that much thought to classical art. Yet as she stood before the sculptures she felt an immediate affinity with them, an irrepressible, inexplicable closeness, even though she was seeing them for the first time. She wondered if there was something to this classical heritage, her distant roots, or if she was identifying with these artworks in some other way.

Victoria paused in front of a time-worn statue of the Greek hero Herakles seated on a rock, the muscles of his extraordinary physique relaxed as he rested from his labours.

Maybe it's a little more primal than that, she thought, and then smiled. She had read somewhere that the favourite internet-search topic on the museum's website was 'naked men'. Looking up, she realised that the tour group was out of sight now. She did not want to get lost so she turned and headed after them.

The group was already heading into the Treasury when she entered the first side gallery. Her attention was drawn to the other side of the room, however, where three magnificent wall paintings caught her eye. She moved closer. In the first painting, an elegantly attired young woman played a large lyre as she sat on an elaborate chair. Next to her, a younger woman looked on approvingly. Another, narrower panel depicted a woman holding a shield with a nude male figure represented on its shining metallic surface. But it was the central and largest panel that captured Victoria's interest. There a muscular nude man sat on a throne next to a veiled woman who looked out into the distance.

The woman's eyes were mesmerising. Her pene-trating gaze had a haunting quality.

Victoria's stomach began to flutter and her skin became clammy. Oh, God, not *that* feeling, she thought as the unmistakable sense of panic rose inside her. She'd experienced this – or something like it – before, and it had terrified her. *Breathe*, she told herself. There was something familiar about the paintings though she could not put her finger on it. It was a different feeling from the one she had experienced in the Roman Court: more visceral, almost a memory dredged up from the depths of time in an instant, dislodged like a pulled tooth.

Her instinct was to move away – quickly. She would ask the tour guide about the paintings when she had a chance. With that in mind, she turned towards the group who had now gathered around a small bronze statuette in its own case near the entrance to the Treasury. The guide seemed to be waiting politely for her to rejoin them. He began to speak as she walked unsteadily to the outer edge of the group. His voice had a deep resonance that caught and held her attention.

'This fine bronze statuette may seem modern to us today but it equally reflects the early Hellenistic milieu of the third century BC, the time when it was created.' He began gesturing towards the statuette. 'It is known as the Baker Dancer after the New York philanthropist Walter Baker, who left it to the museum with the rest of his collection of antiquities. It is an icon of Hellenistic art. The figure is caught in the midst of a dance of the seven veils. Her left foot is raised slightly off the ground and she is pulling her dress tightly around herself. Although only her hands are exposed, and even her face is covered in the sheerest of veils, as you can see we get the feeling of her whole body beneath.'

The group shifted slightly and Victoria now saw clearly the little statuette of a veiled masked dancer. Suddenly she felt her chest constrict, a horrible tightness that pushed her already rising panic into overdrive. Her breathing became shallower, more difficult, until spots started to appear in front of her eyes. *Not here*, she tried to tell herself. *Not now*. She tried to turn away, to distance herself from the statuette, which seemed to have triggered the extraordinary physical reaction that threatened to overwhelm her, but it was as if her body just would not obey her mind. The panic rose higher and higher until, quite suddenly, clasping her hand to her chest, she screamed and fainted.

Museum guards in the two galleries rushed to the scene as Tom Carr took control of the situation.

'Please step back and give her some room,' he said to the other people from the tour. He was on his knees now, checking the pulse of the woman, who was unconscious, her hair fanning out dramatically behind her head. Turning to the guard, he said, 'Gino, radio the nurse's office and tell them to come right away.'

'Yes, Mr Carr.'

The nurse arrived after a short while and began checking the woman's vital signs.

'An ambulance is on its way in case she needs serious treatment. Did she land badly, strike her head or anything?'

'No, no, I don't think so,' Tom said as he stood up and brushed down his trousers, intensely relieved to have a medical expert at hand.

'Well, I think she is going to be all right,' the nurse continued. 'Her pulse is normal and she is breathing fine. I suggest that you continue with your tour.'

'Well, then, ladies and gentlemen.' Tom turned towards the group who had started to mill about the cases in the galleries. 'Everything is under control. Let's allow the nurse to take care of this poor woman. I think that we'll move on to the Augustan gallery if you don't mind and continue with the tour there.'

As Tom Carr led the group into the next gallery, the guard cordoned off the Treasury, closing the space to the public. The nurse sat with the woman, monitoring her condition.

Forty-five minutes later, the tour now over, Tom walked into the entrance hall of the Greek and Roman Department. A receptionist handed him a small stack of messages and asked, 'How did it go?'

It had been such a strange morning that Tom was initially unsure how to respond. 'Well,' he started, 'we had a good turnout of people and it was going very well until we got to the Treasury. But then this woman took one look at the Baker Dancer, screamed and fainted. I've seen all kinds of reactions to that exquisite statuette – wonder, delight, even disbelief – but I've never seen anyone react that way before.' He laughed nervously.

'Is she all right?' the receptionist asked.

'I think so. A paramedic came and they brought her down to the nurse's office. She was unconscious for nearly a quarter of an hour but then came to and seemed to be in a stable condition,' Tom said. He was about to say more, but was interrupted by the telephone.

'Hello, Department of Greek and Roman Art, may I help you? . . . Just a minute.' The receptionist held the receiver to her chest. 'It's the nurse. She wants to speak with you.' She handed the telephone to Tom.

'Hello, this is Tom Carr.'

'Mr Carr, sorry to disturb you. The lady who fainted in the galleries during your talk, she's feeling much better and she insists that she needs to speak with you right away.'

'Is she there with you now?' Tom queried.

'Yes,' the nurse replied.

'Do you think she is okay?'

'Well, she sustained a blow to her right arm when she fell. She's going to have quite a bruise there, but nothing's broken and she seems okay to me. I don't know what caused her to faint but she seems fine now,' the nurse said.

Tom hesitated. He had a ton of work that he was supposed to be getting on with, but he wanted to see the woman to find out what had happened. He had never seen anything like her reaction to the statuette. He made a rapid decision. 'I'll be right down.'

A few minutes later Tom Carr walked into the nurse's office. Victoria was seated in a chair by the water cooler, holding an ice pack against her arm.

'Mr Carr, thank you so much for coming,' she said, looking excited rather than embarrassed about her collapse. 'Is there somewhere we can talk in private for a few minutes?'

She was about to get up when Tom motioned for her to remain seated.

'Are you sure you're okay?' he asked.

'Oh yes,' she said hurriedly. 'It was quite a shock at the time but I feel much better now. Please allow me to introduce myself. I'm Victoria Price.' She held out her hand to him. 'I am just visiting New York for a few days' vacation, and art doesn't usually have this effect on me.' She smiled and her bright blue eyes seemed to light up. 'Actually, I am an aspiring artist myself – a painter.'

'Well, we can talk in my office for a few minutes if you like,' he offered. 'I'm afraid I have an appointment at one p.m., though, for which I mustn't be late.' When dealing with strangers in the museum, Tom always liked to plan his exit strategy. People tended to forget that while they were usually at the museum in their free time, he was working and there was always so much to do. It was all rather irregular but something about this young woman intrigued him and he felt he could at least spare her a few minutes.

'That's absolutely fine. What I have to say won't take long. And, of course, you must be very busy what with the opening of the new galleries and all.'

'Yes, and I'm actually travelling overseas tomorrow,' he explained. 'To Europe on a research trip.'

'Oh, how nice for you,' she said warmly.

'Please follow me,' Tom said, ushering her into the wood-panelled lift that went up to the Greek and Roman Art Department. As the doors of the lift closed, Victoria looked around nervously.

'You know, I couldn't even look at one of these things until recently. I'm very claustrophobic.' Victoria shivered slightly as she spoke.

'It is a very short ride,' Tom reassured her. 'We're just up three floors. We'll be there before you know it. See, we're here.'

The doors opened and they stepped out. Victoria took a deep breath.

'It's just down the hall,' Tom said and led the way.

As they walked together down the hall they passed rows of framed posters from previous exhibitions that had been organised by the Greek and Roman Department. Passing through glass doors framed in maple that marked the entrance, they turned, walked down another corridor and entered Tom's office. Tom motioned towards the wooden chair opposite his desk.

'Please have a seat,' he said as he walked around the other side of his large desk and sat down.

'Now, what is it that you wanted to tell me, Ms Price?'

'Please call me Victoria,' she said as she sat down and clasped her hands in her lap, as if to steady herself. 'Something extraordinary happened to me earlier and it was triggered by some of the artworks on display.' She leaned forward, her breath quickening and her bright blue eyes staring at Tom intently.

He looked at his watch and wondered where this was going. She had fainted in front of the Baker Dancer but what were the other works of art that she was referring to?

'I'm sorry, Mr Carr.' Victoria smiled apologetically. 'You must think I'm nuts. I suppose you get all kinds of characters coming to see you and you may think I'm a little off my rocker but please hear me out.' She stopped for a moment, obviously nervous about what she was going to say, then shook herself and continued, seeming to have collected her thoughts. 'You remember I said that I have a very bad case of claustrophobia.' She paused again, clearly uncertain, and turned towards the window as if lost in thought.

Tom looked at the side of her face. The light from the window illuminated her golden hair, which shimmered around her silky smooth skin. She really was quite an attractive woman. In fact, he thought, in profile her face resembled the statue of Aphrodite Kallipygos in the Naples Archaeological Museum. It was an incredibly erotically charged portrayal, the nude goddess turning back to look down approvingly at her bottom. Most people remembered her bottom but Tom Carr remembered the complete sculpture. He had an extraordinary visual memory; it was one of the qualities that made him a good curator. He made a mental note to look up the statue again and marvelled at Ms Price's classic beauty as she continued to speak.

'Well, I started seeing a doctor about it and she has been helping me tremendously. She uses hypnotism to help me remember instances in my childhood, and even earlier.' She looked over at Tom. 'Instances that may be at the root of my fear of enclosed spaces.'

'What do you mean by earlier than childhood?' Tom asked, confused.

'Do you believe in reincarnation, Mr Carr?' she asked suddenly.

Tom, who was not easily caught off guard by a visitor's questions – he thought he'd heard them all – did not know exactly how to respond. 'Ms Price – Victoria,' Tom corrected himself. 'I don't see what my beliefs have to do with anything,' he said gently but firmly. 'I fear that we are straying far from whatever it is that you wanted to tell me concerning your unfortunate experience in the galleries this morning. And I'm sorry but I really do have another appointment in fifteen minutes on the other side of the museum, so I will need to end this meeting very shortly.'

'This is going to sound strange but the reason that I fainted in the gallery downstairs was because I had a sudden recollection from a past life,' Victoria continued after a slight pause. 'The episode was triggered by some of the objects on display. The statuette you call the Baker Dancer was in my vision; also the three paintings on the far wall of the adjacent gallery. All of a sudden, I was back in time. My doctor calls it channelling. Objects or places can set off memories from past-life experiences that are usually completely suppressed. It was as if I was right there.'

She paused again before continuing after a nod from Tom. He watched her intently as she recounted her vision – if that was what it was – a rapt look on her beautiful face.

'I was in a magnificent tomb but it was not my own. I had the feeling that I knew the man buried there. I had come to rob this tomb together with two other men but they betrayed me and left me inside to die. In my vision, I had been hit on the head and was just coming to when I heard them sealing the stone in the barrel-vaulted ceiling where we had entered. I cursed at them and then pleaded for mercy but soon it was quiet – they had clearly abandoned me. There was a torch on the ground next to me. In the flickering light, I could see in the distance the wall paintings that decorated the chamber. They included the three scenes that you have displayed downstairs, just as they are there. That was the first thing that set my memory off.

'I walked around the chamber,' Victoria continued, closing her eyes as she tried to remember exactly what she had seen. 'The other tomb robbers had taken many things from the tomb but there was more than they could carry. A set of finely wrought armour had been placed in one corner. On a stone bench was the statuette that you call the Baker Dancer, among other personal items. I picked it up and looked at it. It was so beautiful that I began to cry. Since it was made of bronze, not gold, my betrayers had passed it by but clearly it had significance for the deceased. It was that object, which I had touched so long ago, that caused me to faint. I put the statuette down where I found it and moved towards the gold sarcophagus placed in the centre of the room. The flame of my torch was slowly dying and the light grew dimmer. My companions had removed the lid of the sarcophagus. It was too heavy to take, though, and I believe they'd had second thoughts, superstitions, in any case, which had caused them to leave in such a hurry.' She opened her eyes and turned to look Tom straight in the face. 'The last thing I saw was Alexander the Great, his body mummified and lying in the sarcophagus, his head resting on the *Iliad of the Casket* and the dagger that he always kept there in life . . .'

2

THOMAS CARR AROSE early that summer morning, at 5:30 a.m., as he always did on Crete when he was working on the excavation. It was still dark outside, cool, with a light breeze. Stars twinkled brightly in the sky. As he drove down to the site the light was growing and the entire landscape was bathed in a deep red glow. Kastri – a butte-like hill – filled his windscreen view and dominated the bay that spread out around it. The slopes of the hill of Petsophas lay to the east, the ancient site of Dikta nestled below, and the Aegean Sea was beyond. Especially in this light the landscape always looked prehistoric to him, protean, as he imagined the world had looked a billion years ago – except, of course, for the olive trees that covered the land and shimmered in the breeze. It was clear enough to see the outline of the islands of Kassos and Karpathos jutting sharply from the sea off in the distance and it made him think of ancient mariners setting their course by line of sight out across the Aegean.

Tom turned off the main road to the beach onto a rough dirt track that wound through the olive groves to the site. It was still cool and quiet; the cicadas had not yet begun their incessant hum. Swallows darted out from the lower branches of the olive trees that crowded both sides of the road. The delicate little birds flew ahead of the Land Rover as though leading it forward. Tom thought about the wall paintings from the Cycladic town of Akrotiri on the nearby island of Santorini where an artist over 3,600 years ago had captured the graceful flight of these birds and he marvelled at the connectedness with antiquity evident in this small act.

A trail of dust rose up behind the vehicle as it barrelled around the curves of the road. In this remote part of the island at such an early hour Tom could drive like a demon around blind bends and know that there would be nothing coming on the other side. He'd driven this stretch of road thousands of times before and it was a bit like riding a roller coaster, although it was only a few hundred yards long and on relatively flat terrain. It was the quintessential Greek road – without a single straight stretch. Driving along it gave him pleasure and it acted as a liminal zone between the archaeological site and the modern world. As he drove, it was as though he was operating a time machine: the vehicle bumped and rolled but mostly there was an unmistakable feeling of transformation as he whisked through the old wire gate and past the rough stone wall, coming abruptly to a halt at the ancient site of Dikta.

As a seasoned archaeologist and curator of Greek and Roman art, Tom was passionate about the remote past and had travelled all over the Mediterranean and beyond, visiting sites and museums, studying the material culture of classical antiquity and its Bronze Age antecedents. He had been drawn to museum work through his love of ancient artefacts, especially great works of art, which were for him remarkable witnesses from the past that provided a tangible connection to the present, evidence of the achievements of mankind so long ago. Because of the technological advances of the last century, the nature of art today and its future seemed so different from how things had been in classical antiquity where art had played an integral role in society. Yet on many levels mankind as a species, Tom thought, had not changed all that much, which was why he remained so passionate about the study of the past. He also felt a strong personal connection with antiquity. This sometimes manifested itself when he held an object in his hand or visited a site, such as when he had walked into the Greek stadium at Aphrodisias in Turkey: the hair on the back of his neck had stood on end and for a moment he could feel the presence of the crowd and the heat of the competitions that had been held there centuries ago. Certain archaeological sites evoked the classical past very strongly. Dikta was such a place. The past was very much present.

He climbed out of the Land Rover and walked towards the workmen gathered under a large olive tree where simple benches made from field stones supporting wooden planks had been set up. Pickaxes were soaking in a water bucket to keep the wooden shafts swollen and tight within their metal sockets for the work ahead.

'Good morning, Georgos,' Tom said to the foreman, a strong, serious and kind man who knew as much about digging as anyone.

'Good morning, Tom,' Georgos said.

'Let's get started.' Tom could barely contain his excitement.

Georgos nodded. Slowly and methodically, he turned towards the men and blew his whistle. The men stood up, put out their cigarettes and finished their coffees, gathered their tools – picks, trowels, brushes, shovels, and wheelbarrows – and started towards the trenches that were neatly marked out, forming a grid across a flattened field north of the impressive walls of the newly excavated buildings of the Greek sanctuary.

Dikta had first been excavated in 1902. Pioneering British archaeologists had come in search of the legendary sanctuary of Diktaian Zeus. According to ancient Greek mythology, Zeus, father of the Olympian gods, was born in a cave on Crete. Kouretes, young men from the island, took turns watching over the child god and hid his cries from his murderous father Kronos by banging their shields together. The tradition was recalled by archaic bronze shields discovered in Cretan caves where they had been placed as votive offerings to the god, and it continued for centuries as was apparent from a remarkable series of Campanian terracotta reliefs of the Roman period that depicted warriors dancing and clashing their shields around the baby god. His mother Rhea hid him from Kronos to whom it had been prophesied that his son would surpass him. Trying to cheat fate, Kronos set out to kill his children by swallowing them whole. Rhea would not give up Zeus and devised a plan to trick her husband. In Zeus's place, she wrapped a stone in swaddling clothes and gave it to Kronos who was fooled by the ruse. This story is preserved in both ancient literature and art. This very scene was portrayed on a fifth-century BC Greek vase in the Metropolitan Museum.

Whereas most Greeks worshipped Zeus as the father of the gods and head of the Olympian deities, the ancient Cretans also worshipped him as a young god. The sanctuary of Zeus at Dikta was his most important shrine on the island, a major cult centre and pilgrimage site. Like the great sanctuary of Zeus at Olympia, its location had become lost over the centuries and it was the hope of rediscovering this place that was sacred to the thunder god that had led British archaeologists to Dikta over a century ago.

A fruitful decade-long campaign of excavations confirmed that the ancient sanctuary had lain here. The research yielded some important early Greek bronze offerings – shields, large tripod cauldrons, other vessels, miniature sets of armour, as well as an important marble stele of the second century AD bearing a hymn to Diktaian Zeus, the language of which dated back to the third-century BC and perhaps earlier. It also yielded many *membra dissecta* from the upper part of a temple but no clear *in situ* architectural remains of the Greek sanctuary.

These early excavations were conducted at the same time that Sir Arthur Evans was doing his pioneering work at Knossos in the north-central part of the island, uncovering the extensive remains of the foremost nucleus of the first major European civilisation, which he dubbed 'Minoan' after the legendary Cretan king Minos. The British team at Dikta had also uncovered a large Minoan settlement of the Late Bronze Age, with paved streets and splendid houses. In the 1960s the British returned to the site to excavate more of the Minoan town and the refuge settlement on top of Kastri that was occupied in the twelfth and eleventh centuries BC at the end of the Bronze Age when the island had fallen upon troubled times.

By the middle of the 1980s, the field of Minoan

archaeology had advanced considerably. Hundreds of sites had been excavated all over the island. Major Minoan administrative centres, dubbed 'palaces' after Evans's romantic terminology, had been discovered at Knossos, Phaistos in the south-central part of the island, Malia along the north coast, and Zakros on the very eastern edge of the island about thirty kilometres from Dikta. Given the large size of Dikta, the likelihood that it had had a palace or administrative centre like Knossos was high and the prospect of excavating it with current techniques was tantalising. The British undertook a field survey to determine the most likely place for the palace, but the site was so large that there were many promising areas in which to dig and limited time and resources to complete the task.

Excavations in the twenty-first century were much more meticulous than those that had been undertaken years ago and the modern process was extremely slow and painstaking. The new digs unearthed seven more buildings of the town and some important artefacts, most notably an exquisitely carved gold and ivory statuette measuring over half a metre in height. The young male figure – with rock-crystal eyes, an elaborate gold kilt and gold sandals, and with a head shaved at the sides and a braided Mohawk hairstyle – was a masterpiece of Minoan art and quite possibly a Bronze Age forerunner of the young Zeus worshipped by the Cretans during the Greek period.

Tom remembered the day the statuette came to light and the excitement that it had caused. Only a handful of Minoan chryselephantine statuettes were known but, aside from a few remarkable examples from Knossos, most had come out of the art market in the early twentieth century and were suspected of being forgeries. The most famous, of course, was the so-called Boston snake goddess housed in the Museum of Fine Arts at Boston. Scholars wondered now if she had been created by one of the restorers, who worked closely with Sir Arthur Evans on the excavated finds from Knossos.

The thrill of discovery had been palpable and Tom believed that they were now on the verge of another – very different – spectacular find. In the late 1990s a remote-sensing sonar survey of the land to the east of the excavated Minoan town had produced exciting new evidence for walls buried beneath a thick layer of sandy earth. This relatively clean layer of earth had collapsed from nearby Mount Petsophas at some point after classical antiquity and before modern habitation in the area. Consequently, results from a traditional walking surface survey of this area had not looked promising since it yielded very few shards of pottery on the surface. But with sonar-resistivity equipment taking readings in the winter when the water table was high and conductivity was good, an open expanse with massive walls around it became visible underground, suggesting that significant archaeological remains were likely to be undisturbed and in an excellent state of preservation. It also became apparent that there was an ancient spring in this new area and sources of natural water had always been important for ancient settlements. The directors of the dig immediately guessed that this was the site of the long-sought-after Minoan palace at Dikta.

Ironically, a similar situation had developed at the nearby site of Zakros, another important harbour town in Minoan times. The same David George Hogarth who had also tried to find the tomb of Alexander the Great in Alexandria, Egypt, had been the first to dig at Zakros in 1901. Hogarth had hoped to find a palace but instead had discovered many homes that had clearly once belonged to wealthy owners. A Greek archaeologist called Nicholas Platon returned to the site in the 1970s and only twenty feet from where Hogarth had stopped digging he discovered the palace – complete with an archive of linear A tablets, a treasury filled with exquisite works of art such as a rock-crystal vase and a serpentine bull's-head ritual vessel, as well as gold and raw materials such as copper ingots and elephant tusks. Topography also offered significant parallels between Dikta and Zakros. The palace at Zakros was located near a source of water and was nestled down in the valley like the recently discovered site at Dikta. It seemed that at long last the Minoan palace at Dikta was within reach. After prolonged negotiations to buy the land, which was owned by various locals and in some cases by multi-owner families whose members did not see eye to eye on anything, the necessary deal was done. Politics also got in the way of the initial permit requests but after a few more years excavations began in the new area, dubbed Palace Field.

A golden rule of archaeology, however, was that you never knew what you were going to find. Typically, you did not find what you set out to – and Dikta's Palace Field proved to be no exception. A grid of trenches was set up across the area and initial soundings revealed the remains of a massive open-air altar and part of the enclosure wall of the sanctuary of Diktaian Zeus. In fact, the sanctuary lay directly on top of the Minoan palace, so the suspicions about the site of the palace had been correct. In retrospect, this made a lot of sense. The best locations were often reused for obvious reasons and in this case, by locating the Greek sanctuary on top of the focal point of the Minoan settlement, continuity of cult usage might also have been established if the cult of Diktaian Zeus stretched back into the Bronze Age as was suspected. Even more remarkable was the final stratigraphy of the sanctuary. It was clear that the massive collapse of earth from Mount Petsophas had actually occurred while the sanctuary was still in use, not at some much later date as had been initially believed. In fact, the altar was covered with the charred remains of a massive bull sacrifice to the thunder god. The ritual had probably taken place on a feast day of Zeus in the spring of AD 365 as part of the god's ritual rebirthing ceremony, and was cut short by a cataclysmic event, a massive earthquake, that caused a landslide from Mount Petsophas that covered the sanctuary in more than a metre of earth and rubble. Because only a few decades later Theodosius I decreed the abolition of pagan religions, the sanctuary at Dikta was never rebuilt and its location slipped into oblivion.

Every excavation season brought to light more of the sanctuary and increased the researchers' understanding of this major religious centre. This year the outstanding discovery was something within the sanctuary: a shrine dedicated to the divine Alexander the Great. Alexander became king of Macedonia in 334 BC when his father, Philip II, was assassinated, some say as part of a conspiracy devised by Alexander's mother, Olympias. He was undoubtedly one of the greatest leaders of all time. In nine short years he and his armies overcame the Persian Empire and continued his conquests as far east as the Indus River valley. In the end, his own armies convinced him to turn back and he eventually died of a fever, possibly malaria, in Babylon. On his deathbed, when he was asked to whom he would leave his vast kingdom, Alexander replied 'To the strongest'. But his successors divided his vast empire into smaller kingdoms: Ptolemy reigned over Egypt and its neighbouring territories, Antiochos ruled much of the Near East, and Perdiccas ruled Macedonia. The newly discovered shrine at Dikta could contribute much to modern historians' understanding of the later history of the cult of Alexander and its enduring popularity into Roman times.

The area that Tom, Georgos and their team were now excavating was in front of the shrine, a building comparable in size to the jewel-like Temple of Athena Nike on the Acropolis in Athens. Inside the shrine was a colossal marble statue of Alexander, the most remarkable find of the season. From stylistic details it appeared to be a Hadrianic copy of the original cult statue that had probably first been placed within the shrine in the third century BC. Although the sculpture was still encrusted with earth, one could already see that traces of the original gilding and brightly coloured paint were still preserved. It would be a stunning addition to the local archaeological museum in the nearby town of Siteia. The statue was massive and must have weighed more than a ton. The decision had been made to undertake preliminary conservation *in situ* until the area was fully excavated and the necessary riggers and heavy machinery could be arranged to move it safely. After the remains of the collapsed ancient roof had been removed, the workmen had built a makeshift scaffolding with a new covering to protect the masterpiece from the heat of the sun and to provide shelter for the conservators. It was imperative to attempt to stabilise the pigments and remove the earth that encrusted the statue, since the soil's high acid content was often damaging to the paint. Archaeology was, indeed, a destructive process. When works of art first came to light, removed from their stable environment where they had lain for centuries, the vestiges of their original appearance were often apparent but quickly faded perceptibly. The *Tales from the Crypt* image of an object, or person, turning to dust before an observer's eyes was a cliché but closer to the truth than many people might have imagined. Fortunately the statue of Alexander was made of marble, a durable material, but the delicate paint that covered nearly every part of its finely carved surface was another matter entirely.

While the conservators tended to this delicate task, Tom and his team worked on the area in front of the shrine. Two rectangular stelae, stone slabs covered with inscriptions, still stood where they had been set up centuries before. The older one had been excavated earlier in the season. It stood on the right of the temple's entrance and recorded the building's initial dedication in the early third century BC during the reign of Ptolemy II, when this part of Crete had been under Ptolemaic control. The text was formulaic but was especially remarkable for mentioning the tomb of Alexander the Great, known as the Sôma, which Ptolemy I had built for him in Alexandria. References to Alexander's tomb were rare and such an early reference was notable indeed. The second stele, set up on the right as you exited the temple, was being fully uncovered now. Tom told the workmen that he would finish cleaning it off and sat down in front of the slab. As he dusted off the letters with his brush and trowel, traces of the red paint commonly used in antiquity to bring out the shapes of letters were becoming visible. The sun's morning rays were producing a nice raking light and Tom, with his note-book on his lap, began to record the inscription. The stone exhibited unusual wear patterns. Much of the wording was nicely preserved but some of the text was worn away almost completely. Since the sanctuary had been destroyed probably less than fifty years after this stone had been erected, and the stele had presum-ably been covered at that time, such wear seemed strange. He thought that abrasion by the roots of nearby olive trees and the actions of the elements over centuries must have been responsible for such erosion. As it turned out, the stele was much later in date than the first one they had discovered near the entrance of the temple. Its later origin was apparent from the forms of the letters and its text, which appeared to record a late refurbishment of the sanctuary during the reign of Trebonianus Gallus in the third quarter of the third century AD. What was stunning for Tom to see was the repeated formula from the first stele, only with a significant change. Instead of mentioning the tomb of Alexander in Alexandria, it stated: 'the tomb of Alexander, which is no longer in Alexandria but which has been moved through the divine sanction of the Emperor Trebonianus Gallus . . .' – and the rest of the text was too worn to read. The reign of Trebonianus Gallus had been short-lived, during the time of the so-called soldier-emperors, and provided a close dating of sometime between AD 251 and 253 for the transfer of Alexander's remains. The new inscription extended the modern world's knowledge of the tomb of Alexander into the middle of the third century AD, long after the reign of the emperor Caracalla who considered himself to be a reincarnation of Alexander the Great and whose visit to Alexander's tomb in Alexandria was the last known on record. Here was a new, if tantalisingly incomplete, clue to the final resting place of Alexander the Great, king of kings and conqueror of the world. Tom could barely contain his excitement. This fresh piece of history recovered from the earth reopened the question of the location of Alexander's tomb, one of the greatest unsolved archaeological mysteries of all time. They would have to wrestle the remaining text from its worn stone.

It was a typical Saturday night in Dikta. Excavations had ceased for the week and everyone was on their own for the remainder of the weekend. Dikta was a small town, a village really, and the dig team's social options were limited. They tended to hang out together and the younger members in particular liked to let their hair down a bit and party. Claire, a student from Columbia University, had a feeling that it was going to be a magical night but she had no idea what surprises lay ahead. The evening began at the raki hut, formally known as 'Kali Kardia' or 'The Good Heart', in the neighbouring village of Hieronero. This tiny bar served raki – the Cretan moonshine distilled from grape stems – beer, and soft drinks and was the principal local supplier of a public telephone and cigarettes. In summertime the door was always open. The proprietor, Barboyannis, and his wife, Georgia, could usually be found sitting at a large square wooden table just inside the door, ready to serve a cold drink or gossip about the goings-on in the village. This bit of authentic Cretan life, sitting out on the street in front and having a raki and chatting about the day's events while watching the setting sun change the colours of the Cretan landscape, was a great pleasure for the dig team. The evening drink was followed by dinner at the place where they lodged and where everyone sat outside eating by candlelight at the long table in the pit, as the lower terrace of the dig house was called. Afterwards, Claire and her friends headed out on the town, heading first to the Why Not? pub.

It was hot, even long after the sun had gone down, and there was a slight warm breeze. The wind always blew at this time of year here. The bar was open to the street with a veranda in front that was set off by a low bamboo divider. The atmosphere was a bit heavy but was inviting in a goth kind of way: the room was darkly lit and had tall ceilings from which hung fans to keep things cool. Heavy acid-rock music blasted from the speakers that hung at either side of the bar. Several young Greek men were sitting at the bar in colourful cut-off T-shirts, smoking and talking.

'Can't they change the music?' Claire asked her friend Sarah.

'Sure, I'll ask. The bartender is from Zakros and he's really into this headbanger stuff. What do you want to hear? I bet I can sweet-talk him,' Sarah replied.

'Anything else. Well, how about some Springsteen or U2?'

'Okay, I'll try.' Sarah went over to talk to the bartender.

Sarah and Claire danced to the music for an hour or so and then decided to move on to the Enigma music bar with the rest of the dig crowd.

The Enigma was located on the outskirts of town near the dig house and was a favourite weekend haunt, especially at the end of the night. A large sphinx perched over the entrance on a *kafeneion*, or traditional Greek coffee shop-style sign. Terracotta satyr masks hung inside on either side of the door and on the brightly coloured walls were hung black and white photographs of a beautiful nude woman in various poses on a moonlit beach. The Enigma definitely had its own vibe. The owner loved the dig's business and pretty much gave its members free run of the place. Even the excavation directors and the architect would sometimes come out earlier in the evening. It was amusing to watch the place fill up after the dig girls arrived. They liked to dance together as a group, occasionally going in for slam dancing or flamboyant disco dancing. The Greek men followed them around like a pride of lions circling fresh meat. The local Greek girls came out only once a week and arrived all together. This was the social mechanism for traditional dating in the village, and it was dying out slowly since Greece had entered the European Union. The bars in town were truly male bastions and it was easy to see that the fraternity system adopted in American universities was actually based simply on the Greek social system in which young Greek men hung out together at bars, drinking, fraternising and hitting on foreign women tourists.

There were six young women working on the excavation and they received a lot of attention. Claire, for her part, had been resisting the numerous come-ons that were thrust upon her daily by many of the workmen on the dig as well as the flirtatious approaches from some of her male colleagues. She was not that kind of girl, she thought, but there was something about this country – and especially this place – that made you want to fuck! Tourist posters in Athens and Herakleion showed a pudgy Eros shooting arrows at a foreign woman relaxing in a pool with a handsome Greek man but out here in the country she seemed possessed not so much by the playful sensual love of Aphrodite and her sidekick Eros as by the wild animal lust of Pan the goat god. Claire had been here for four weeks – the dig season was already coming to an end – and she had been practising sexual abstinence. She was about ready to explode. Her hormones were driving her crazy. So she decided to review her options. Tonight would be the night that she would give in to her carnal cravings, she thought, but who would be the lucky guy? One of the Greek boys caught Claire's fancy. It was the pickman, Yannis. He wore a tight light-blue collared shirt with several buttons open at the front so she could see his chest. The sleeves were rolled up to expose his toned arms and beautiful olive skin. He had on faded tight jeans, which accentuated his crotch, and slip-on shoes with tassles and no socks.

His hair was brown and straight, combed to the side and fixed with gel so that it glistened, and he had the most piercing blue eyes and a broad smile that he flashed frequently during conversation. He had a very easy way about him and his laughter was infectious. Claire was a pretty girl herself but much less confident when it came to boys, and she envied the way he was so comfortable with his body. Yannis immediately sensed that Claire was watching him and came over to her.

'To be looking at you, is to be making me very happy,' Yannis said to Claire in his best *kamaki* voice. 'But seriously, Claire, I've got my *papaki* outside – want to go down to the beach for a swim?' he said, smiling at her.

'Sure,' she said.

'Let's go.' He squeezed her arm. As they were leaving, Claire's friend Sarah came up to her with an approving look on her face and said, 'Have fun. But whatever happens, don't let him take you into the banana groves!'

Yannis winked at Sarah and kept pulling Claire along. When they got outside Yannis started up his moped and Claire climbed on behind him. Yannis took the back roads through the olive groves down to the sea. The dirt road was bumpy as Yannis sped along and Claire hugged him tightly so she wouldn't fall off and rested her head against his strong back.

At one point, Yannis pulled up to the entrance to a hothouse and asked if Claire wanted to go inside. By the light of the moped's headlamp, Claire could see the rows of banana plants growing inside, bunches of the diminutive Cretan fruit hanging from the stalks, which also produced a wildly phallic-looking flower. The air was warm and pungent with the smell of ripe bananas and dark shadows swung to and fro as Yannis moved the headlamp around. 'No, thank you. Let's go to the beach,' she said, and they roared on down the road.

A few minutes later they came to the main road to the shore. Yannis cut across a fork in the road and continued down past the archaeological site to a secluded beach that looked back out to Kastri and across the bay. He pulled off the road onto a field that served as a makeshift parking lot and cut the moped's engine. As the illumination from the headlight faded, Claire looked up and the brilliance of the night sky with its myriad stars came into focus. The sound of the gentle lapping of the waves that broke over the fine sand was so inviting. Claire jumped off the bike and ran down to feel the temperature of the water. Kicking off her sandals she dipped her toes into the edge of an advancing wave.

'It's gorgeous,' she called back to Yannis as she ran along the shore. After twenty-five feet or so she climbed across some rocks to the more secluded section of the beach. She slipped out of her dress, which she let fall in the sand, and then her underwear, and ran into the water with a scream of delight, diving under when she was in far enough. The water was invigorating and she wiped it off her face when she surfaced, kicking her legs, and paddling with her arms to stay afloat.

'The water is glowing around me! It's like pixie dust!' she exclaimed.

Yannis was on the beach opposite her now and after dropping a blanket and towel on the sand he started stripping off his clothes.

'It's phosphorescence,' he said. 'It's magical, isn't it?' He was completely naked now and stood there in full view of Claire. She was amazed how self-confident he was – and at how beautiful he was to look at. She could feel herself getting aroused.

He ran into the water with a whoop and dived straight towards her, emerging just a few feet away. He swam right up to Claire and they kissed. The taste of salt water was on their lips and the particles of light glowed around their moving limbs. Claire gently pushed away from Yannis and floated face up, looking at the stars.

'The stars are magnificent, aren't they?' she said. 'Try floating like this, it's great.' As she looked up all she could see were thousands of stars with the dense swathe of the Milky Way like a thick brushstroke across a speckled canvas.

SEÁN HEMINGWAY

'I think it would be a bit cold for me right now,'
Yannis said, smiling sheepishly. 'I bet if you look hard
enough, though, you'll see a shooting star. You know,
Dikta has always been a place sacred to Zeus. It is
true that we have more than our fair share of shooting
stars and lightning storms, lingering remnants of the
thunder god's ancient power.'

Claire looked intently and, sure enough, a minute
later a fiery ball streaked across the sky. She squealed
with delight.

'You're right. I just saw one! It was magnificent,'
Claire gushed.

'Don't forget to make a wish. Let's sit on the beach
for a while,' Yannis said, swimming towards shore.
'There is something I want to show you and it could
happen at any minute.'

'Okay.' Claire followed him to shore where she
grabbed the towel and wrapped it around herself.
They both sat down together on the blanket that
Yannis had brought, his arm snug around her shoulder.

'So what's the show?' Claire said.

'Look out across the water, out past the peninsula.
Do you see anything?'

Claire turned and looked to where he was pointing
but there was total darkness on the horizon and she
couldn't see anything. Then, a few minutes later,
suddenly there was a small prick of light. Moonbeams
travelled across the sea and struck Claire's face in an

instant – she was astonished. There was no warmth as there would have been in the sun's rays and the quality of the illumination had its own peculiar radiance. The light grew in an arc whose rays lit up the waves of the Aegean Sea, which reflected the moonbeams into endless shimmering cascading waves of silvery motion. It seemed in that first moment as though the tide increased its power, responding to the moon goddess Selene's charms, and the play of the light on the waves was almost hypnotic in its effect. It was one of the most breathtaking sights of her life. Claire was amazed by how big the moon looked as the great crater-filled ball revealed itself and continued to climb up the sky. The entire panorama grew brighter and brighter and now she could see clearly across the bay. Soon the moon was high in the heavens and the sea had calmed but Earth's satellite's radiant glow continued to hold Claire's attention.

Claire turned to Yannis and asked, 'If you could lasso the moon, would you climb up to it or bring it down to you?'

'You think I'm an American cowboy? We don't use lassos in our country,' Yannis said.

'Well, you know what I mean.' And as she nuzzled closer to him, Claire suddenly noticed a boat motoring towards them from across the bay. It was still quite a way off.

'Yannis, do you see that boat?'

'Yes, it came from the large yacht moored on the other side of the bay. It has been heading this way for a little while now.'

'Do you think they can see us?' Claire suddenly realised that she was naked. 'What can they be doing out at this time of night?'

'We're pretty well hidden in this cove,' Yannis said. 'But the main beach nearby is one of the best spots for landing a boat on this side of the bay. They might just be heading this way to come ashore and not simply be out for a moonlit jaunt.'

Sure enough, the boat continued on its course towards the main beach.

'Do you know who owns that yacht?' Claire asked.

'It sailed into the bay earlier today. They registered with the port authority. My friend is the harbour master. Of course, everyone in the village has seen the boat at anchor there. It was the talk of the town today. It is a nice-looking yacht. We don't get so many of those here. The waters around this part of the island can be a bit treacherous, as anyone will tell you. My friend told me the boat is registered in Malta but it is an American man who owns it. He appears to be cruising around the Mediterranean on holiday with his family,' Yannis said.

'Let's not attract their attention – just keep quiet and see what they do,' Claire said as she nestled in Yannis's arms.

From their vantage point they had a good view across the beach if they looked over the rocky outcrop that separated them from the main stretch of sand. As the boat drew closer it was clear that there were several men aboard. One sat at the front and held a lantern out over the bow. He was directing the man who was steering, a tough-looking sailor with a sallow face that became visible whenever the helmsman turned the lantern back so he could speak to the others. In the middle was an older man, dressed in a tweed jacket and gaberdine slacks like an English gentleman on a Sunday walk. He had a shock of bright white hair and he was smoking a cigarette. Next to him on the central bench of the boat was another burly man who sat silently, his big arms crossed in front of his broad chest.

'Doesn't look like your typical family outing, if you ask me,' Claire whispered to Yannis.

'It's a strange sight, all right,' Yannis said. 'I wonder what they're up to?'

The steersman cut the engine as they approached land, raised the prop, and they coasted towards the beach. When the bow of the boat ran aground, the man with the lantern jumped out into the water and pulled the craft up onto the beach. One of the burly men jumped ashore, carrying an anchor that he fixed in the sand further up the beach to secure the boat. The older man stretched his legs on the beach and lit another cigarette as the others began to unload two large bags and some digging equipment, a pickaxe and a shovel.

'Where can they be going at this time of night with all that stuff?' Claire was absorbed in the goings-on.

'Looks like they're heading up to the site,' Yannis said as the men headed up through the fields.

Oskar Williams was not a man to be taken lightly. In another age he would have been a pirate captain. He had flair and abundant charm but also a darker side, a swashbuckling nature that was never too far below the surface, even now that he was getting on in years. To be successful in his business you had to take risks, make split-second decisions, and you had to be able to trust your judgement. In one sense it was a gentleman's profession and above all Oskar considered himself a gentleman. He'd been well schooled as a boy. He attended Exeter where he studied classics and then went on to do his first degree at Harvard University. His family had money, and this allowed him to pursue his interest in classical studies. Oskar started a Ph.D. programme at Princeton University but during a prestigious fellowship at the American Academy in Rome he realised that the traditional path to academia was not for him. He had come to his awareness of ancient history through the study of classical languages but Rome awakened a love of antiquities in him that became a passion. After all, in Rome ancient works of art were everywhere around you: they were something to be experienced, not just read about in a book deep in the library of the American Academy.

Oskar decided to move out of the Academy and rent a flat just down the hill in Trastevere. He began to collect antiquities, and soon learned that he had an excellent eye but a limited amount of capital. He realised that in order to satisfy his craving for new works of art he would need somehow to turn a profit on his passion. So he started a small antiquities business in Rome and shipped things back to the States where he set up a second shop in New York. This was in the mid-1960s and the art market was a wild and woolly place. It suited Oskar perfectly. There weren't too many rules and regulations and there was pretty much a continuous supply of antiquities. A good number of items could be had from other dealers, from flea markets and from collectors who were trading up or selling out. People had been collecting antiquities for centuries and these legitimate sources made up much of the market.

Oskar, however, saw in his infinite wisdom – and he often thought that he had infinite wisdom – that there was another side to the market. With his entrepreneurial talents, he would carve a niche for himself by trading in newly discovered works, objects that had been dug up out of the ground recently. Sometimes this happened accidentally, but Oskar came to know a growing number of suppliers who were digging clandestinely for a profit – tomb robbers, essentially. At first this seemed like a rough crowd for a gentleman like Oskar to get involved with, and many dealers steered clear of them. But Oskar found that he could handle them and a part of him even enjoyed the danger. Most importantly, these *tombaroli*, as they were called, often obtained the most exquisite works of art for him to enjoy before he passed them on to someone else at a tidy profit.

Oskar's business grew and word of his interests spread through the grapevine. He made connections in Greece, Albania, Turkey and North Africa, anywhere that Greek and Roman antiquities might surface with a little help from a spade and a lantern. As his interests grew, he dabbled further afield in Ancient Near Eastern antiquities and Egyptian works.

But in the early 1970s laws started to change, making it more difficult to buy and sell antiquities. Export permits and paperwork were now required. Oskar and his suppliers had no trouble finding ways around this. Switzerland with its free port became a useful place to traffic antiquities and its common border with Italy only made it that much easier to get the objects across. Oskar had had a good run through the 1980s and 1990s, and his dealings had landed him only the occasional rebuff from a country. Once he'd been stopped bringing ancient coins out of Turkey and on another occasion had been fined by the Greek government for not registering some antiquities in his house on Naxos, but these were relatively minor incidents.

In recent years, though, it had become increasingly difficult to get hold of genuine antiquities. There was even more red tape and, frankly, there had been so much looting in various countries that the sources were not as readily available as they'd been before. As with so many species of fish in the ocean or supplies of oil around the world there was only so much in existence and the pressure of demand was showing its effect on the market. In many ways, Oskar was by now at the top of his game, and he did not really need the money. If he were prudent he would have retired some time ago but he still kept up with his myriad contacts and when word of something special got out he acted on it. In truth, he could not bear to get out of the game, despite the increasing dangers involved, and there was always a buyer for exceptional works of art.

It was the pursuit of just such a find, perhaps the crowning achievement of his career, that had brought him to eastern Crete this evening, he thought as he stood on the beach in the moonlight and took a deep drag on his cigarette. Last week, while docked at

Mykonos, he'd been reading the *International Herald Tribune* and had happened to see a brief article announcing that an important archaeological discovery had been made at Dikta – a cult statue of Alexander the Great and two stelae with inscriptions that provided tantalising new information about the location of Alexander the Great's tomb.

Archaeologists were always keen to get the word out when they discovered something important since such announcements helped them get funding for their excavations. However, Oskar knew too that they were also painfully slow in publishing their finds. It could be years before the details of this discovery would be published in some obscure archaeological journal or monograph. He wanted to come and see it for himself. The statue sounded impressive but it was the stelae that he was really interested in. Alexander's tomb was the holy grail of antiquities. If it still existed unplundered – admittedly a big if – Oskar could only imagine what wonders it contained. With his connections in Egypt and around the Mediterranean, he'd have no problem getting to it before the archaeologists. With their permit applications, grants, and so forth, even if these stelae said exactly where the tomb was located it would be months before the archaeologists would be able to act. Oskar could have a team of diggers ready to move by next week if necessary. It was a long shot but the more he thought about it the more he realised that he had to come and see what it was all about. The newspaper article had given no specific information about the text inscribed on the stelae.

As the group of men walked up the fields towards the site Oskar listened to the rustle of the olive trees, their silvery leaves shimmering in the moonlight. They were lucky that it was a full moon that night – they hardly needed the torches. Soon they came to a fence with an old metal gate and passed through it onto the site. Dikta was not a very well-known site and consequently the gate was usually left unlocked. A small guardhouse stood near the entrance but it was empty now and was in any case usually only manned in the off-season to protect against illicit digging. As Oskar and his team came into the site, the olive groves gave way to the ruins of a large town. There were low walls of buildings all around. These must be the houses of the Minoan settlement, Oskar thought, with their fine ashlar masonry and paved streets. Life couldn't have been so bad here in Minoan times.

Oskar turned to the burly local man who was their guide and said in Greek, 'We want the area they've been digging recently, the place where they found the statue of Alexander the Great. It is in the ancient Greek sanctuary dedicated to Zeus. Take us there.'

The man motioned to the left and they headed in that direction, following him as they walked through the Minoan streets. Soon they came to another gated area. This time the gate was locked. Beyond were the remains of the sanctuary of Diktaian Zeus. A shed-like structure in the distance had to mark the location of the statue, Oskar thought, and the stelae . . . He took out his skeleton keys and got to work on the lock. There was no need to draw any attention to their visit if they could avoid it. With his nimble fingers at work on it, the lock soon sprung open, the thick link chain fell to the ground, and the metal gate swung open gently on its squeaky hinges.

Oskar turned to his motley crew and said, with a flourish, 'Gentlemen, I give you the sanctuary to Diktaian Zeus, legendary birthplace of the thunder god.' Without waiting for a response, he headed straight for the little temple to Alexander the Great. As he approached it, he expected to see the stelae set out in front but, to his surprise, they were not there. Getting nervous, he then realised that they must be inside the modern shed. The doors to the shed were closed with a heavy chain secured by a large lock. Oskar got out his skeleton keys again and started to work on the lock. After several minutes, though, he still was not able to get it open.

'Well, so much for remaining discreet. I did not come all this way to turn back now,' he muttered to himself. He turned to the burly man next to him and told him to shoot open the lock. Oskar stood back as the man took out a 9mm Walther pistol with a long silencer screwed into its muzzle and took aim at the lock. After two shots the lock busted open, the chain fell to the ground, and the doors swung open.

Oskar let out a gasp as the statue of Alexander looked out at him. It was magnificent to behold. The once-great king of the ancient world sat enthroned with a benevolent look on his face and cradling a sceptre in one arm. The moonlight cast an eerie glow. Standing before the entrance to the temple were the two stelae. Oskar got down on his knees in front of the first stele to have a closer look. He ran his fingers along the engraved letters and the smooth surface of the marble. The text was quite long but it seemed to be all there. He took out a small camera from his pocket and took a few quick photographs. The inscription was too long for him to decipher now but he'd have some fun puzzling over it back on the boat.

He called to one of his assistants, 'Give me the canvas bag. I'm going to make a squeeze of the text. While I'm doing that you have a go with the metal detector inside the perimeter of the sanctuary. See if you can get any readings, there are often metal votive objects dedicated at sanctuaries like this and we might come across something good.' The man brought the bag over to Oskar and then took out the metal detector from the other bag and set out, scanning the surface as he walked. Oskar took out several sheets of thin paper, a spray bottle filled with water, and his squeeze brush. He moistened the first sheet and pressed it against the surface of the marble over the area of the inscription. He placed a second and a third sheet over the first. Then he took his thick brist-led brush and systematically applied pressure to the surface of the stone, pushing the sheets of paper deep into the engraved letters. While the paper was drying he went over to the second stele. It was not as well preserved as the first. Parts of the surface were worn and one corner was missing. Unfortunately, the broken area included part of the text. He took more pictures and made a squeeze of the second inscription. They would have to wait for a half-hour or so while the paper dried.

In a moment of weakness Oskar thought about lopping off the head of the sculpture of Alexander and taking it with them. But he had not brought a mason's saw and with his boat anchored in the bay it was too risky to go back for one now. He could have his man check later and if the archaeologists were careless enough to leave the statue unguarded for another couple of weeks he could have him come back for it with the proper equipment.

'They will have cleaned more of it by then, too,' he chuckled to himself. Yes, keep your cool, Oskar, he thought, and had another cigarette as he waited for the squeezes to dry.

After the allotted drying time he peeled off the squeeze paper from each stele and held in his hands perfectly formed one-to-one copies of the inscriptions. 'We've got what we came for. Let's get out of here.' He called to the man who was still searching for objects with the metal detector and together with their guide and the other fellow they headed back down towards the boat.

3

TOM LOOKED ACROSS his office desk and thought, 'Who is this woman?' He was intrigued, to say the least. There was something amazingly serendipitous about her coming to him at this time, given that he was, in fact, hard at work trying to locate the tomb of Alexander the Great. For a moment, he wondered if a friend of his had put her up to this but it seemed clear from the way Ms Price was looking intently at him, as though she expected him to respond to her incredible story about being inside Alexander the Great's tomb over 2,300 years ago, that she was quite serious. If Tom worked anywhere else in the world, it might have seemed too great a coincidence but experience had shown him anything could happen during a workday at the Metropolitan Museum.

'Would you join me for a coffee upstairs on the Roof Garden?' Tom asked, smiling at her. 'I think the fresh air would do us both some good and there is a bench there with a wonderful view over the park. If you don't mind, let's continue our conversation there. It's on the way to my next meeting, and I'm dying for a cup of coffee. We've just about got time.'

'Okay, Mr Carr,' Victoria replied.

'Please call me Tom.' They walked together out of Tom's office and through the museum to the Roof Garden. Tom bought them each a cup of coffee and they sat down on a bench on the broad terrace veranda that looked out over Central Park. The trees were still in peak foliage and the park was a sea of red and yellow with patches of green where open expanses of grass poked through. Just in front of them on their right was the tip of Cleopatra's Needle, the great stone obelisk that was brought to New York in the early twentieth century and set up behind the museum.

The sun was warm on their faces. Tom put on his sunglasses, took a deep breath of the fresh autumn air as he gazed at the view, sipped his coffee, and then turned to Victoria Price and said, 'Well that's quite a story, Victoria.'

Tom had not been quite sure how to react but he was intrigued by her story and decided that it was best to take it with a straight face and respond rationally. There were so many historical improbabilities in what she had said. He could point these out to her, and then end the meeting gently.

'I'm not sure what you expect me to say, but let me offer a few thoughts. First, about the objects in our collection that you saw downstairs and which you believe figured in your dream,' Tom continued. 'The wall paintings are from a Roman villa at Boscoreale, a site near Pompeii that was destroyed during the eruption of Mount Vesuvius in AD 79. These paintings were made for that villa, *in situ*, some time in the middle of the first century BC. So you see, it is impossible for you to have seen them in a tomb centuries earlier, much less in the tomb of Alexander the Great. Now, it is generally agreed among scholars that the Boscoreale frescoes are copies of lost Hellenistic paintings from one of the great palaces of a successor king and were commissioned in the years after Alexander's death. The owner of the villa at Boscoreale was probably emulating the opulence of Hellenistic royalty in his own home, displaying his knowledge of earlier masterworks to impress his visitors. In light of the many newly discovered tomb paintings that have been found in Macedonia, notably those at Vergina, I will admit that it has been suggested the paintings downstairs could be copies of paintings that adorned the tomb of Alexander the Great, and perhaps you read this somewhere. But there is, in my opinion, no compelling evidence to support this.'

Tom then turned his attention to the Baker Dancer. 'With regards to the bronze statuette of a veiled and masked dancer, it has been much studied, beginning with an outstanding article in the *American Journal of Archaeology* in 1950 by Dorothy Burr Thompson. It is true that the statuette is linked with Alexandria, the city where Alexander's tomb was located, but this is based primarily on a rather good stylistic argument as well as the hearsay of the dealer who sold it to Mr Baker in the 1940s. This statuette is an icon of Hellenistic art and it has been studied intensively. Scholars generally agree that the naturalism of the figure is a stylistic trend that did not begin until the third century BC, well after the death of Alexander the Great. Based on our current knowledge of Hellenistic art, there is no basis for dating it as early as you suggest, that is to say the late third or early fourth quarter of the fourth century BC, or that it was made before Alexander's death.' Tom paused for a sip of coffee.

'I admit, though, that some of the other details you provide are most interesting. Your remark that Alexander's head rested on his dagger and the *Iliad of the Casket* seems to come straight from Plutarch, but his comment refers to Alexander while he was on campaign. Alexander always kept with him his cherished copy of Homer's *Iliad*, which had belonged to his tutor Aristotle. The knife most probably alludes to the uncertainties of monarchy – it seems an apocryphal anecdote to me, the kind of embellishment that good ancient historians employed to spice up their text. In any case, I am afraid there is no preserved ancient source that states these objects were buried with Alexander.'

Victoria thought for a moment, then asked, 'Has the tomb of Alexander the Great been excavated?'

'No, no – its actual location remains one of the greatest unsolved archaeological mysteries.'

'Do you mean that if I could prove to you that what I dreamed was true, that my body could be discovered in the tomb just as I described it?' Victoria said excitedly.

Tom smiled. 'Well, I'm afraid I doubt that very much, but not simply because I personally don't believe in reincarnation. You see, we do know *something* of the history of the tomb. Alexander died in 323 BC in Babylon and after his death there was considerable debate over where his body would rest. Given its importance as a tangible relic of the great king, his generals realised that the tomb could function as a symbol of the authority and legitimacy of any king in whose kingdom it resided. His remains were mummified and laid in state in Babylon while his successors decided on his final resting place. The body was eventually placed on a magnificent cart of delicately wrought gold. As his body was wheeled in procession, people from all over the known world came to mourn the loss of their great king. It was quite a spectacle and the funerary cart was accompanied by hundreds of marching soldiers. Originally the body was to be brought to Macedonia according to Perdiccas's plan but Ptolemy took it to Egypt instead. It is thought that a monumental Macedonian-style tomb was built for the king at Memphis, south

of the Nile Delta, where he was first buried. That is
the place where your dream would have taken place.
However, sometime early in the third century BC
Ptolemy moved Alexander's body to Alexandria, the
seat of his new kingdom in Egypt. So even if you had
died in Alexander's tomb your body would have been
discovered long ago and removed. Ptolemy built
another monumental tomb for the great king's remains
within the city walls of Alexandria. That tomb became
known as the Soma, the Greek word for body, probably named after Alexander's own body. In subsequent
centuries, though, the tomb was reopened and it
became a pilgrimage site.' Tom paused, took another
sip of his coffee, and then continued.

'Alexander was buried in a gold sarcophagus as
you describe but that sarcophagus was removed in
the second century BC and melted down to fund the
war chest of another Ptolemaic king. It seems that at
that time the body was placed within a translucent
alabaster, or possibly glass, sarcophagus that allowed
visitors to view the body without disturbing it. I
imagine it was something like a museum case. The
ingenuity of Hellenistic artisans is quite extraordinary.
Still, the lid of the sarcophagus seems to have been
removed from time to time for especially important
visitors. For example, the first Roman emperor,
Augustus, came to pay his respects after his victory
at Actium, where he defeated Mark Anthony and

Cleopatra and gained control of Ptolemaic Egypt. It is said that Augustus placed a crown of gold upon Alexander's head and that he touched the king's nose, accidentally crushing it as it turned into dust. The eccentric and unusually cruel Roman emperor Caligula is said to have taken Alexander's armour from the tomb and to have worn it from time to time in his Palatine palace in Rome while he conferred with the god Jove, whom he believed was his ancestor. Alexander, of course, also claimed descent from Zeus, the Greek version of Jove, and was declared a god himself shortly after his death – if not before in some regions.

'The last clear record of a visitor to the tomb was in the third century AD when the Roman emperor Caracalla paid homage to Alexander sometime around AD 215. Like many rulers before him, Caracalla saw himself as Alexander's successor and cast himself in that light in his imperial propaganda. After Caracalla, the history of the tomb is pretty much unknown – at least until very recently.'

The location of Alexander the Great's tomb was a subject of great interest to Tom. He realised he had been jabbering on at great length so he looked at Victoria Price to gauge her interest.

She was still holding his gaze so he continued, 'Well, there are various stories of the tomb in later times but none seem to be based in truth. The writer E.M.

Forster, who incidentally spent time in Alexandria, recounted a marvellous tale of an eighteenth-century guard at a mosque who claimed to have come upon a buried chamber in which Alexander was encased in glass, wearing a gold diadem and surrounded by old books – presumably priceless texts from the famous library at Alexandria. According to another tradition, the remains of Alexander were removed from his tomb prior to the sack of Alexandria in the sixth century AD and were brought to a monastery in the desert for safe keeping along with other holy relics. A recent book has suggested that Alexander's remains were actually taken from the tomb even later, in the ninth century, and placed in Saint Mark's Cathedral in Venice where they are revered as the body of Saint Mark himself. Tantalising as these stories and theories are, they lack any real factual basis. However, a clue did come to light recently in an excavation, actually the excavation that I work at on Crete. The evidence suggests a very different fate for the remains of Alexander the Great.' Tom looked at Victoria who was quite fascinated with what he was saying.

'For some years we've been excavating a major sanctuary of Zeus at Dikta in eastern Crete. Recently, we discovered a shrine to Alexander the Great within the sacred precinct. Such shrines are known to have existed in various places around the Hellenistic world, most notably in Macedonia and Asia Minor. The one at Dikta seems to have been especially important because it had a very long life, having first been erected in the third century BC, when Crete was under Ptolemaic control, and then refurbished at least twice, in the second century AD, probably during the reign of the emperor Hadrian, and again in the third century AD when the entire sanctuary seems to have had a renaissance. As I mentioned to you earlier, Alexander cultivated strong associations with Zeus, so it's not surprising that his successors would have set up a shrine to him at one of the most important sanctuaries to Zeus in the Greek world. Also, with Crete under Ptolemaic sovereignty at this time it would have been a savvy political move since the greatest shrine to Alexander was in Alexandria itself, the Ptolemaic capital. In fact, a marble stele set up in front of the shrine mentions the location of the Soma in Alexandria, a new independent reference to the location of the tomb in the third century BC. This past excavation season we also uncovered a second stele dating to the time of a third-century refurbishment of the sanctuary. This stele was set up next to the other and earlier one. The text is quite worn in places but it nonetheless records an amazing new piece of information for the trail of the Soma. It states that Alexander's remains were removed from Alexandria in the third century during the reign of Trebonianus Gallus, who reigned from AD 251 to 253.'

'That's amazing, Mr Carr. Does it say where the Soma was moved to?' Victoria asked excitedly.

'Unfortunately, that part is very worn and difficult to read but we are still studying it.' In fact, there was more that Tom could have said at this point but he didn't really know this woman and the implications for the discovery of the tomb were so great that he thought it best to keep quiet. 'So you see it's my turn to sound a bit crazy.' He laughed. 'I am actually trying to locate the tomb of Alexander the Great. You can imagine my surprise when you told me about your vision. Still, considering the facts, as far as we know them, it seems most likely that your vision was the result of something other than the recollection of your past life.'

Tom looked at his watch. 'It's 1:15, and I'm afraid that I am now late for that appointment. I really must go. Thank you for sharing your experience with me. It was a pleasure meeting you, Victoria. Do take it easy with that arm of yours. The nurse said that you have quite a bruise.'

He stood up to signal that the meeting was over and smiled at Victoria.

She said: 'I know what I've said must sound crazy to you and, in a way, I guess I didn't really expect you to believe me, no matter how real the experience was for me. It's just that I had an overwhelming sense that it was important for me to tell you while the details were still fresh in my mind. Frankly, before working with my psychiatrist, I would have been inclined to agree with you about the vision but I am not so sure now. To my knowledge, I've never had any previous thoughts on Alexander the Great in my life. I want to learn more about him. Since you are an expert, can you recommend any reading materials for me?'

Tom thought for a moment and then replied, 'Well, I'd suggest you start with the primary sources. Unfortunately, practically nothing survives from Alexander's lifetime but there are later ancient biographies. I'd begin with Arrian and Plutarch. There's a modern biography by Peter Green that is also quite good. If you are in town next week, a new exhibition is opening at the Morgan Library, featuring a magnificent manuscript of the Alexander Romance that they have in their collection. It has marvellous illustrations of Alexander's life and later legends. Because of the recent conservation that the library has undertaken, they've had to unpick the book's binding and have taken the opportunity to exhibit all the individual illustrated pages. It is probably the only time that anyone will get the chance to see the book like that since it will be rebound after the exhibition. I've been down to the Morgan and seen some of the pages while they were being given the preservation treatment; they are breathtakingly beautiful. I intend to catch the show myself when I return from Europe.'

Tom's phone buzzed in his pocket and he took it out and answered it, motioning to Victoria Price to wait one minute.

It was the receptionist from the Department of Greek and Roman Art. 'Arthur is waiting for you in Objects Conservation. I've got him holding on line one. What should I tell him?'

'Tell him I'm on my way,' Tom said and he ended the call. 'That was my next appointment. Look, here's my card. I really do have to go but if there is anything that I can do for you with regards to the collection, please don't hesitate to contact me. It really was a pleasure meeting you, Victoria. Good luck.'

'Thank you for these suggestions. I'll look up the books and will definitely catch the exhibition at the Morgan Library next week. Thank you for hearing me out, too, Tom. It meant a lot to me.' With that Victoria looked him straight in the eye, slipped his card into her purse and offered him her hand. 'I think I'm going to sit here for a little while. It's such a beautiful day and the view is amazing.'

Tom took her hand, shook it warmly and said 'Goodbye' before he turned to head off to the Objects Conservation Laboratory.

4

As Tom walked away from Victoria Price, his thoughts turned back to the Tomb of Alexander and his work. He felt that he could be on the verge of a breakthrough with the help of the new technical device that Arthur Peebles had developed for him and he was very excited to see how the thing worked. Finally, he was going to get to test it out – and just in time, too, since he was leaving for Greece tomorrow. Arthur had performed miracles for him in the past. In fact, Arthur had been at work on the device since Tom had told him about the discovery of the second Diktaian inscription in the summer. From their discussions together over the past several months, it now seemed possible that Tom might actually be able to read its worn text and bring to light the location of Alexander the Great's tomb.

This was not the tomb of Victoria Price's dream, Tom thought, but the actual final resting place of Alexander the Great, perhaps the greatest military leader of all time. Victoria's story did have a haunting quality to it, but Tom was not convinced that her vision was a true recollection, even though she clearly believed in it. It just showed what a hold the mere thought of Alexander's tomb had on the imagination. It was no wonder that it should exert this fascination since the royal tombs of ancient Egypt were known to contain untold treasure. In fact, the only unplundered royal tomb ever discovered in Egypt was that of the boy king Tutankhamun. What riches it had held – and King Tut had been a relatively minor pharaoh. Alexander the Great, though, had conquered much of the known world, including the kingdom of Persia with its king's vast treasury in Babylon. People had been searching without success for the location of the tomb in Alexandria for centuries. But the inscription at Dikta clearly indicated that Alexander's tomb had been moved, which meant that they all might well have been looking in the wrong place.

To locate and excavate the Tomb of Alexander would be the crowning achievement of Tom's career. What wonders it might contain! What more could be learned from it about Alexander and his remarkable life? It got Tom's adrenalin pumping every time he thought about it.

The labs of the Objects Conservation Department were set up at different locations within the museum, in the basement and on the roof respectively, where at any rate in the latter location they had good access to natural light for their work. Tom was heading for Arthur Peebles's upstairs office. Arthur was the senior conservator and a brilliant man with an extraordinary command of his field. In the old days, the conservation lab might well have been called the repair shop and while much of its work still revolved around the cleaning and restoration of works of art, the museum was also at the forefront of conservation research. Arthur Peebles was constantly exploring new scientific techniques for the examination of artworks.

Tom came to the Department's main entrance and rang the bell. The receptionist buzzed him in. 'He's expecting you,' he said.

Tom continued down the hall and seeing that Arthur's door was open, he walked straight in. Arthur was seated at his desk, holding up a radiograph of a bronze Buddha and studying it intently. Tom dropped into the chair opposite him. Arthur still hadn't noticed that he'd come in. Tom cleared his throat and said, 'Hello, Arthur.'

Arthur lowered the X-ray image and looked across his desk.

'Oh, Tom. Hello. Good to see you. I was waiting for you and then got absorbed in this X-ray. It's the damnedest thing. Quite amazing. Here on inspection for purchase. The piece looked too good to be true, so I thought I'd better give it the full treatment, just to be sure. I'm still waiting on the metal analyses. You can't be too careful these days. I think it's going to be okay, though, which will please the curator no end since she never had any doubts to begin with.'

Tom returned Arthur's gaze and waited for him to continue.

'But you're here about your inscription.' Arthur had a way of downplaying even the most important topics – he was always working on something important – and he could see that Tom was eager to see the device that he had created for him.

Arthur continued, 'I know you're off to Greece tomorrow so I won't hold you up with shoptalk. I think you're going to be pleased, though. We've been testing out the instrument and it is finally ready for you. I think that it will do the job. Of course, these are not exactly field conditions . . .'

Arthur looked at him and smiled. Since he probably ran the world's most sophisticated laboratory for the study and conservation of works of art this was some-thing of an understatement.

'Follow me and I'll show you how it works.'

Arthur flipped his longish salt-and-pepper hair from his eyes and headed out the door. He had a slight limp and a lazy eye, endearing features that together with his unmatched knowledge of the inner workings of things, how they were made centuries ago and his understanding of the effects of the passage of time on works of art, caused Tom to think of Hephaistos, the lame god of bronze-working. People like Arthur were an essential component of the museum's staff. After all, one of the primary missions of the museum was to preserve its collections for all time. This was a tremendous responsibility as minimising the ravages of time could be a constant battle. To do this effectively, you needed to know what you were up against, and Arthur, through the years, had made many important contributions to the field of conservation studies.

They walked into the main lab, a large clean white room with tables set up at regular intervals. Conservators were working busily at stations throughout the room. Large ducts were set up over some tables to carry noxious fumes away from those who were working with hazardous chemicals. At other tables microscopes and large magnifying glasses had been set up to assist in the close examination of artworks. Various dental picks and other surgical instruments were carefully arranged and ready for use. Arthur led Tom to the far corner of the room where an ancient stone inscription had been placed.

'Without getting into the science of it, this device is quite simple to operate.'

Arthur picked up a small instrument, which was not much bigger than a point-and-shoot digital camera attached to a framework with adjustable straps that extended from its sides.

'You just affix the straps to the sides of the stone. Since your stone at Dikta is broken and you provided us with an outline of the contours of the break, we've created a template for you that you can fit onto the stone to get a square edge for attaching the instrument.'

Arthur held up the template for Tom to see.

'Just fit the template into place and secure the device with the straps. When you turn it on allow it some time to power up. When the light turns green, it's ready. Press the scan button and move the device across the face of the stone, following the lines of the inscription.' Arthur paused. 'For the best results do one line at a time. It will collect the data and then you can download it to your computer through the USB connection. We've installed the software on your hard drive – it's called "Red Phantom". The icon is in the form of a Casper-like red ghost.'

Arthur pointed to Tom's laptop set up on the table. Tom had left it with the department the day before.

'Yes, very cute,' Tom said.

After double-clicking on the icon, Arthur continued, 'Okay, I've already downloaded the images of the stone that you sent up for us to test the device. Nothing too surprising but there are some worn letters as you can see, here and here.' Arthur pointed to a photographic image of the stone on the computer screen.

'Yes,' Tom replied. 'It's a Hellenistic dedicatory stele. So the text is not very long. The first part of the patronym, or family name, is missing. We have [. . .] OLEMOS. The first three letters are worn away. There are numerous possible restorations.' Tom instinctively turned back to the actual object, which was sitting on the table. 'Also the last part of the inscription is worn but we know the formula. It must be AN[ETHEKEN] or DE[DICATED (this)].'

'Okay, let's look at the scanned inscription.' Arthur clicked the mouse and a different image of the inscription appeared. Tom was amazed to see that there was considerably more of the writing visible on the screen than was visible on the stone itself.

'It's fortunate that most stone inscriptions from antiquity were painted red to make the letters more readable. This device picks up the composition of the paint that was used to fill the letters. You can see that where the paint has faded on the surface it has leached over the millennia into the stone itself, leaving a ghost impression that's often not visible to the naked eye. The scanner is able to read this information and reveal, in most cases, the form of the missing letters.'

'That's amazing, Arthur,' Tom said as he looked at the inscription on the screen. The extant carved letters were very distinct and then in the worn places the images of the remaining letters were now also visible, less sharp but quite distinct. The name was EUPOLEMOS, a common Greek name in Hellenistic times, and the last word was ANETHEKEN as Tom had predicted.

Arthur smiled, 'You know that old tailor's joke,

"Euripides, Eumenides"? Then, of course, there was the great fifth-century BC Athenian statesman, "Testicles" . . .'

'That's Perikles, Arthur. Please, stop it. This is serious. Names are important. To know the name of the person who dedicated this stele, even if we don't know anything else, takes away the anonymity. It provides us with a human connection.'

At that moment, the department's receptionist walked up to the table and spoke to Tom.

'Your office is on the phone, Tom. They said it was urgent. I've put the call through to the line here. Just pick up the receiver and press the button by the blinking light.'

Tom picked up the receiver.

'This is Tom. What's up?'

'Sorry to interrupt your meeting, Tom, but your neighbour called. He says that your apartment has been broken into. He's called the police, but he said you'd better come right away.'

'Okay, I'll grab my things and leave immediately.' Tom hung up the phone.

'Arthur, I'm so sorry, but something's come up. Apparently, my home has been burgled.' Tom tried not to look too concerned but he was. It was a bad omen, having this happen just before his trip. His thoughts raced for a moment to the break-in at the temple of Alexander at Dikta during the summer . . .

but he was jumping to conclusions. It would be too much of a coincidence for this burglary to be related to that event. He dismissed the idea.

Tom was sweating a little now as he spoke to Arthur. 'I've got to go. I think I understand the basics, though. It's a fantastic new analytical tool and it is going to prove very helpful indeed on this trip. I can't thank you enough for all your hard work to get this ready in time for my return to Dikta. I know I don't need to lecture you on the importance of being able to read the inscription there and what it may tell us about the tomb of Alexander.'

'Good luck, Tom. We'll be here rooting for you. With any luck, traces of that illegible text will emerge like the Lady of the Lake with Excalibur held high in her hand, showing us the way to the tomb of Alexander.' Arthur liked to make analogies with Arthurian legend whenever possible. He continued, 'We were just about done here, anyway. There are some ways of refining the image, tweaking it, but we can help you with that when you get back. Don't give it another thought. If you have any problems in the field, you know where to reach us.'

'Sounds good, Arthur,' Tom replied. 'I'll be back in a couple of weeks and I'll give you a full report then.'

Tom took the laptop computer and the device, packed them into their cases and headed back to his office where he picked up his briefcase. When he got to his car, an Aegean-blue vintage Carmen Gia, he opened the boot and carefully put everything inside. He slipped into the driver's seat, started up the engine and pulled out of the parking garage. There was no time to lose.

5

SOON TOM CARR was barrelling down FDR Drive along the East River. It was a beautiful crisp autumn day and he had the windows open to catch the breeze. Traffic was light and he made good time.

'What the hell is going on?' he thought, as he crossed the Brooklyn Bridge and headed down Court Street towards his home in Carroll Gardens. He had never had a break-in at his home before. It was considered to be a safe area. In fact, it was an old Mafia neighbourhood, so people always joked that it was very secure.

Tom turned onto Union and then made a right onto Hoyt. A few blocks later he pulled up at his home on President Street. Carroll Gardens, a small, charming district that bordered the Gowanus Canal, had originally been primarily an Irish blue-collar working-class neighbourhood in the early nineteenth century when it was first built. Over time it had become predominantly Italian and a favourite hangout of the Mafia before they moved out of the city to New Jersey. According to local legend, one *capo* had kept a lion in his basement in the 1970s for intimidation purposes.

There was a police squad car parked in front of Tom's house. Two policemen were talking with Tom's neighbour Sal on the sidewalk by the iron fence that enclosed his front garden. Sal was known informally as the mayor of President Street. A born leader, he knew everyone and everything that went on. Retired, and a spritely eighty years old, he always watched out for everyone on the street, especially their cars, making sure that no one got a parking ticket: the local laws required that cars be moved several times a week for street cleaning.

When Sal saw Tom, he called to him. 'Oh Tom, it's good that you've arrived. These officers want to speak to you. I've told them everything I know.'

Sal proceeded to repeat the story again for Tom. 'I saw the guy coming out of your apartment and thought something was wrong. You didn't say you were expecting any visitors or having any work done. You see, this guy was a tall fella, some muscles, you know. He wore a bike shirt, and some kind of coat. He was hiding something in his jacket – I could tell. So I walked up to him and was about to ask who he was, but when he saw me coming he started walking real fast to a car that was double-parked by the hydrant. I smelled a rat, and it wasn't no four-legged rat either.' Sal looked at Tom and winked.

'Some guy was at the wheel and he fired up the engine. He was wearing sunglasses and a hat so I couldn't see him too good. The tall fella jumped in the back seat and they sped off down the street. It was a big old Buick, a sedan, black, with New York plates. My eyesight isn't so good any more, though, so I didn't catch the numbers on the plate. It was the kind of car you still see plenty of in Brooklyn but less and less these days with these crazy gas prices. I wouldn't be surprised if they boosted it from some-where around here. You know, a lot of people park their cars in this neighbourhood and then take the subway to the city for work.' Sal had said his piece.

One of the police officers spoke up, 'Thank you for your statement, Mr Angelo. You've been very helpful. If you think of anything else important, here's my card. Please give us a call at the precinct. We need to speak to Mr Carr now.'

Turning to Tom, the police officer said, 'Can we continue this inside your apartment, Mr Carr?'

'Yes, officers. Please follow me. Let's see what the damage is. Sal, I'll see you later, okay?'

'Okay, Tom, you know where to find me,' Sal said.

Tom opened the little iron gate and he and the cops walked down the long pathway that was bordered by perennials still in bloom. Tom walked up his front steps and unlocked the door. There were no signs of a forced entry. Tom occupied the top three storeys and rented out the basement to an old woman whom he rarely saw. She was basically an invalid these days and never left the apartment, though a nurse checked on her every day. The basement had a separate entrance under the porch steps. When Tom had bought the place over fifteen years ago she and her rent-controlled apartment had been part of the deal. He'd thought she'd be long gone by now but she was still hanging on and was determined not to move into a nursing home.

They walked into the hallway and Tom placed his jacket on the coat rack. The hallway opened into the living room with its tall ceilings and elegant late-nineteenth-century mouldings. A large Piranesi engraving of the Classical Greek temples at Paestum in southern Italy hung in a gilt frame over the fire-place. Bay windows looked out onto the garden in the front. An overstuffed couch and two antique chairs were placed round a glass coffee table that was supported on a massive marble Corinthian column capital. The catalogue of the new Greek and Roman Galleries at the Met lay on the coffee table, together with several other large art books.

'Everything seems to be in order here,' Tom said and they passed through the dining room and into the kitchen. He noticed that the sterling silver candlesticks were still at the centre of the dining-room table where they always stood. He made a mental note that this didn't seem to be a 'smash-and-grab' burglary for immediately fenceable items. He checked the kitchen door that opened onto the backyard, and it showed no signs of being tampered with. The police officers checked all the windows, and every one of them was locked.

Next they went upstairs to the second floor, the policemen following close behind Tom.

'There are two bedrooms, a den, and two bathrooms on the second floor,' Tom explained. 'The entire third floor is devoted to my study.'

Again, everything seemed in order. The three of them made their way upstairs to the study. Tom had restored the building when he'd bought it and had tried to adhere to the original architectural layout. Carroll Gardens was a landmarked area so there were limitations on what kind of renovations could and could not be done, but the top floor was the one space that he had changed dramatically. He had knocked through the interior walls, turning the space into one large room. Floor-to-ceiling built-in book-cases lined the two long walls. Three large circular fans hung from the tall ceiling. Tom's massive mahogany desk was situated at the back and faced inwards so that the light from the rear windows streamed in from behind. At the front end of the long room, an oak library table benefited from the light provided by the front bay windows. On either side of the table stood two eighteenth-century globes, one terrestrial and the other celestial, each set on carefully tooled wooden stands. Next to the reading table two glass vitrines contained assorted antiquities and unusual stones and shells from around the world. In the middle of the room two leather-upholstered chairs and a couch stood round a low table. As Tom's gaze turned to his desk, a growing feeling of horror gnawed at his insides. He saw that the drawers of the desk had been pulled out: things were in disarray and he saw immediately what was missing. His personal laptop, which usually sat open in front of his chair, was gone. It had all his computer files on it. Everything he was working on now and years of earlier research.

'My computer's gone!' Tom shouted as he ran over to the desk to double-check. 'I always keep it here.' He pointed at the centre of the desk. The power cord was still lying where it would have connected with the laptop.

'That must have been what the man had under his jacket when Sal saw him leaving the house.' Tom was visibly agitated now and was pacing back and forth as he spoke to the policemen. 'I have to say that I find it very strange, officers. There are plenty of things in this house that would bring a thief more money than my computer, and yet it seems that's all they were after. It's not even the latest model, but it had a lot of personal files on it and all my archaeological work. Thank God I keep a backup of everything at work.' Tom was sweating now, his face turning red.

'Why don't you sit down for a minute, Mr Carr?' The officers motioned to the nearby couch and they all sat down. 'We have a few questions for you. It is strange that there are no signs of forced entry. Does anyone else live here with you, Mr Carr? Does anyone have the key to your place?' one of the officers asked.

'Does the description of the man Sal saw match anyone you know?' the other officer added.

'Only Sal, the man you just met, has a spare key to my place. No one else lives here. There's an old lady who rents out the basement but she doesn't have a key to the rest of the house. The man he described doesn't sound like anyone I know. I can't imagine why he broke into my place and stole my computer.'

'Anything else unusual happen recently? Anything out of the ordinary?' the first officer asked.

'Come to think of it, I did have a strange telephone message about a month ago. My name was in the papers over the summer. I work at an archaeological excavation in Greece, on the island of Crete. We made a remarkable discovery, a shrine to Alexander the Great. In front of the shrine we discovered a sacred text with a reference to the tomb of Alexander. Actually, it's now the last secure datable reference to the tomb, the location of which remains one of the great unsolved archaeological mysteries. It caused a mini-sensation in the press: articles ran in the *New York Times* and the *Herald Tribune*, and the Associated

Press picked it up so the story appeared all around the world. Well, as I mentioned, I came home to a message on my answering machine about a month ago. It was a man's voice and he said he belonged to an organisation, a secret society, whose origins stemmed back to Alexander. He said that the preservation of Alexander's tomb was very important to them and was something not to be desecrated by archaeological investigations. He urged me to call him back at a California number, asking me to provide him with any information that I had learned.' Tom paused. 'I figured it was a practical joke or someone a little off their rocker so I just deleted the message and haven't heard anything since.'

'Sounds like a crank call to me, Mr Carr. What do you think, Charlie?' the first officer said, turning to his partner.

'Oh yeah,' replied Charlie. 'I wouldn't give that another thought. Probably some whack-job getting his jollies off at your expense.'

After the officers left, Tom grabbed a beer out of the fridge and sat upstairs in his study. He was worried about what he had lost on his computer. Was *everything* really on his work computer? The more he thought about it, the more it started to make him mad. It was such an invasion of privacy. Then his thoughts turned to the break-in at the site during the summer. Could someone be after his research on

Alexander? It seemed too incredible. Scholars didn't go to such lengths to steal information. At least, he didn't think they did.

All his finances were on the computer, too. Now he was worried as he realised that practically his whole life was filed on that computer, from photos to tax documents. Should he cancel his credit cards? There wasn't time before his trip to do all that; he couldn't leave without any financial plastic. He'd just have to monitor the situation. He thought again that it was not a good omen for his trip to Europe.

6

THE BLACK VOLVO station wagon sped down the highway. Traffic was starting to build on the Long Island Expressway as people left New York City for the weekend. Victoria Price sat in the front passenger seat and looked across at her old college room-mate, Cynthia Madden – now Cynthia Madden Wilmerding. It was good to see her old friend again. They corresponded now and then and spoke on the telephone once in a while but they had not spent any real time together in ages. In fact, Victoria had not seen Cynthia since her wedding four years ago last summer. She was looking forward to this weekend and the chance to relax with Cynthia and her family in East Hampton, eat good food, drink good wine, and have soulful walks on the beach.

'What a relief! The kids have finally settled in back there. They look like angels when they sleep,' Cynthia said as she glanced in the rear-view mirror.

'Now you can tell me about your visit to the Met,' Cynthia continued. 'I am so jealous. I think I haven't been to a cultural institution in at least three years. With two children under three, I'm lucky if I ever get out of the house to do something for *me*. Cultural institutions, unfortunately, are not as high on the list as they used to be when I was single. I am happy if I can get a mani-pedi and my hair coloured, for goodness' sake.' Cynthia paused.

Victoria had so much to tell her friend but she was not ready to talk about her past-life experience at the Met this morning. She was still figuring out what it meant to her. She needed to talk to her therapist about it before she talked to any friends or family. The whole experience had been unnerving for her. She was a Catholic, for heaven's sake. Reincarnation was not part of her belief system. Her parents definitely would not understand and she was not sure that Cynthia would, either. It had taken her a long time with her therapist even to be open to the idea. Now she had just had a breakthrough. She had vividly recalled a past-life episode. It was mind-blowing. She needed to choose her words carefully with Cynthia, though. She was just not ready to open up about it with her.

'I went to see the new Greek and Roman galleries. It was extraordinary, revelatory even. I really connected with some of the works of art.' That was as far as Victoria would go about revelations.

She continued, 'What an amazing space. The light on the sculptures was incredible. What a beautiful collection. They have some absolutely exquisite things. I wish I had brought my sketchbook. I took a tour with one of the curators. He and I even had coffee afterwards.'

'You had coffee with a curator from the Met? How did you do that?' Cynthia's jaw dropped. 'You're incredible, Victoria,' she continued. 'You always amazed me, you know, with how you get people to warm up to you. And it's not just because you are drop-dead gorgeous. Doors opened for you at college. You had the nerve to ask, too.'

'Actually, *he* asked *me* to join him for coffee,' Victoria replied, leaving out the fact that it was she who had made the initial contact.

'Really . . . So what was he like? Was he handsome?'

Victoria surprised herself as she answered, 'Yes, he was.' She paused and then continued speaking with a thoughtful look on her face as she described Tom Carr. 'I'd guess he was about five, maybe ten years older than me.'

'An older man.' Cynthia smiled approvingly as she drove.

'He was tall, about five foot eleven, broad-shouldered, dark hair, tan with piercing grey-blue eyes and a kind, strong face.'

'Sounds positively dishy,' Cynthia exclaimed.

'But we mostly talked about the art,' Victoria continued. 'It was not the kind of coffee that you are thinking of. It wasn't a date. We share an interest in Alexander the Great. He recommended that I go see an exhibition that opens next week at the Morgan Library.'

'I didn't know you were interested in antiquity. As I remember, you tended towards modern art in college,' Cynthia replied.

'That's true. It's something that I started fairly recently, since I've been living in Rome. Antiquity is all around you in Rome. It has become a part of my life in a way that it never was before. It's been inspiring for my painting.'

'Well, maybe this is the kind of guy you *should* be dating. Not that hot Italian lover you wrote me about who turned out to be a mama's boy. What was his name? Lorenzo?'

'Lorenzo, Lorenzo,' Victoria sighed. 'He *was* a great lover.' Victoria paused for a moment as she thought of the passion that they had shared. Even the mention of his name still brought a feeling of pain to her heart. 'But he was a terrible partner. He definitely had his own issues – besides his mother and don't get me started on her. He had a wandering eye and when I found him cheating on me with another woman that was the end. It took me months to get over him.'

Victoria had been saying this for weeks but now was the first time that it actually felt true. 'I'm finally feeling like myself again. That whole thing threw me into a terrible depression. My painting took a rather dark turn. You'd laugh if you saw all the still lifes I did of skulls and rotting, overripe fruit.' Victoria smiled, thinking of it and how transparent it had seemed after she had talked to her therapist about it.

'But it was good for me,' she continued. 'It helped, I think. I'm no longer in such a dark place. I'm not sure that I am ready for a serious relationship, not just yet. Still, maybe you are right about Tom Carr – that's the curator's name. There was something about him that was attractive to me. I'm going to send him a quick message to thank him for taking the time out of his busy day.'

She pulled out Tom's card to read his e-mail address, typing it into her BlackBerry. Then she wrote a short message and sent it off.

Victoria looked out the window and indulged the fantasy for a few more moments. She thought about sitting in the Roof Garden with Tom Carr in the bright early-afternoon autumn light, the slight chill in the air counteracted by the warm coffee mug in her hand as she looked intently at Tom and listened to him, entranced by his stories of Alexander the Great. She realised that she was daydreaming and thought out loud. 'But I don't think I could do a long-distance relationship. And I'm not planning on moving back just yet. I know I won't live in Rome for ever but I am enjoying it. It has been great for my work. I think that I have matured as a painter.'

'You never know when love is going to strike,'

Cynthia replied, not realising that Victoria was talking to herself. 'Look at me. I met my soulmate here in New York right after college and I couldn't be happier. The last thing I was looking for was a serious relationship right out of college but I really believe that Newt and I were meant to be together. That it was our destiny. You'll know when you meet Mister Right. Of course, there's no hurry. Once it happens and you start having children, wow, your life will change like you don't know what. It's all for the good – but what a difference.' Cynthia looked in the rear-view mirror again, checking on the children.

'Well, I'm not ready for all that just yet. Don't get too serious on me, Cynthia,' Victoria chided, looking out the window again and smiling. 'This weekend is supposed to be an escape. *Que sera, sera*. Whatever will be, will be. That's my philosophy.'

7

OSKAR WILLIAMS SAT at the large desk in his study, staring intently into the screen of Tom Carr's stolen laptop computer, scrolling through entries while smoking a little Dutch cigar. He clicked on a document detailing the travel arrangements for Carr's European trip and moved closer to the screen to read it. Then he sat back in his chair and exhaled smoke as he thought to himself.

So Carr is off to Athens today and he'll be in Rome in a week. After a week in Rome he flies to London and then back to New York. When he is in Greece he's going to Crete to sign off on the conservation of the Alexander statue at Dikta. That does not give me much time. Surely they'll move the piece to a more secure location once they have finished working on it.

Oskar turned to the computer screen again and got into Carr's e-mail. He opened a recent message from the Greek conservator and downloaded the attached images.

Well, well, well – the conservation has gone well. A detailed image of the head of Alexander filled the screen. It looked magnificent. *I was right to wait,*

Oskar thought. *Even the blue of the eyes and the golden eyelashes are preserved. Cleaning can be such delicate work. It's so easy to make a mistake and lose what was there or alter it irrevocably. I don't have anyone who can do work like that on marble.* Oskar put his head right up to the screen to take in all the detail. The light from the screen gave his face an eerie glow.

After a minute, he sat back again and took another long drag on the small cigar. *I have not had a head of Alexander for years,* he mused. *Not since that fine life-size terracotta portrait from Afghanistan. I was lucky to get that out during the Afghan war between the Soviets and the mujahedin in the 1980s. They so rarely become available . . .*

Oskar wondered what price such a monumental head of Alexander the Great would bring. Of course, he could not sell it on the open market. But he knew of people who would be interested. People who didn't care about provenance as long as it was the real thing. Oskar looked at the image on the screen again. And this time it was the real thing, all right. Oskar thought back to the night he had stood before the imposing statue in its temple, the moonlight illuminating the chiselled features of the legendary king. It would take a lot of arranging and there were risks involved. He needed to think more about it before proceeding.

Oskar picked up his mobile phone from the desk and called a number in Greece.

'Manolis, it's Oskar. Look, I need you for a job. There's a man arriving in Athens on Sunday. His flight gets in during the late morning: Delta Flight 88 from New York. He'll be staying at the American School of Classical Studies. That's in Kolonaki, right above the hospital. Do you know it? Good. I want you to keep an eye on him for me, okay? Follow him wherever he goes. I want full, regular reports. Don't do anything stupid. We need him alive and what's more I don't want him to know he's being tailed. Be discreet. It will be the usual arrangement. I'll wire you the money. Call me on Monday – or sooner if you have any news.' Oskar ended the call and turned back to the computer.

There was a new e-mail message from a woman named Victoria. It was entitled 'Tomb of Alexander'. Oskar raised one eyebrow excitedly, a wicked smile coming to his lips. He looked across his desk at the squeezes he had made at Dikta of the inscriptions on the two stelae that stood in front of the temple to Alexander the Great. He had studied the inscriptions carefully but the later reference to the Tomb of Alexander was not complete. It only stated that the tomb had been moved from its location in Alexandria to somewhere else. The crucial part of the text was too worn to read. It was SO typical. Archaeologists would announce in the papers that they had made an important new discovery that awaited further study but in fact their information was woefully incomplete. It was a tease. Still, perhaps Carr had made better headway or had some ideas for restoring the lost part of the inscription that were buried somewhere in his computer's excavation files. Oskar needed more time to see what was there and if it was any help. Perhaps this woman's e-mail would save him some time. He clicked on the message to open it and read:

Dear Tom: It was so nice to meet you earlier today. Thank you for taking the time to hear what I had to say about the Tomb of Alexander. It's funny that in very different ways we are both searching for the same thing. I appreciated your insights and I will definitely go see the Alexander exhibition at the Morgan Library on Tuesday morning. I'll keep in touch and I hope that your research trip to Europe goes well.

Yours sincerely, Victoria Price

Not so illuminating, Oskar thought, *but a fellow seeker of the tomb. Why can't people express themselves more clearly?* Oskar was getting angry. He called to his assistant: 'Nestor, come in here.'

A minute later a compact, wiry, but muscular brown-haired young man entered Oskar's study.

'Yes, boss?' Nestor asked.

'I need you to trace this e-mail. Find out who this woman Victoria Price is and where she lives. I want a photograph of her by Monday morning.'

'Okay, boss.'

'Also find out what this exhibition is at the Morgan Library. I'll go there myself on Tuesday morning and kill two birds with one stone. Why am I only learning about this Alexander exhibition now, Nestor? You know of my passion for Alexander. I must be kept informed.'

'Sorry, boss. I'll get right on it. There is a man here to see you, boss. His name is Luigi. He's brought something to show you. He said that you'd want to see him.'

'Here? Why didn't you tell me before now? Where is he?' Oskar's blood was beginning to boil.

'He's waiting downstairs in the lobby. Shall I send him up?'

'Yes, you idiot. I can't have people like that loitering in the lobby. Supposing a client comes in. It doesn't look good, Nestor, does it?'

'Sorry, boss, right away boss.' Nestor turned and headed straight for the door.

Oskar walked into the living room and waited for the man. A few minutes later Nestor came back in, accompanied by a rough-looking Italian man. The man was wearing a heavy peasant jacket and workman jeans and was holding his cap in one hand and a paper shopping bag in the other.

'Luigi, what are you doing here? You know I told you never to come here.'

'I'm sorry, Mr Williams. It's just that I've got something important. Something that I thought you'd want to see right away. It's a Greek cup with very fine painting.'

Oskar controlled his expression so as to reveal no discernible interest. 'Well, since you're here, out with it. I might as well have a look but I haven't got all day. I am very busy.'

The man sat down on the couch and took a bubble-wrapped package out of the shopping bag. He started to undo it.

'You know the economy is terrible these days. No one is buying antiquities. I barely make ends meet. And look at the overheads I've got.' Oskar lapsed into his usual bargaining gambit.

Luigi pushed the bubble wrap aside and opened the cardboard box that it had concealed. Inside, fragments of pottery were individually wrapped in tissue paper. He started to uncover each piece and lay them on the coffee table in front of him.

Oskar paced back and forth, appearing to be deep in thought. Then he turned to Luigi and said, 'My God, I forgot I've got a client coming in fifteen minutes. I can't do this now, Luigi. I think you'd better come back another time – maybe next week. You can leave the piece here if you like. It will be safe.' Oskar could see the look of horror on the man's face. It was clear that he had planned on walking out of there with some cash.

'No, no, Mr Williams. This won't take long. It is an extraordinary piece. I know that you will want it. I would not have come all this way myself otherwise. It's something my cousin came across in his night-time explorations. My grandmother brought it over from the old country. She carried it in this box, which was labelled "personal medical supplies".' Luigi smiled at the ruse. 'She is very frail and the sweetest lady you'll ever meet.'

'You mean to say it was not exported legally?' Oskar feigned surprise. 'You know that brings the price down significantly. It looks like it was dug up recently, too – not acquired from an old collection, which is more desirable these days.' Oskar marvelled at the freshness of the painting on each shard. It was exquisite.

'It looks very broken.' Oskar knew that Luigi would have some outrageous sum in mind so he continued to add to reasons why it should be less although the more he looked at the fragments the more he could not take his eyes off them. 'How much of it is actually there? It looks like a lot is missing,' Oskar continued, sitting down on the couch to get a better look.

'Oh, it's all there. It wasn't broken when my cousin found it. He broke it to make it easier to smuggle out of the country.' Oskar winced when he heard this, thinking of the cup complete as it would have been on the day it was made. Luigi continued, 'He practised on two modern pieces first and then had a go at it. He did a pretty good job, too. He only put a fracture across one of the figures and then not near the face. The pieces will rejoin together perfectly. Don't worry, Mr Williams.' Luigi beamed, detecting Oskar's interest.

As Luigi finished putting the fragments on the table, Oskar could see that, in fact, most if not all the cup was there. He had to be careful because sometimes his suppliers left out key pieces and then came back later to him with them, asking for more money. The breaks on the pottery were fresh, though, and Oskar could see the distinctive red buff clay that was so characteristic of the painted pottery of Classical Athens. Oskar picked up two pieces from the main scene on the body of the cup and placed them together. Two Greek warriors were locked in combat and their names were inscribed next to their heads. They were Achilles and Hector, the two arch-enemies of the Trojan War. The scene portrayed had to be that of their climactic battle on the plain of Troy in Book XXII of Homer's *Iliad*. It was a magnificent painting and it was so rare to be able to link an ancient image with a famous ancient work of literature. The cup did not seem to be signed but Oskar thought it must be the work of one of the Pioneers, the group of early Red-Figure Athenian vase painters, such as Euphronios or Euthymides, who had taken the art to a new plateau in the late sixth century BC.

'You did right to come to me first, Luigi,' Oskar said. He knew his competitors would give their left eyes for such a piece. 'I really do have someone coming in a few minutes. Let me give you this now.' Oskar took out his wallet, counted out ten crisp one-hundred-dollar bills and put them into Luigi's eager hands. 'Leave the piece here with me and come back tomorrow. We'll settle on a price then. Okay? I don't have enough money here now to cover the purchase in any case. Let's say one p.m. tomorrow. Return here and we'll settle it then.'

'Okay. *Grazie*, Mr Williams – thank you.'

8

THE TRIP TO Athens was a journey that began at JFK Airport with a long line of Greeks, all waiting impatiently to get to the ticket counter. Their baggage, piled high, often consisted of bulging cardboard boxes and vast suitcases strapped together with packing tape. An old lady, dressed completely in black, clutched the small gold Greek cross that hung around her neck as she pushed Tom forward with her stomach, acting as though this was the most natural thing in the world to do. At least there were only non-smoking flights these days. Tom remembered flying from Greece once on the Greek national airline and being seated towards the back of the non-smoking section. The man in front of him lit up and proceeded to chain-smoke merrily. When Tom complained to the stewardess, she simply moved the non-smoking sign two rows forward and went to smoke her own cigarette in the rear of the plane. That had been one long transatlantic flight.

The late-night flight brought Tom into Athens the following afternoon at the new international airport that the Greeks had managed to build well before the Athens 2004 Summer Olympics. Every four years, it seemed, friends had sent Tom bogus, or rather optimistic, T-shirts with logos for the 1992, 1996 and then 2000 Athens Olympics. But their time had finally come and the Greeks rose to the occasion in style and on a grand scale. The new airport had been a small but nonetheless important part of the Olympic effort.

Tom took the new subway train into Syntagma Square, and stopped to look at the archaeological exhibition cleverly displayed in the station. Finds made there during construction offered a glimpse of the area's rich history. You could not build anything in Athens, much less dig a large underground station, without hitting remains of the ancient city and its environs. After emerging from the metro station, Tom hailed a cab that took him up Lycabettos Hill and through Kolonaki Square to the American School of Classical Studies at 54 Souidias Street. The cab screeched to a halt in front of the school's entrance. The smell of rubber from the tyres melded with that of the hot asphalt of the street, producing an acrid odour. Tom passed through the heavy-barred iron gate, smiled and waved to the security guard, and walked up the gravel driveway to the main building. After Tom had introduced himself, the receptionist handed him an envelope that contained his room key and a note of welcome.

Tom walked across the street with his luggage to Loring Hall, a fine old neoclassical building. Using the keys he found inside the envelope he opened the iron gate, freshly painted green, and headed up the marble steps and into the building. His room was in the south wing on the second floor. Tom opened the tall wooden door to his room, dropped his suitcase next to the hospital-style bed and went to the bathroom down the hall to splash some cool water on his face. Back in the room, he opened the window to let in some fresh air.

He lay down on the bed, listening to the rustle of the pine trees and the cooing of the doves in the grounds outside his window, and his thoughts drifted to Victoria Price and her remarkable vision. It had seemed so improbable at the time but the more that Tom thought about it the more he wondered about how she had recounted it so clearly and with such detail.

Tom was physically exhausted from the trip. He considered heading down to the *saloni* for afternoon tea. He was a great believer in the restorative powers of tea. He knew that he had to try to stay up and not give in to jet lag, otherwise he'd wake up in the middle of the night – and he had a busy day tomorrow. His appointment at the Gennadeion Library was at nine a.m. the following day. The librarian had promised to bring out all their illustrated manuscripts that had to do with the Alexander Romance and he wanted to make the most of this extraordinary opportunity to study the material first-hand.

Instead of tea, Tom decided he needed something a bit stronger and strolled down to Kolonaki Square for a frappe, the frothy iced-coffee drink that – together with cigarettes – kept a large portion of the population functioning. He sat at an outdoor cafe on the west side of the square and ordered his frappe, *metrio me gala*, with one sugar and milk. It was much more expensive to sit at a table than to drink standing at the bar, but Kolonaki Square was the place to see and be seen and the people-watching there was very good. Cafes crowded both sides of the street. As Tom watched beautiful people happily strutting their stuff, his thoughts returned to Victoria Price and her account of Alexander's tomb. He had never given much thought to reincarnation and he wondered what the ancients had thought about it. Perhaps he could gather some gen at dinner tonight. He finished his frappe, feeling refreshed, and left the hard buttery biscuit served with it on the small white saucer next to his tip.

He walked back and breezed into the *saloni* at the American School, moving purposefully towards the bar. There he poured himself an ouzo, pausing to add three cubes of ice and a small amount of water to his glass. He nibbled on a vine leaf stuffed with rice as the clear liquid turned a smoky white from its interaction with the ice and water. Gently rolling the ice in the glass and sipping the cool drink, he surveyed the scene in the *saloni*. A tall bearded man sitting in an overstuffed armchair opposite the bar was talking loudly to a young woman.

'Protagoras said, "Man is the measure of all things." Some think that he was placing special significance on the individual, maintaining that everything is seen or filtered through an individual's eyes. It is his theory of perception. Some took it to mean that Protagoras did not believe in the gods.'

Tom sauntered over and said, 'There are those of us who choose to believe that art, great art, is the measure of all things.'

'Oh, it's you,' the man said. 'What else would we expect to hear from a museum curator? They've let you out of the museum, have they?'

'Just for two weeks' research here and at Dikta and then elsewhere in Europe. I'll be working in the Gennadeion tomorrow and then I'm off to Crete the day after.' Tom turned to the young lady. 'Please allow me to introduce myself: my name is Tom Carr. I am a curator of Greek and Roman art at the Metropolitan Museum of Art in New York.'

The young woman looked Tom straight in the eye, offered her hand limply and said, 'Hi, I'm Sandy Milken, I'm a fellow here at the school this year. I study classics at the University of Michigan.' Before she could continue the bell rang in the dining room. 'I guess dinner is served, gentlemen. Shall we continue our discussion there?'

The three of them and others who had gathered in the *saloni* made their way across the hall to the dining room where long wooden tables were set for dinner. Candles were lit along the tables, creating a pleasant ambience that together with dimly flickering sconces added a slightly medieval air to the sparse decor. It was a congenial bunch of scholars and there were seldom pauses in the conversation. This was not a group who were at a loss for words. Over the first course of lentil soup and a hearty Peloponnesian red wine from Nemea, Bruce, a classics professor from U. Cal Berkeley, reflected on the value of beans. 'You know, of course, the lentil has a long history here in Greece. It was a staple of the ancients. Pythagoras for one waxed lyrical on the health benefits of the bean.'

'I believe he also was the first to observe that they make you fart,' John, another bearded professor, chimed in quite seriously as he raised his glass to drink.

'Well, Pythagoras was obviously a brilliant mathematician – his theorem still holds water – but he was also a bit of a quack in my opinion, and not because he was a vegetarian. His mystical views on life and reincarnation seem very borderline to me,' said Sandy.

Tom spoke up. 'It's interesting that we know Pythagoras visited the sanctuary of Zeus at Dikta in the third quarter of the sixth century BC. Porphry tells us that, in the course of his journey from Asia Minor to Italy, Pythagoras came to Crete. He landed on the beach at Dikta where he underwent a purification ceremony administered by one of the priests using a so-called thunderstone, a Neolithic axe thought to have been left by one of Zeus's bolts of lightning. After his purification, it was required that Pythagoras don a wreath of black wool and lie on the beach with his face towards the sea for one night, symbolising a kind of rebirth. He visited the Diktaian sanctuary, and then made a pilgrimage to the cave of Zeus, the legendary site of the god's birth, where he spent an entire lunar month. You know the mystic rites of Diktaian Zeus have some parallels with Egyptian religion, which we know interested Pythagoras. And it's no wonder, given the strong connections between Egypt and his own home island of Samos where there are amazing Egyptian finds from the great sanctuary of Hera from the seventh and sixth centuries BC. But, Bruce, tell me more about the ancients' views of reincarnation.'

'The idea of reincarnation was not central to Greek religion, and in that sense I think that Pythagoras was not in the mainstream. The more popular belief is expressed clearly in Homer's epic poems. After you died, your spirit, or soul, made the journey across the river Styx to the underworld, the land of Hades. In the *Odyssey*, when Odysseus goes down to Hades to visit the spirits of the dead, Achilles, mightiest of warriors, tells him that he would prefer to be the lowliest man alive on Earth than to be the king of Hades. And then there's the passage in Homer's *Iliad*, when Achilles is deciding his fate: whether to live a long and dull life at home or a short and glorious life as the mightiest hero of the Trojan War, followed by immortal fame.' Bruce paused to draw breath.

He was on a roll now, Tom thought.

Bruce continued: 'The Greeks got it right with the Furies – or the Fates, as they were known. Sure, chance and luck play a part but human will is more often the determining factor. There's more than one fate that we can follow. We make our own fortunes. Achilles knew well that once he was dead, once his life's breath had left him, there was no coming back. Yet he chose a short glorious life and immortal fame.'

Bruce cleared his throat. 'It is true that Pythagoras was not alone in believing in reincarnation. Plato, for example, reflects deeply on the soul. There's that marvellous passage in *The Republic* where he describes the recently deceased drinking from the River of Forgetfulness. Plato writes that those who were imprudent drank more than their measure and forgot everything. It's as though a deep draught of this magical water keeps us from remembering our past lives, which could otherwise be recalled. When the deceased go to sleep by the river, they're reborn like shooting stars. According to Plato the soul is an entity distinct from the body. It's immortal and endlessly reborn. He even argued that it encompassed both one's intellect and one's personality.'

Bruce paused to eat some of the main course that a waiter had just placed before him. It was a savoury chicken dish seasoned with rosemary, olive oil, sea salt and a little tomato, accompanied by roast potatoes sprinkled with oregano.

Victoria's recollection seemed to follow the Platonic view, Tom thought. It was as if she had drunk less water from the River of Forgetfulness and recalled this vision from a past life so clearly as if it were her own memory.

Bruce was enjoying his monologue, and Tom was looking at him encouragingly, so he continued. 'What's more, forty million Hindus can't all be wrong, as they say. In fact, scholars recently have suggested that Hindu beliefs in the afterlife might stem from Platonic philosophy, brought east by Alexander the Great during his conquests in the late fourth century BC. The Roman writer Arrian describes a meeting between Alexander and a group of naked philosophers in India who began stomping their feet as he approached them. When Alexander asked through an interpreter what they were doing, they replied in kind, asking him why he spent his time conquering vast lands when ultimately every man owns only the small plot of land where he is buried, hence the stamping of the feet. You can't take it with you was their message.'

'Why is it,' said John, 'that every time I meet someone who believes in reincarnation they've had a past life as someone famous like Cleopatra or Henry the Eighth?' Tom thought of Victoria Price. John continued, 'What are the odds? It's like in that book *Archy and Mehitabel* – you know, the one about the cockroach and the cat – which I found entertaining but not believable.'

'But the ancient Greeks did not believe in coming back as anything other than human, though,' Bruce responded.

John wasn't convinced. 'But the Romans sometimes wondered about people being reincarnated as animals. Plutarch, in his excursus *On the eating of flesh*, states that even though the migration of souls from body to body had not been demonstrated beyond a doubt, he believed there was enough evidence to make him cautious, even fearful of eating meat,' he said as he began to gnaw gingerly on a chicken leg.

Tom continued to ponder on Victoria Price's story as the conversation continued over dessert, flitting from topic to topic, such as recent field trips to ancient sites, the plans for the new Acropolis museum, and what film was playing down at the local winter cinema.

After a small Greek coffee, Tom excused himself from the table and headed upstairs to his room. The effects of jet lag were hitting him hard and he found that by the time that dessert was served, it was difficult to stay engaged in the conversation. He washed himself in the bathroom at the end of the hall, collapsed on his bed, and drifted into a deep sleep.

9

VICTORIA GOT OFF the Hampton Jitney at Grand Central Station and looked at her watch. It was just before ten a.m. The Morgan Library opened at 10:30 a.m. She had just enough time to leave her suitcase with the doorman at her friend's apartment on Park Avenue and head over there. She thought that she'd get to the Morgan as soon as it opened; the exhibition was less likely to be crowded then. It would be a perfect end to her visit since this was her last day in New York before she flew home to Rome that evening.

She had spent a relaxing long weekend with Cynthia and her family. Because Victoria had been living overseas she had not spent time with an old girlfriend like that in too long a while. It had been wonderful to stay up late drinking good wine by the fire, sharing their college stories and laughing themselves silly after the children had gone to sleep. Of course, seeing Cynthia so happily married with two children and a loving husband made her think of her own situation. Still, she would not have wanted to change her life. Yes, in Rome she was rebounding from a relationship with Lorenzo but she was also learning about herself, especially through her painting and this new work with her therapist about channelling and past lives. Although Lorenzo was very handsome, he was not the right one for her. That was for sure. After several months she was finally in a good place.

Victoria felt liberated once she had dropped off her bag at her friend's apartment. The doorman hailed her a cab and told the driver to take her to the Morgan Library. The taxi pulled right up at the main entrance on Madison and 36th Street. Taut colourful banners hanging on the side of the building above the pavement signalled the presence of the museum and announced the special exhibition about Alexander the Great. The Morgan Library was housed in a complex of buildings that had belonged to the great American financier J. P. Morgan, the core of which had once formed his private home. Victoria walked up the steps and through the glass doors to the admissions desk. There were only a dozen or so people queuing in front of her. Her timing was perfect. After getting her ticket, she made her way directly to the Alexander exhibition, which was located in the main temporary exhibition space through the great atrium and off to the right.

As Tom had told her, the exhibition centred on a single illustrated manuscript that told the story of Alexander the Great's remarkable life and legends. Victoria learned as she read the introductory wall panel that the manuscript dated from the twelfth century but that it drew from much earlier versions of what was called the *Alexander Romance*, a work that was probably first composed in the third or second century BC. The original was attributed in antiquity to Alexander's contemporary and friend Cleisthenes, but was almost certainly not by him. It was probably begun sometime soon after Alexander's death, although the earliest extant copy dated from a much later period. The *Alexander Romance* was rewritten and enlarged many times throughout antiquity and in the medieval and Byzantine periods, resulting in a range of divergent texts. It was translated into a multitude of languages and Victoria was amazed to learn how widespread its influence was. Its stories were incorporated into the Talmud, the Old Testament, and the Koran. They also inspired ancient Persian writers of the tenth to twelfth centuries. A Latin version translated in the late third or fourth century AD helped to spread the fame and adventures of the great king throughout medieval Europe where various Alexander traditions flourished in local lore and in the visual arts. The edition exhibited here had been a treasured possession of J. Pierpont Morgan and was, in fact, an extraordinary work of art in its own right, lavishly illustrated by a French master miniaturist painter. It must have taken years to complete.

Victoria was fascinated by the individual manuscript pages. Each illustrated page was laid out, one next to the other, in flat-topped cases that allowed very close scrutiny. The story began, naturally enough, with Alexander's birth, which had been accompanied by many omens predicting that he would become a great king. On the day when Alexander was born in 356 BC, his father, Philip II of Macedon, won the prestigious horse race at the Olympic Games held in honour of Zeus. Alexander's mother, Olympias, had had a dream on her wedding night that she was visited by Zeus in the form of a thunderbolt. In the manuscript illustration that Victoria was now looking at, Alexander's birth was depicted like the Nativity of Christ, signalling once again the importance of Alexander as a future saviour and hero. Victoria peered closely at the tender image of Olympias holding her newborn son in swaddling clothes and she marvelled at the detail that filled the small page around this focal scene. In the far-right corner the temple of Artemis at Ephesus, one of the seven ancient wonders of the world, was in flames. According to some legends, this terrible event occurred on the day that Alexander was born and it foretold to the priestesses of Artemis a dire future for all of Asia. The artist of the manuscript depicted a fiery comet streaking high across the sky, suggesting that a celestial event like this was yet another portent from the heavens that the birth of Alexander was no ordinary occasion.

When Oskar Williams entered the exhibition he recognised Victoria Price immediately from her photograph. She was not hard to spot. Quite a beauty, Oskar thought. She was wearing a short camel-coloured wool jacket, a white blouse, a paisley scarf and skinny black jeans that accentuated her fine form as she bent over to look at the manuscript illustrations. He did not approach her right away but continued to look around the room, noting the security stations: he did not want to attract any attention. The exhibition filled two rooms but the cases were low and there were no obstructions. Victoria was looking at the first illustration – she must have just arrived, he thought. Oskar turned to the introductory text panel, occasionally glancing nonchalantly over at Victoria as he read.

Victoria moved on to the next page where a particularly charming illustration depicted Alexander in his youth when he first tamed his famous steed, Bucephalus. Alexander had been only eight or nine years old when a Thessalian horse breeder had brought a magnificent stallion to King Philip. The horse was a chestnut-brown colour with a white blaze on his forehead. He had an ox's head – *bucephalos* in Greek – branded on his thigh, the symbol of the breeder. The man wanted thirteen talents for the horse, a vast sum. Philip and his men tried to ride the horse but none could master him. As Philip was about to tell the breeder that the horse was no good, Alexander spoke up and said that he could break him if he was given a chance. The king questioned his son's audacity and asked him what price he would pay if he were not successful. Alexander replied that he would pay for the horse himself.

In the manuscript illustration the artist had chosen to represent the critical moment in the story. Alexander stands before Bucephalus, holding his reins and staring him straight in the eye. He turns the horse away from the sun, which sends his shadow behind him. Boy and horse face each other, each proud and strong, measuring the will of the other. Already there is a calmness about Bucephalus, and soon Alexander will jump up on his back and ride him across the wide plain into the distance. Philip and his companions stand to one side watching in wonder and admiration.

So impressed was Philip with his son's achievement that, according to Plutarch, he told him, 'You will have to get another kingdom: Macedonia is not big enough for you.' Alexander and Bucephalus would be constant companions throughout Alexander's campaigns as he rode the horse into every major battle. Bucephalus carried him across central Asia and into Afghanistan. It was only after Alexander's major battle against the Indian king Porus and his elephants that Bucephalus finally died, whereupon Alexander gave his steed a magnificent royal burial and named a city after him.

After studying the scene and the artist's incredible talent not just with the brush but also with his colour palette, which was remarkably vibrant, Victoria moved on to look at another early scene in the book in which Alexander was shown being taught by Aristotle in the open air. Alexander's father Philip II had invited the famous Greek philosopher to tutor his son in 343/2 BC when Alexander was just thirteen. It was said that Alexander was a precocious young boy and, here in the manuscript illustration, he was seated cross-legged on a cool green patch of grass underneath a tree as he listened to his tutor lecture on the subject of nature. The tutor's long beard, carefully draped cloak, and hand gestures identified him as a Greek philosopher. Alexander's association with the great Aristotle was an important part of the *Alexander Romance* and the later tradition as it helped to establish Alexander's role as a sage and wise man. Victoria noticed how delicate birds that were perched in the olive trees also seemed to be listening to Aristotle's lecture.

A man seemed to crowd Victoria in slightly as she looked at the illustration, brushing against her unnecessarily, she thought, and she noticed that more people were coming into the exhibition. It was time to move on. She decided to go to the last section in the next room. She never felt the need to follow an exhibition strictly according to its layout anyway and after looking at these incredibly detailed images she realised that she was not going to be able to pay the same level of attention to all the illustrations on display; it would be too exhausting. She could get the cata-logue and read about them later. She'd just see a few more and then go on to have lunch and do some shopping uptown before she would need to pick up her bag again and head to the airport. It was fascin-ating to her, though, to think that in some way in a former life she had actually known Alexander and had been inside his tomb. She felt that she needed to know more about him. Perhaps new information about Alexander would trigger more memories of her past life, she thought.

The last section of the exhibition looked at a number of later legends about Alexander. Victoria decided to look at the series of illustrations depicting the story of Alexander and his daughter Nereida, which drew her interest. As with the Ancient Near Eastern hero Gilgamesh, who sought out the plant of immortality, or any of a number of Greek myths in which mortal men wished for eternal youth and immortality, it was not surprising that stories of Alexander searching for the Fountain of Youth – or the Water of Life, as it was sometimes called – came to be a part of his lore. This legend was especially popular among the Arabic texts and was featured in the Koran. It also became a theme that resonated with painters in the Middle Ages.

Victoria looked at the first illustration in the series, which showed Alexander and his troops at the Fountain of Youth. Dressed like medieval knights in shining armour, Alexander's soldiers rallied around him, the high-domed tents of their camp stretching out into the distant landscape. To the right was a clear spring where Alexander's cook held in his hands a fish, which seemed to be flopping around. According to the story, when they reached the spring that was the source of the Water of Life, Alexander's cook was cleaning a dried fish and it came to life. However, he chose not to reveal the miracle to Alexander, but drank of the water himself and Alexander missed his opportunity to drink and gain immortality. The cook then fell in love with Nereida, one of Alexander's daughters, and shared the Water of Life with her. In this illustration the stories were conflated. Alexander's daughter stood in the spring with only her upper body visible, the contours of her breasts showing through her wet blouse, next to the cook who held the wriggling fish.

In the next illustration the cook and Nereida stood before Alexander who was seated on a throne and had just learned of their betrayal. Alexander, visibly upset, pronounced their punishment; a court scribe stood to his left, taking notes. Alexander banished his daughter Nereida, who became a mermaid or water nymph, and he had his men tie a heavy stone to the cook and then cast him into the sea, where he too became a water spirit, giving his name to the Adriatic Sea.

As Victoria turned to look at the final illustration, her pulse started to race. She felt as though she was about to have a panic attack. The scene before her was one of farewell between Alexander and his daughter. Nereida stood before Alexander, tears rolling down her cheeks, her long blonde hair parted in the centre of her forehead and flowing down over her chest. She held an amulet in her hand and she was handing it to her father as a peace offering. It was the famous Amulet of Nereida. Carved from the clearest crystal, made from the Water of Life itself, Nereida gave it to Alexander to protect him and to show her love for him even in the face of dire punishment. Victoria pressed her face close to the glass case to see the detail more clearly. Her heart was racing as she realised that this image had meaning for her. She had to sit down. She was feeling very dizzy. She might faint at any moment.

There was a bench against the wall just behind her. She stepped back and sat down, resting her head against the wall. How could this be happening to her again? Her vision grew blurry and she lost consciousness.

When Victoria opened her eyes again she thought she must be dreaming – but it all seemed so real. She was inside the tomb of Alexander the Great again and it was moments after her last vision. She felt over-whelmed with sadness. The torchlight cast a flickering eerie glow. She was looking at the mummified remains of Alexander the Great, but she realised that it was not the body itself or the king's face that her gaze was focused on. It was fixed on something else that hung around his neck: the Amulet of Nereida. It was, in fact, this object that had drawn her to the tomb in the first place, hoping to achieve her own immortality. It was while her attention was focused on it that her cohorts had hit her from behind and abandoned her. The amulet had magic properties and was said to protect whoever wore it, even to stop the ageing process and to grant immortality to its owner. It was exquisitely carved in the shape of a great ram's head, the Egyptian form of the god Zeus Ammon, Alexander's legendary father. It was set in gold and hung on a finely wrought gold chain. Victoria approached closer and removed the amulet from Alexander's neck, clutching it tightly in her hands, thinking somehow that it might save her from this awful predicament.

She felt bitter, betrayed, and ultimately inconsolably sad as she realised that she would die here with no food or water, or even air as the torchlight grew dimmer and dimmer. Sometime later the torch went out and she was just sitting there in the dark, still holding the amulet tight. In the total darkness, she could see that the amulet glowed faintly and she could feel power emanating from it. It did have a calming, almost soothing effect on her but without food and water she became steadily weaker and weaker. She had no sense of time. She became frailer and frailer, barely able to move or speak from lack of food and water. Then she heard the flutter of wings and she felt a slight breeze on her face. Suddenly she knew that Death was there to take her to the Underworld. When she felt his cold hand on her shoulder she tried to scream for help at the top of her lungs, but nothing came out of her parched mouth. It was at this moment that Victoria awoke, screaming, and pushing away a female guard who was holding her up and trying to calm her.

10

THE VEILED DANCER twirled slowly before Tom with measured steps, as if in slow motion, her supple and sinuous body revealed beneath the thin layers wrapped tightly about her. Two musicians stood in the background. The eerie sound of a double flute accompanied by a tortoiseshell lyre filled the air. Tom sat on a gilded throne whose armrests were supported by seated sphinxes. The back support he leaned against had a gentle curve and was crowned with lions flanking a globe against which a soft cushion was suspended to rest his head. He was naked, with the body of a Greek god, and wore only a crown of golden oak leaves upon his head. In his left hand he held a sceptre and in his right a gilded glass goblet filled with red wine. As the dancer moved closer Tom became more and more entranced with her. She wove her way across the dance floor, her body one fluid motion, enticing, erotic, smelling of sweet jasmine. The music grew louder and cymbals crashed. It was only when the dancer lay prostrate before him and looked up at him that Tom recognised those bright blue eyes. It was Victoria Price.

* * *

Tom awoke in a cold sweat. It was early in the morning, almost six a.m., and he knew that he wouldn't be able to get back to sleep. His body clock was still set seven hours earlier on New York time. He went down the hall to the bathroom and splashed water on his face. After brushing his teeth and shaving, he got dressed and decided to walk to the little church at the top of Lycabettos Hill. There was a funicular that climbed the steep slope but it was not running at this early hour. He made his way purposefully up the stone path to the summit, the highest elevation in the city. The sun was just coming up and the air was cool. It was a clear day and you could see straight across to the Acropolis with its gleaming white temples, and its Greek flag flying in the slight morning breeze. The city stretched pretty much as far as the eye could see – to the mountains and to the Aegean Sea beyond the Acropolis, one vast urban sprawl. There were many days in the summer when an observer couldn't see the Acropolis from here, when the *nefos*, or cloud of pollution, was thick and low like a pea-souper fog over the city. Athens was situated in a deep broad valley, and the air pollution built up whenever there wasn't a breeze. Tom was thankful this was not one of those days.

Entering the little church at the summit of Mount Lycabettos, Tom said a prayer and crossed himself. He then dropped a euro in the offering box and took up a thin beeswax candle that he lit from a lamp hanging above an icon of Saint George. Tom placed the candle firmly into the bowl of sand that was set up for such devotions. On the marble step to the iconostasis, a silver incense burner emitted a steady narrow wisp of smoke that trailed up before the icon. The room was filled with the heavy scent of myrrh. Tom reflected quietly for a moment, before glancing at his watch and realising that he would have just enough time for a coffee and perhaps even a plate of warm *loukoumades*, fried dough balls covered in sweet syrup and sesame seeds, before his appointment at the Gennadeion Library. He headed back down the hill taking two steps at time.

It was now just nine a.m. and Tom was right on time for his appointment. As he entered the forecourt in front of the library, he paused briefly to look up at the stark but striking neoclassical façade. Then, walking up the white marble steps, Tom entered the building and went straight to the receptionist seated at the entrance to the main reading room, a grand spacious hall two storeys high and lined with book-shelves and with an arcade around its perimeter. Here the most valuable books were kept in cabinets behind locked glass doors.

'Good morning, my name is Tom Carr. I have an appointment to see the librarian regarding some of your illustrated manuscripts of the *Alexander Romance*,' he said.

'Yes, of course, Mr Carr – we've been expecting you. Please come this way.' The receptionist led Tom to a nearby table where a number of old books were set up on wedge-shaped reading stands that kept the bindings from cracking.

Tom took out his pencil, a small notebook, and the file with his original list. There were specific manuscript pages that he wanted to see, those that he had seen illustrated in scholarly articles and books. But he also wanted to leaf more casually through the manuscripts to see what other illustrations might be of interest.

The literature on Alexander the Great was immense. It had started in Alexander's lifetime with his official journal and the letters that he wrote during his military campaigns. However, there were no known copies of the works written during his lifetime or shortly thereafter by people who actually knew him, such as his generals Ptolemy and Nearchus. Instead, scholars had to rely on later works, like those by the Roman writers who lived centuries after Alexander – Arrian, Diodorus, Curtius and Plutarch, whose life of Alexander was compiled from a myriad reliable and unreliable sources. The most interesting of the later works was the *Alexander Romance*.

Tom Carr was particularly interested in the visual

representations of Alexander's life and the associated stories. As he sat down at the large library table he decided that he would begin by looking at some of the later adventures that were added to Alexander's story: tales of the flying machine, the diving bell, the wonder stone, and the Unclean Nations. These legends transformed a great military general and leader into a wily hero and adventurer revered as one of the great sages of antiquity, and even depicted him as a Christian saviour.

Just as Tom was about to begin his work, the librarian appeared and introduced herself. 'Mr Carr, my name is Maria Olympias. I am the librarian. We have prepared everything for you, and I've put out all the manuscripts you wanted to see on this table. As you can see, the books are laid out on special stands and I've already opened them to the illustrations you requested. Since you yourself are a museum curator, I know that I do not need to remind you how fragile this material is. Please use the gloves provided and handle the texts as little as possible. But with that proviso you are welcome to leaf through them after you are finished with the images to which they have been opened. If you need any assistance do not hesitate to ask me. My office is just over there and I should be there for most of the morning. There will also be a receptionist by the entrance at all times and she knows how to find me if for some reason I am not at my desk.'

'Thank you very much,' Tom replied. 'It is a real treat for me to see this material first-hand, as there really is no substitute. I greatly appreciate your letting me look through the manuscripts for other illustrations. I'm excited to see if there are others that will be of use to me in my research and there is quite simply no other way for me to do this.'

'Well, one day we hope to digitise the collection and make it accessible through our website so that scholars like yourself can see the material without coming all the way to Athens. But I am afraid those plans are still some time away from fruition. I wish you every success in your work,' Maria said, reiterating her statement in Greek: '*Kali doulia.*' And with that the librarian left Tom to proceed with his research.

With a magnifying glass in his hand, Tom stood up and leaned over a manuscript that had been opened to the page he had requested. Before him was a fourteenth-century representation of Alexander the Great in his flying machine. The mighty king on a journey to the ends of the Earth sits on a gilded throne of his making to which are harnessed two griffins, mythical winged beasts that are part eagle, part lion. In front of the beasts, Alexander holds out two long spears with pieces of meat – described as horses' livers in the text – skewered on their blades. The ravenous creatures fly towards the meat, taking Alexander in his throne up into the air along with them. According to legend, by manipulating the spears Alexander was able to direct the flight of the griffins and fly high enough to see all of the lands that he had conquered. Details of the scene recalled for Tom the great twelfth-century mosaic on the floor of the cathedral in Otranto in Southern Italy, where this very image was prominently placed amidst a variety of scenes including a depiction of the Tree of Life and episodes from the Old Testament and Arthurian legend. Tom thought it was amazing how Alexander had made his way so prominently into such a major Catholic compendium of religious images.

Then he turned to look at a twelfth-century representation of Alexander's exploration of the ocean in a glass diving bell. The illustration had been set up on a stand next to the scene showing the flying machine. In this exquisitely detailed manuscript illustration Alexander is shown at the bottom of the sea inside a glass bell with a rope extending up towards the surface: another account of Alexander's ingeniously devised travels to the ends of the Earth. Monstrous fish swim past him and a mermaid, holding the ends of her split tail, looks at Alexander in wonder. Inside the glass bell with Alexander is a rooster. According to the legend, when Alexander finished his underwater exploration and was ready to return to land, he killed the rooster and released its blood into the water, whereupon the sea spat him out in distaste.

One of Alexander's greatest challenges in the

Alexander Romance was his containment of the
Unclean Nations, a feat that placed him squarely
within the sacred history of Christianity as related in
Bibles of the late Middle Ages. The Unclean Nations
were fabled countries that lay beyond two mountains
in the great unknown region called the 'Breasts of the
North' and contained the very spawn of Satan. It was
foretold that these nations would join together with
the dark angel and make war on mankind at the End
of Days. The scene Tom beheld now showed these
foul beings enclosed by a giant circular wall of
Alexander's making with the great king standing
outside, his task of containing them completed.

After another hour Tom had finished looking at the
illustrations that he had come to see and he spent the
rest of the time gingerly leafing through the manuscripts, looking at other scenes that were portrayed.
An image of Alexander, dressed like a knight of the
Round Table and standing at the gates of Babylon with
his army behind him, caught his eye. In another scene
from a Persian manuscript the legendary king did battle
with a dragon whose form, with its monstrous head,
big furry ears and long sinewy scaly body, lay somewhere between a Greek *ketos*, or sea monster, and a
Chinese dragon. In another medieval scene, Alexander
and his army came upon the race of Amazons, a
legendary tribe of warrior women who lived beyond
the edges of the known world. Alexander was portrayed

at the head of his army offering the Amazons his spear for them to revere, a phallic symbol of his power.

There was also a fine representation of Alexander coming upon Darius, king of Persia, in the mountains. After Alexander defeated Darius and his army at Gaugemela, the Persian king escaped and fled. It was essential that Alexander capture Darius himself so that there could be no doubt about Alexander's legitimate ascension to the throne, and no chance of Darius returning to claim his empire. Ancient historians relate that Alexander hunted Darius down, but arrived only after Darius's own men had slain him. In some versions of the *Alexander Romance*, though, Alexander arrived just before Darius died. In the illustration before Tom, Alexander was shown kneeling and holding in his arms a dying Darius who utters with his dying breath that Alexander is now king of the world.

But nothing prepared Tom for a scene depicting the first meeting of Alexander and his future wife Roxane, whom Alexander married in 327 BC. It was a famous moment in Alexander's life and one of the few, besides his relationship with his friend, the nobleman and general Hephaestion, where Alexander's love was on display. After taking his army deep into Afghanistan and conquering the region he was toasted by the local Bactrian baron, Oxyartes. As part of the dinner entertainment, Oxyartes presented a performance of dancing girls, among them Oxyartes's own daughter Roxane. Alexander was smitten by Roxane from the moment he laid eyes on her, and they were married soon after. The marriage did not make political sense since Bactria was hardly an important region for Alexander, being at the very edge of the territories under his control. Instead, it truly seemed to be love at first sight for this young man who at the age of twenty-nine had conquered much of the known world. In fact, in some of the later versions of the *Alexander Romance*, Roxane was introduced as the daughter of the Persian king Darius, a legend that served to legitimise Alexander's conquest of the Persian Empire and maintain an unbroken bloodline of Persian kings.

Very little in the way of hard information about Roxane and Alexander's relationship has survived the ravages of time. It is said that they had a child, Alexander IV, who was born shortly after Alexander's death in 323 BC. In fact, it is likely that the boy was conceived not long after Hephaestion's death, when Alexander was distraught and contemplating his own mortality. The boy – the legitimate heir to all of Alexander's kingdoms but too young to rule – and Roxane became pawns in the political struggles between Alexander's generals after his death. Initially, they were protected by Perdiccas, the most senior of Alexander's generals. We do not know what Roxane did after Alexander's death but it is likely that she remained in

Babylon awaiting the proper funeral of her husband. She probably would have accompanied the funeral cart on its long trek to Egypt, the duty of a widow in mourning. However, it is recorded that in 320 BC, after Alexander was buried, Roxane and Alexander IV were with Perdiccas when he marched on Egypt against Ptolemy. It is said they came to a sad end, having been poisoned by Cassander at Amphipolis in Macedonia in 309 BC and buried in unmarked graves.

Tom had always tended to think of Roxane as mysterious and exotically beautiful, the way her ancestor was portrayed in the movie version of Rudyard Kipling's masterpiece *The Man Who Would Be King*, or like the haunting photograph of a young woman from Afghanistan featured on the cover of an issue of *National Geographic* in the 1980s. Consequently, he was all the more surprised to see the illustration before him, depicting Alexander on an elaborate throne with Hephaestion and his companions around him. A Bactrian lord, who must represent Oxyartes, sits to his left. Musicians play flutes, beat on a drum and shake tambourines on one side while a chorus of dancing girls look on as a heavily veiled woman performs an alluring dance for the Macedonian king.

Tom's dream of the night before immediately flashed into his mind. 'That was pure fantasy, though,' he said quietly to himself. 'Nothing more than a figment of my imagination induced by jet lag, perhaps a little too much wine at dinner, and a wild story told by a beautiful woman.'

Nonetheless, the figure of Roxane in this illustrated manuscript was undeniably and strangely reminiscent of the Baker Dancer. Was it possible that the bronze statuette was commissioned to commemorate that historic event, either during Alexander's lifetime or at some point afterwards? The thought was breathtaking. After all, Lysippos of Sicyon, perhaps the greatest sculptor of the fourth century BC, was Alexander's court sculptor and was renowned for his sculptures in bronze. Pliny stated that Lysippos produced more than fifteen hundred bronze sculptures legendary for their grace and elegance. Tom jotted a few notes and decided that when he got back to the museum he would do some research on dance traditions in Hellenistic Bactria to see if he could find more evidence to support this intriguing hypothesis.

11

VICTORIA WAS DISORIENTATED when she awoke screaming. It took her a few minutes to realise where she was, that she was at the exhibition at the Morgan Library. The guard had called a nurse who was now tending to her. People had gathered around but two more guards had come and they were cordoning off a wide area around Victoria to give her breathing space. She was upset but she did not feel sick or hurt in any way. What she did realise was that she needed to get out of there – and not to a hospital. She needed to get outside, into the light. She needed to breathe fresh air and feel the sunlight warm on her face. To have been so close to death, even in a previous life, was utterly draining, stifling, terrifying.

After sitting quietly with the nurse and working on her breathing till it was at a normal pace again, Victoria thanked the nurse for her help and insisted gently but firmly that she was okay and that all she needed was to get out of there. Reluctantly, the nurse walked her to the main entrance and said goodbye. Victoria sat outside by the steps for a few minutes, taking in the fresh air and recovering. Her mind was racing. She needed to get in contact with Tom Carr.

She could send him an e-mail but she wanted to talk on the phone or even better speak face to face. She wanted to see him, to tell him about this latest revelation. It could have significance for his search for the tomb, for the world. What if the amulet was still there? It could be a tangible link to the Fountain of Youth.

But Tom had told her that he was leaving for Europe. He would not be at his office, she remembered. Still, they would know how to get in touch with him. She knew they were not likely to give her any information over the phone. She could be very persuasive in person, though. She thought she should try, at least. She hailed a cab in front of the Morgan and asked the driver to take her to the Metropolitan Museum of Art.

Oskar Williams watched Victoria Price from inside the museum. It was one of the strangest episodes he had ever witnessed and he'd seen plenty of odd things in his life. She had moved into the second gallery after he had approached her. She'd been looking closely at one of the manuscript illustrations when she'd reeled back unsteadily from the case and sat down on a bench. A moment later she was leaning her head against the wall and then she was out cold. If he had not been watching her closely it would have looked like she had just taken a rest. It was eerie.

Oskar had walked up to see which manuscript it was: a scene from the Amulet of Nereida myth. He felt like someone at a party who is left out of a joke. He did not get it. The guards had only rushed to the scene when Victoria regained consciousness a full fifteen minutes later, screaming. In fact, when she'd started to scream Oskar had turned to alert a guard, wanting to seem an ordinary bystander, but they were already walking towards her as he approached them.

All Oskar could do now was wait and watch as Victoria sat outside in front of the museum. He called his driver and told him to wait outside. He was sure when Victoria went outside that she would take off pretty soon. He wanted to be ready to follow her. Sure enough, he was right – after a few minutes she hopped into a cab. He followed right away, his driver pulling up as soon as he stepped outside. When he jumped in the back seat, he leaned forward and said, 'Follow that cab. Don't lose it. I mean it.'

'Yes, Mr Williams,' his driver replied and stepped on the gas to pursue the yellow taxi, which was already up at the next light.

About twenty minutes later Oskar watched as the cab pulled up in front of the Metropolitan Museum of Art. Victoria got out and walked purposefully up the main steps.

Well, there is not much hope of following her in there, thought Oskar. *It's too big and the security is too tight. Where is she going? Carr is in Europe. Is someone else involved?* Oskar sat there wondering for a few minutes. Then he turned to his driver and said, 'Okay, you can take me home. We're done here.' And the black sedan lurched forward, merging into traffic as they sped down Fifth Avenue.

It was a busy day at the museum and there were lots of people milling around the Great Hall, getting tickets, checking their coats, standing and waiting to meet friends or getting ready to venture into the galleries. Victoria remembered how to get to the Greek and Roman Department and headed straight there after she got her admission button. She walked up to the receptionist and introduced herself.

'Hi, my name is Victoria Price. I am an artist visiting New York from Rome and I am returning home this evening. I was here speaking with Tom Carr last week. I know that Tom is away on a business trip in Europe but I really need to speak with him. Can you give me a telephone number where I could reach him?' Victoria wanted to express urgency but did not want to seem unhinged. She flashed the receptionist a warm smile.

'I'm sorry, Ms Price, but I am not allowed to give out any information. If you'd like to leave a message, I'd be happy to pass it along to him. I can't guarantee that he'll get it today, though, but he usually checks in every few days and I heard from him yesterday.'

Victoria thought for a moment. She did not want to leave a message about her vision. The receptionist was liable to read it. It was too private.

'No, thank you. He gave me his e-mail – I suppose I can contact him through that and get his telephone number directly from him.'

'He checks his e-mail regularly. That would be the best way to reach him.' The receptionist paused, making her own judgement of Victoria, and then added, 'He will be in Rome at the end of the week staying at the American Academy. Perhaps you could see him there.'

'Oh really? Thank you, that would be ideal. I'll e-mail him about the possibility of our getting together. Thanks so much for your help.' Victoria smiled again and then turned to leave the reception desk.

She decided to go up to the Roof Garden for a cool drink and to think. She sat down on the bench where she and Tom had sat the week before. It was another beautiful autumn day. She got out her BlackBerry, wrote Tom a quick e-mail and sent it off. She took a sip of her drink and looked out at the bright colours of the foliage. She had now experienced two episodes of channelling, both from the same moment in a previous life. She had given Tom all the archaeological details of the first episode but she had not shared with him how traumatic it had been. The second episode had been much worse. She realised that what she really needed was to talk to her therapist. She scrolled through the contacts on her BlackBerry until she came to Dr Ilse Winter's name. It was already late in the evening in Rome so Victoria knew that Dr Winter would not answer the telephone but she could leave a message requesting an appointment.

The call went straight to the answering machine.

'Dr Winter, it's Victoria Price. I am in New York City. I've had a breakthrough. I had two extraordinary past-life visions. I must talk with you right away. I return to Rome this evening and will arrive early tomorrow morning. Can I *please* meet with you sometime tomorrow? I know it's short notice but it's an emergency. I'll explain when I see you. You can reach me at this number. Thank you.' Victoria looked at her watch. There was just one other thing she needed to do at the museum before she left. She still had time before going to the airport.

12

IT WAS TOM'S last day in Athens and he planned to go to the Agora to see the marble portrait head of Alexander that was found on the Acropolis. Temporarily displayed in the Agora Museum while the new Acropolis Museum was being built, it was one of the earliest existing portraits of Alexander and one of the very few that dated from during his lifetime. Tom knew the head but he had not seen it recently, and he wanted to see it again with his own eyes so that he could compare it with the new statue discovered at Dikta.

It was slightly ironic that one of the very few early portraits of Alexander to survive came from Athens since the democratic Athenians of the fourth century BC were quite opposed to the idea of monarchy and the growing power of Macedonia. Their opposition to Philip II came to a head at the Battle of Chaeroneia in 338 BC when Philip, with Alexander at his side, defeated Athens and the other city-states of the Greek mainland and effectively became ruler of all Greece. Philip showed extraordinary leniency to Athens, though, and even sent his son to bring this good news to the city, which was the one and only time that

Alexander was known to have actually visited Athens. It must have been an awkward welcome at first, but Alexander handled it with his usual panache.

Tom walked down to the Agora along the same path he had used to take when he had dug there as a volunteer field archaeologist many years ago. His route passed through Kolonaki Square. It was relatively quiet in the square at this early hour, free from the bustle that usually grew steadily as the day progressed, but the traffic was already getting heavy. He came to Syntagma Square as the *Evzone* guards were just changing their watch in front of the Tomb of the Unknown Soldier and the Parliament building. The tall men in their striking traditional costumes of tights, clogs, a short kilt-like skirt, jacket, and colourful tasselled hats marched with high synchronised steps, their rifles held at the port-arms position, as a few tourists and passersby stopped to watch the carefully coordinated spectacle.

As Tom walked purposefully, he had an uncomfortable, undeniable feeling that he was being watched. When he had worked as a photographic safari guide in Zambia years ago he had taken people out on walking safaris to look at the wildlife and experience the bush first-hand. On those walks through the mopane woodland, Tom was the observer and teacher, explaining to tourists the unique flora and fauna of the place and the web of life within the complex ecosystem of the Great Rift Valley. On such walks, he usually did not get very close to animals, unlike when he did game watches by car, because the creatures recognised a man on foot as a dangerous predator. Once, however, he had had this same uncomfortable feeling of being watched himself. It had turned out, as he scanned the landscape, that there was a great black-maned lion stalking his group. When he looked into the fiery yellow eyes of that young beast from only fifty yards away through a thicket and became aware of the precarious situation he and his party were in, it was a terrifying moment of realisation. He found it hard to believe that he was having the same unsettling feeling here in Athens. He had known what to do when he saw the lion. He had acted right away, not giving it the chance to strike on its own terms. He had motioned silently to the gun bearer who had immediately fired off a warning shot in the lion's direction. The beast had let out a mighty bone-chilling roar and looked as if it would charge but then turned and ran away.

Tom stopped in front of the Parliament building and took a long look around the large open square. A few dozen people were walking in different directions across the square. He was ready to act but he could not locate the source of his anxiety.

In the heat of the summer Tom usually walked through the old royal gardens, which were lush and afforded some shade from the oppressive heat. Once or twice he stopped at the little zoo but found it depressing with its emaciated lion in a small iron-barred cage forlornly pacing back and forth. A colourful parrot in a domed mesh cage whistled at the girls who walked by and squawked '*Malaka*' at the men. *Malaka*, modern Greek for 'one who mastur-bates', was an activity that one might unwittingly observe in the secluded garden if one's timing was bad. Tom could only imagine the dedication of the person who must have spent years training that bird. The gardens would be the wrong route to follow today. They were too secluded, just the kind of place where he might get cornered by a stalker. He needed to stay out in the open where he was safe. He continued across Syntagma Square on his way towards the Agora Museum, the hair on the back of his neck up on end.

Tom went straight down Mitropoleos Street past the little Greek Orthodox church where Melina Mercouri, the actress and minister of culture who had championed the return to Greece of the Parthenon Marbles, had lain in state for three days while thousands paid their respects before her funeral. Tom crossed the marble paved square in front of the church and walked down Pandrosou Street, crowded on either side by tourist shops. In the old days there had been a good number of antique shops here that had sold all manner of things from prehistoric pottery and Cycladic figurines to Greek vases and Hellenistic gold jewellery. It had been a thriving centre for the antiquities business. Now there were just one or two small shops that carried very modest objects and these places were mixed in among the many tourist shops selling leather sandals and trinkets.

Tom tried to enjoy the walk down to the Agora as more and more people began to go about their daily business and the city came to life. Still, he could not shake the strange feeling that he was being followed. He stopped at shop windows periodically, glancing back to see if anyone was watching him. There was a man several yards behind him: average height and wearing a tan suit. He looked Greek, with deep olive skin and a thick moustache. He had a hat pulled low down on his head and he was smoking a cigarette. Each time Tom stopped, the man also seemed to be looking in a window a safe distance away. *That's strange*, Tom thought, *but maybe just a coincidence. If he follows me into the Agora Museum I'll know something's up*. It was not a typical destination on an October morning.

Soon Tom had reached the entrance to the Agora excavations and museum. Before entering the site he crossed the street and looked down on the area of the recent excavations in the north-east corner of the ancient marketplace. It was the location of the famous Painted Stoa where paintings on wooden panels by outstanding fifth-century BC painters had once hung. They had depicted scenes of the Athenians' victory over the Persians at the Battle of Marathon as well as mythological episodes. Although nothing of the great paintings survived, it was known from literary sources to have been a major art form. The Painted Stoa was described by many ancient writers as a kind of early art gallery where the public could view the illustrations. Next to it stood an altar to Aphrodite, which, when it was excavated, had yielded thousands of pigeon bones, the bird of choice for sacrifice to the goddess. This was the area that Tom had helped excavate years ago and it had been good training. Digging in Athens was like excavating a piece of Swiss cheese since the place had been inhabited continuously from antiquity and the foundations of later buildings, wells, and Ottoman-period long-drop toilets intruded on the remains of the earlier periods. What was amazing, though, was that thanks to ancient descriptions of the buildings that were located in this important district of the city it was often possible to identify these famous places even from their fragmentary remains. American archaeologists had been working steadily at this site for over seventy years. By now a large portion of the Agora had been uncovered down to its Classical remains and the buildings were all carefully identified. It was indeed a grand archaeological park.

Tom turned to take in the fine view of the Hephaisteion temple that stood on a low rise at the western end of the Agora. The Hephaestion was the best-preserved temple of the Classical period in Greece. It was named after the god Hephaestus, the master craftsman who was patron of this part of the city where many goods were manufactured. The temple had been converted into a Christian church dedicated to Saint George at least as early as the seventh century AD, which accounted for its remarkable state of preservation. In the nineteenth century it had been turned into a museum under the first king of Greece, Otto I, and had remained as such until 1934 when it was designated an archaeological monument.

Returning to the entrance to the site, Tom showed the guard his identification card that allowed him free entrance into archaeological sites and museums. He walked towards the Stoa of Attalos, which was the only other largely intact building on the site. It was originally commissioned by Attalos II, King of Pergamon who ruled between 159 BC and 138 BC, as a gift to the city in recognition of the education that Attalos had received there in his youth. It was a magnificent building serving as a museum and a headquarters for the ongoing excavations. The collection comprised the most significant finds from the Athenian Agora.

Tom looked around to check if he could see the man in the tan suit. He did not seem to have come into the Agora, which put Tom more at ease. He entered the museum gallery. The display followed a general chronological progression. Just beyond the material from the Classical period of the fifth and fourth centuries BC was the head of Alexander, prominently displayed on a marble pedestal.

It was an extremely impressive portrait. When Alexander had come to Athens in 338 BC the Athenians made him and his father honorary citizens. According to literary sources the Athenians set up bronze statues of Philip and Alexander in the Agora probably in commemoration of their new citizenship and to honour their beneficence to the city-state. Alexander presumably sat for that bronze portrait while he was in Athens, and consequently it would have been a good likeness. The marble portrait that Tom looked at now was uncovered in 1896 on the Athenian Acropolis, near the Erechtheion. It was an original portrait commissioned during Alexander's lifetime and almost certainly would have been influenced by the bronze portrait that stood in the Agora. From its style and context, it too could have been a commemorative image commissioned by the city itself in honour of Alexander. The legendary leader sent to Athens 300 sets of Persian armour, trophies of war, to be dedicated to Athena on the Acropolis in commemoration of his victory at the Granikos River in 334 BC, the key battle at which Alexander routed the Persian king Darius. This marble head could well have been set up by the Athenians to recognise that major dedication at the sanctuary and to acknowledge Alexander's crusade against the Persians who had desecrated the Acropolis and burned the city to the ground in 480 BC.

What Tom noticed as he looked at the powerful stone image were the mixed messages conveyed in the portrait. The sculpture had the signature leonine hair with a tousle at the centre of Alexander's forehead and exuded a youthful aura. Traces of red pigment in the hair were the remains of an undercoat for gilding that would have given the effect of golden blond hair. The highly idealised face and deep-set eyes, however, gave a mask-like effect as if to ask 'What do we really know about this young man?' The portrait seemed to reflect the ambivalence, bordering at times on hostility, that Athens had felt throughout Alexander's sweeping military campaign. This portrait was a very different image from the much later statue at Dikta where Alexander had become a god and a symbolic ruler of the world. In that powerful larger than life-size image Alexander looked aloof, also idealised but no longer human; here he was still portrayed as a young, albeit enigmatic man.

Tom contemplated how far Alexander had come from his visit to Athens at the age of eighteen and the adversity that he must have faced at every step along the way but had overcome against all odds. Indeed, just months after his visit to Athens, Philip had married another woman who bore a male child, an act that might have signalled to Alexander and his mother Olympias that Philip was considering other dynastic plans for his kingdom. Nonetheless, it was remarkable to be able to stand in Athens in the early twenty-first century, over twenty-three hundred years later, and see an image of Alexander that had been made when he was still alive. Tom walked around the sculpture and took it in for quite a while, making notes in his journal.

As he walked out of the gallery and into the cool breeze of the porch of the Stoa, Tom couldn't believe his eyes. There was the man he had suspected was following him. He was smoking a cigarette and strolling around outside the museum near the azalea bushes. For an instant, their gazes met and the man quickly stubbed out his cigarette and turned to leave. Tom started after him but the man had about a fifty-foot head start on him and once he exited the archaeological park Tom soon lost him among the crowds in the street. Tom made a mental note of what he looked like, though, and then hailed a cab back to the American School. Once again he found himself wondering what the hell was going on.

13

TOM SPENT THE rest of the morning and afternoon in the Blegen Library at the American School. They had a very fine research section and there were several books on Alexander which were only available here and a few other places in the world. In the afternoon, Tom packed his things, tossed his two bags into the boot of the car that he kept at the American School during the year, and drove down to Piraeus to catch the ferry to Crete. When he got down to the harbour, he lined up with all the other cars until he was finally waved onto the large Minoan Lines ferry. He drove aboard and parked in the hold before heading up to the concierge's office to find out where his cabin was. He'd taken a berth in a third-class cabin that slept four. Since he could leave his things locked in the car, it was the most economical solution. With luck he would not be sharing the room with any loud-snoring Cretan men. As it was no longer the height of tourist season, there were mostly locals on the boat.

Tom went up on deck to see the boat leave Piraeus. As he was looking down at the pier, to his amazement, by one of the large bollards used to secure docked ships was the man in the tan suit. He was talking on a mobile, a cigarette in one hand, and was looking up at the ship. Tom wondered if he was talking to an accomplice on board. He must have followed Tom to the boat, but it seemed clear that he himself was not embarking. The crew were packing up the gangplank and had already closed the hull door where the cars and trucks drove into the hold.

The Greek took a long drag of his cigarette, then dropped it on the ground, stubbed it out with his shoe and continued speaking to Oskar Williams. 'He's on board the *King Minos* headed for Crete this evening. I'm standing across from the ship now, in Piraeus. The *King Minos* stops first in Herakleion, then Agios Nikolaos and finally Siteia. I am not sure where he will disembark.'

'He'll get off at Siteia, I'm sure of it. He's heading to Dikta to approve the conservation work that they've been doing on the statue of Alexander. When does the boat dock at Siteia?'

'About twelve noon ferry time,' the Greek replied.

'You've done good work, Manolis. That's all for now. Goodbye.' Oskar Williams terminated the call on his mobile and then looked up the number for his contact at Dikta. He did not have any time to lose. As he dialled the number, he gazed at the large colour prints he had made of the head of the Alexander statue from Dikta, images that he had hacked into on Carr's computer.

It really is a masterpiece. I've got to have it, Oskar said to himself as he waited for Georgos to answer the phone.

'Georgos, it's Oskar. Carr is on his way to Crete tonight. He'll be in Siteia by noon tomorrow. We need to act quickly. Are you ready?'

'I can't do it, Mr Williams. The conservator and her boyfriend are camping out on the site. It's too dangerous. I can't risk being recognised. This island is too small and I couldn't live somewhere else.'

'What's the matter? The money isn't good enough? Because I can improve our arrangement . . .' Oskar replied. In Oskar's experience, it almost always came down to money.

'Look, I'm sorry. When we talked about it before it was just a matter of stealing it from the site when no one was around. It's just an old stone sculpture. But now there are people guarding it day and night. It is a whole different situation. It's not the money. I can't do it. I'm too well known around here. My involvement would leak sooner or later.'

'Okay, Georgos, I see your point. I am sorry that I can't give you the business. Goodbye.' Oskar ended the call. He thought for a minute. *So they have a couple of people sleeping out on the site at night. So what? That's not an impediment. The Greeks can be so dramatic. Of course, there are risks involved but if you are going to do something, do it right. Plan B,* Oskar said to himself as he got out his Rolodex and dialled the number of his German associate.

'Max, it's Oskar.' Oskar switched to German. 'That little plan that we hatched the other night. I want it to move forward. It needs to happen in two days. I know the timing is tight. Are you still available? Good. There will be two people sleeping at the site in a tent, a man and a woman. They won't be armed but be prepared for them. We don't want them alerting the authorities. Remember, I don't want anyone hurt. That would complicate matters unnecessarily. Okay? We understand each other? Good. Let me know when it's done.'

14

TOM WAS UP early the next morning and was walking the deck when the ferry approached the harbour of Herakleion, Crete's largest city. Herakleion was an old settlement, founded according to legend by the hero Herakles himself, a son of Zeus. It had a renaissance during the Venetian period when it was the capital of the island and when Crete was an important trading point along the maritime route between Venice and Constantinople – modern-day Istanbul. Candia, as the town and the island were known then, in the fourteenth and fifteenth centuries, had been a beautiful city and the wealth that was generated from the taxes levied on sailing ships that passed through it made the inhabitants rich. The harbour was built during the Venetian period and it was one of the few parts of the city that was not destroyed by heavy bombing during the Second World War.

Crete has a remarkable topography consisting mostly of mountains and a coastline dotted with beautiful beaches. As the ferry came through the entrance of the harbour, which was flanked by a man-made causeway creating an area of calm water for anchorage, Tom was reminded of Evelyn Waugh's description of the port when he had made a brief visit in the 1920s. Waugh described rugged men loading and unloading goods from the quay onto small boats, especially barrels and large goatskins filled to capacity with the local red wine, which was then as now an undistinguished vintage. It was quiet this early morning in October and, as the ship docked, a rosy-fingered dawn bathed everything in a soft reddish hue.

Tom would have liked to spend the morning at the Herakleion Archaeological Museum looking at its vast treasure trove of antiquities but there was not time during this trip. He watched from the deck as many people disembarked and a few more got on before the boat continued on its way along the north coast towards Siteia. As the ship chugged along Tom gazed out at the mountains and thought about the fabled Tomb of Zeus. The presence of Zeus's tomb on Crete was one of the most confusing legends associated with the thunder god. Ancient sources referred to the existence of the tomb at least as early as the sixth century BC when Pythagoras of Samos visited it and even wrote an epigram entitled 'Pythagoras to Zeus' cut right into the stone lining of the tomb. The Hellenistic poet and scholar Kallimachos of Cyrene, writing in the third century BC, mentioned the Tomb of Zeus on Crete in his *Hymn to Zeus*, where he accused the Cretans of perpetrating a mighty falsehood since a god does not die. Kallimachos's accusation might be why Saint Paul famously also described the Cretans as liars.

Some scholars interpreted the tomb as an indication that the origin of Zeus stemmed from the deeds of a living person who was deified upon his death, much like Alexander the Great. Other scholars maintained that the cult practices of Zeus stretched back to Minoan times. The tomb of Zeus then would not have been a grand charade or unseemly tourist attraction as many later came to think, but a sacred cenotaph where annual rituals were performed according to time-honoured traditions. Whatever the case, Tom thought that the monument itself must have been substantial and that it was remarkable how it seemed to have disappeared without a trace over the course of time. It made him think of the seven wonders of the ancient world and how little was preserved of them – except, of course, the Great Pyramid of Giza. The Hanging Gardens of Babylon, the Temple of Artemis at Ephesos, the chryselephantine statue of Zeus at Olympia, the Maussoleion of Halicarnassos, the Colossus of Rhodes, and the great Pharos or lighthouse at Alexandria were all gone or only the barest traces of them remained.

It was known that the Pharos was once located on an island of the same name near Alexandria – the first and greatest city founded by Alexander the Great and dating from 332 BC. A mole had been constructed from Alexandria to the island to create a safe harbour for the city. In some versions of the *Alexander Romance*, the construction of the Pharos is attributed to Alexander the Great, although it actually was begun later under his successor in Egypt. In fact, it was probably built at the same time that Alexander's mausoleum, the Soma, was constructed in Alexandria. Foundations of the lighthouse were recently identified by underwater archaeologists in the harbour of Alexandria and some images on coins of the Roman period give an idea of what the grand structure looked like. However, they give little sense of the wonder it must have inspired. Its great beacon of light, made of firelight reflected from giant mirrors, was a stunning technological achievement for its day and must have made a lasting impression on all who visited the city. Although ancient writers differed on the distance its light carried, the building itself was immense and visible for miles across the water, warning any approaching ships.

As Tom looked out across the deep blue waters of the Aegean Sea, he reflected on the marvels that the ancients had accomplished. Thinking about these great architectural and sculptural feats of antiquity and how little remained of most of them today made him wonder what he would find if and when he discovered Alexander's tomb. Like the Tomb of Zeus, would the Tomb of Alexander remain undiscovered? He just could not think that way now. If the inscription at

Dikta yielded more information about the location of the tomb, he had a reasonable chance of renewing the quest. He would know soon enough.

When the boat docked at Siteia, Tom drove straight off and travelled on through the Cretan countryside to Dikta. After about forty-five minutes, a little after one p.m., he pulled his car into the shade of a Cretan palm tree by the entrance to the dig house. The old Ford Fiesta that belonged to Evangelia, the conservator, was parked nearby and Tom surmised she was probably working inside. Walking up the main steps, he entered the main room where the conservators worked. Evangelia looked up from her desk where she was mending a pot and smiled warmly as she saw Tom come through the door.

'So you made it. Welcome.' She got up and gave Tom a big hug. She was a petite woman with olive skin and short dark black hair and a calm inner strength that matched her fit physique.

'Good to see you, Evangelia. All is well here?'

'Yes, we've been preparing for your arrival. I just came up from the site. The conservation of the statue is nearly complete. I'll finish it this afternoon after lunch. We can look at it tomorrow if you like.'

'Definitely. I've got an appointment with the abbot at Toplou in the morning but we can do it in the afternoon. Would two p.m. suit you?'

'Absolutely. You know that Yannis and I have been

sleeping down at the site just to keep an eye on the statue. After the break-in during the summer, it seemed like the prudent thing to do. We've set up a tent. We've got our two dogs down there, too. I am pleased to report that there have not been any more break-ins. I'll be glad to move back into my house, though, once the statue is moved into the museum. The romance has worn off and it is starting to get cool at night.' Evangelia smiled at Tom.

'Well, I'm sure that you've done an excellent job. Judging from the photographs you sent the results are quite spectacular. Are they ready to receive the statue in the museum?'

'Yes, I was speaking with the museum director only this morning and the statue can be moved on Friday if you are happy with my work tomorrow.'

'That sounds great. It's going to be a fabulous addition to the museum,' Tom replied.

'Nikos and his team are working out at the back on the material from their recent excavation up at Modi. He has some things he wants to show you. I think you are going to be surprised. They have some finds that are important for your research on the cult of Alexander the Great.'

Nikos was excavating a new site called Modi, situated on a high mountain plateau between Siteia and Dikta. They had discovered the site during a field survey the previous summer. Since the excavation was a joint Greek-American undertaking, they were able to get a permit to excavate. Nikos and his team had begun digging in September, only a month ago. He had told Tom over the telephone that they had already identified an open-air altar to Zeus with quite a number of votive dedications, including some that clearly related to Alexander the Great. What was so remarkable about the shrine was its date. It was still early in their investigations, but it seemed that the main period of the site had been during its latest use, in the late fifth and sixth centuries AD, long after the official outlawing of pagan religions in Greece and everywhere else in the Roman Empire. Nikos wouldn't say more over the telephone, but he had insisted that Tom stop by to see the finds for himself since he would be on Crete soon enough.

Tom walked around to the back of the dig house where he saw about a dozen people standing over tables filled with pottery fragments, working on restoration and conservation. Tom spotted Nikos talking with a young woman as they leaned on a table and looked together at some pottery shards. Nikos was an old friend from graduate school, a tall Greek man with a warm personality and a tremendous knowledge of the island and its archaeological history. Since the Dikta dig team had finished for the season, they had let Nikos and his team make use of the dig-house facilities for their work.

Tom walked up to them and said, 'Good afternoon.'

'Well, hello, Tom! Welcome. It's wonderful to see you,' Nikos said, clapping him on the back and shaking his hand warmly.

'Have you got a minute?' Nikos continued. 'Come over here. I think you'll find what I'm going to show you of great interest. Follow me.'

Nikos led Tom back into the conservation lab where Evangelia was working. Inside the large room were a series of tables covered with archaeological objects, which several conservators were busily working on. Pots restored from many broken fragments sat in tubs of uncooked lentils that allowed the newly joined parts to dry properly and hold fast. One area was devoted to the conservation of metals and in another section a conservator worked carefully on some Roman glass. Pieces of marble sculpture sat on another table awaiting conservation. Nikos walked over to a table and greeted Evangelia.

'Evangelia, do you mind if I show Tom one of the pieces you finished with recently?'

'Of course.' She put down the object she was working on, pulled a plastic tub from under the table and opened it. Inside, sitting in a pile of silica gel that served as a desiccant to keep the bronze at a stable relative humidity, was an exquisite bronze trident.

Tom gasped. 'It's perfectly preserved! Is this from your new site at Modi? It's not exactly what I would expect to find at a mountain sanctuary dedicated to Zeus. It looks as though it could have belonged to Poseidon himself.'

'It's amazing, isn't it?' Nikos never could contain his excitement. 'We excavated it at a site near the coast over the summer. Look how the barbs curve like an oyster curls when you pour lemon juice on it. It feels alive. Pick it up. You can still feel its energy.'

Tom hefted the trident in his hand. His friend was right. You could feel energy emanating from it. An ancient life-force, old but strong, palpable. Shivers ran down Tom's spine.

'Its archaeological context is a foundation deposit in the corner of a Late Minoan IB building. It was probably made in the middle of the fifteenth century BC. Judging from its perfect state of preservation, it was made shortly before it was buried. In fact, it might never have been used.'

'Maybe that's why it feels so powerful, like it's been waiting to strike but has never had the chance.' Tom was beside himself. 'It's so Minoan, though, isn't it, with those barbs that curl and hook?' he continued. 'The artist who fashioned it gave it life, the same kind of energy that we see in marine-style pottery of that period.'

Nikos smiled, 'Imagine how I felt when I picked it up, knowing the last person to handle it had put it in the ground thirty-five hundred years ago.'

Then Nikos took it back from Tom and placed it in its silicon-filled box.

'Now come over here,' Nikos said, walking over to another table at the far end of the room. A number of small metal objects and terracotta fragments were laid out on a piece of thin foam board.

'These are the pieces from Modi I wanted to show you, and I admit it may not have been fair to have shown you the trident first. There's no comparison. Technically speaking, these objects are rather crude, but I'll let you look at them before I say anything more.'

Tom walked over to the table and stood over a group of small medals. Some were round and others were oval in shape. They looked like they were made of bronze. One highly corroded example appeared to be made of silver or possibly lead. On their broad flat surfaces in relief was a portrait bust of Alexander the Great. An inscription above the head read 'Megas Alexandros' – 'Alexander the Great'. Each medal was pierced at the top so that it could be strung and worn.

'Late Roman medals of Alexander! I've seen similar things on the art market. They were often used as talismans to bring the owner luck. Beyond the *Alexander Romance*, objects like these attest to Alexander's continued importance as a folk hero, but I'm not aware of any other excavated examples that come from an explicitly religious context like yours.'

Nikos picked up a small coin and held it to the light.

'This is a sixth-century AD bronze coin minted at Itanos.' Itanos, the main town near Dikta in Late Roman times, governed the sanctuary to Diktaian Zeus until its destruction in the late fourth century AD. Remains of a fine sixth-century Christian basilica still stood on the site, which was situated on two adjoining hills overlooking the sea.

'We found this coin in the same context as the medals, in a fill not far from the central open-air altar in the sanctuary. It provides a *terminus ante quem* for their deposition sometime in the late sixth century AD.'

Tom looked at the small coin. It was very worn but turning it in the light he could make out the bust of an emperor and an inscription on the front of the coin. On the reverse side was a standing male figure wearing a cuirass. He could barely make out the city name: Itanos.

'As you know, when Crete became a Roman province in the early first century BC, Gortyn, north of Knossos, was made the capital. The island was an important stop along the Roman trade route to the Ancient Near East and Egypt. And when the Roman Empire was divided in AD 395, Crete naturally fell to the Eastern Empire.' Nikos looked at Tom before continuing. 'Have you been to the little abandoned village on that high mountain plateau at the base of Modi? Our site's not too far from there, just around the other side of the mountain.'

Tom nodded. He knew the area that Nikos was talking about. Modi was the most impressive of the three mountain peaks near Dikta. The abandoned village that Nikos spoke of was along one of the main footpaths between Dikta and Siteia during the Ottoman period and it remained a remote area well into the twentieth century until roads were built. Tom had walked it himself many times and it took several hours. Modi was a natural spot for a sanctuary to Zeus, he thought. The mountain formed an almost perfect cone that dominated the landscape for miles around.

'I've been up there quite a few times,' Tom said. 'It's a beautiful hike from Dikta. I'll never forget approaching that abandoned village one hot summer afternoon and seeing a shepherd sitting under a big plain tree, like the one at Gortyn where Zeus seduced Europa.' He laughed. 'The shepherd watched me approach from almost half a mile off, staying perfectly still in the heat of the day. A hound sat at his feet and his goats milled about, their bells making a wonderful sound in the mountain air that carried across the valley. When I got to where he was sitting, which happened to be the best-shaded spot around, he said, "Hello" and I said "Hello" back to him, smiling.' Tom paused and smiled again to think of it. 'It was the antithesis of New York City where I was living at the time. Two solitary strangers meet on an ancient road in the mountains and exchange pleasantries. I know that shepherd was wondering what the hell I was doing up there since no Greek would hike during the heat of the day, but he did not want to pry and appear rude. Ordinarily, only shepherds and hunters venture into the countryside.'

Nikos laughed, 'Yeah, we hardly ever saw anyone up there when we were digging. I had to get workmen from Roussa Ekklesia, which is about the closest inhabited village but still not close.' Nikos continued, 'Well, so far, we've defined most of the sacred *temenos*, the boundaries of the sanctuary, demarcated by large rectangular stones with Zeus's name cut into them. At the centre of the sacred space is an open-air altar made of reused ashlar blocks and fieldstones. I'm not sure where they got the ashlar blocks; they could even be Minoan. The top of the altar is big enough for an entire bull to be placed on it. The faunal remains are still being analysed, but we've got large deposits of bones, many charred and with evidence of butchery – cutting marks still preserved in the bone and so forth. There are bones from bulls, cows, goats, sheep and pigs. They sacrificed all kinds of animals, and it appears that they dined up there as well, perhaps during feasts in honour of the gods. We have drinking cups and bowls, too. I didn't pull out all that material but you can come back another time and I'll show it to you.'

Nikos looked at Tom and continued, 'We know

eastern Crete was home to the Eteo-Cretans, the oldest continuously living inhabitants of the island. There has long been evidence to show that communities continued to live on the island even in the so-called Dark Ages of the eleventh through ninth centuries BC. Praisos, for example, became a leading city in the ensuing Geometric and Archaic periods. The Eteo-Cretans were well known for hanging on to old traditions, some of which may have gone back to Minoan times. Your sanctuary dedicated to Diktaian Zeus was undoubtedly the most important cult centre for Zeus in the eastern part of the island for over a millennium and until the fourth century AD, as you've shown with your recent excavations. This newly discovered sanctuary at Modi is especially interesting, to my mind, because it provides evidence for continuity of the cult to Zeus after the official outlawing by Theodosius of pagan cults, and into the Late Antique period.'

Nikos paused and then asked, 'You haven't commented on the terracotta votives. Any thoughts?'

Nikos looked at Tom with a grin that caused Tom to look more closely. The pieces were very worn and for the most part unpainted. There was not a lot of detail and the material was quite fragmentary. But, as Tom took a closer look, he began to recognise various body parts of animals and people. One piece in particular caught his eye and he held it up to the light, feeling the coarse texture of the clay in his hand. The head and legs were missing, only the torso and arms were preserved. Judging from the lack of breasts and the sculpted physique the figure was male. The arms were bent at the elbows and held to the chest with the fists clenched.

'The pose of this piece is remarkably reminiscent of our Minoan chryselephantine statuette.' Tom was amazed at the similarity.

'The evidence is too fragmentary to be certain but it's a tantalising thought. The parallel is striking. I hope that we find more of the figure during conservation or while studying all of the material for our publication,' Nikos replied. 'I know you've only got a few days here and you must be tired from your trip so I won't keep you.'

'Thank you, Nikos. This is amazing stuff – congratulations. I'll let you get back to your work. I'll see you later, I'm sure.'

Evangelia joined Tom as Nikos left to go back outside to his pottery-shard tables, and said, 'I've also cleaned that statue base from the Roman wall on that farmer's property down by the sea. It is ready for you if you want to have a look.'

'Excellent. Yes, let me get my things.' Tom went out to his car and returned a moment later with his briefcase. Evangelia led Tom to the statue base, which was set up outside in a gated area behind the dig house. 'It was not difficult to clean. The inscription is in very good shape.'

Tom knelt down in front of the statue base. It had been discovered at the end of the dig season during the dismantling of a Late Roman wall near the sanctuary. He took out a small brush and dusted the surface, running his fingers along the letters of the inscription. The statue base, with its finely cut letters neatly spaced one next to the other, dated to the late fourth century BC, although its archaeological context was much later. It had been separated from its bronze statue, which had probably been melted down, and the base reused as building material for the Late Roman wall.

In fact, the inscription on the base indicated that it had been made to support a statue dedicated by Nearchos, Alexander's Cretan general. Nearchos hailed from Lato, a small hill town in the north-eastern part of the island, not far from Agios Nicholaos. Tom knew the ancient town of Lato well, and he remembered the sunsets visible from the archaeological site as some of the most beautiful that he had ever seen.

Tom was interested in the statue base that stood before him for two reasons. Nearchos was one of Alexander the Great's inner circle. As Alexander's commander of the navy, he wrote about their infamous expedition down the Indus river and, although his account was no longer preserved, it remained the source for numerous later works and was referred to by many ancient scholiasts. When Alexander braved the desert and returned to Babylon by land, he had Nearchos lead the rest of his army by sea along the north coast of the Indian Ocean. Not much known about Nearchos after the time of Alexander's death. This statue base, however, indicated that he had made his way back to Crete and that he had commissioned a statue of himself, an offering of thanks for his safe return. The statue was dedicated to Diktaian Zeus and had, almost certainly, been set up originally in the sanctuary at Dikta that Tom was now excavating. How its base got built into a Roman wall hundreds of years later was anyone's guess, although such reuse was common. Here was a tangible if indirect connection to Alexander from the time when he had lived and it was further evidence for the importance of the sanctuary dedicated to Zeus at Dikta in the late fourth century BC.

Tom recorded the inscription in his notebook, took some photographs and made some further notes. Before he knew it, it was four p.m. when Nikos appeared again and came over to see how he was getting on.

'So, how is it going?' Nikos asked.

'Great. I've just finished. It really is an important find for the history of the Diktaian sanctuary since it provides evidence for a dedication by a known historical figure. As you know, Nearchos of Lato was one of Alexander's most trusted companions. The cuttings in the top of the stone indicate that he commissioned a standing bronze figure, probably of himself. It's a shame that we don't have any remains of the statue, but that's not surprising. They presumably melted it down and had already reused the metal during the Roman period by the time the base was built into a wall.' Tom paused to show Nikos the cuttings for anchoring the statue in place through its feet, the outlines of which were clearly visible on the stone.

'You know, I always assumed that the cult of Alexander the Great at Dikta was initiated by the Ptolemies, who controlled this part of the island at the time. But, given this new evidence, I can't help but wonder if there was also a personal connection with Nearchos. He might well have been involved in the early formation of the cult. At the least, he would have taken great interest in it.'

'Yes, I am not surprised that Alexander the Great had a Cretan admiral for his fleet,' Nikos replied. 'The Cretans have always been great seafarers and it would make a lot of sense that Nearchos would have wanted to pay tribute to his commander-in-chief and friend once he returned to retire in Crete.' Nikos said goodbye and packed up his things for the day.

Tom's thoughts turned to the work ahead. What

would Arthur's red-phantom device reveal on the stele? Would the stone yield its original inscription or had all trace of the missing words been obliterated, erased by the ravages of time? Perhaps it would be something in between – a bit more of the inscription but not everything – and he would need to supply a probable translation. It was exciting to think about and Tom had a good feeling that there was an important discovery to come.

15

TOM HAD A siesta in the late afternoon. Ordinarily, he would have stayed at one of the rooms for rent in town but it was the off-season and there was a vacant room at the dig house so he set himself up there. The dig house was a wonderful old Cretan stone building that had once served as an olive press and then for a long time had been home to a family of goats. The dig had brought in a wrecking crew of volunteer students who helped to clear the building and then local contract workers undertook its careful restoration, creating living and working spaces as well as a pleasant garden. It provided a congenial working environment for the excavation team, especially when the season was on and there were a good number of team members in residence.

Tom unpacked his things, took a shower, and put on a fresh set of clothes for the evening. He went into the kitchen, poured himself a cold glass of water from the fridge, and sat out on the veranda to enjoy the drink. He didn't want to have a late evening, but thought he would set out on foot to the nearby village of Hieronero for a sundowner and then a quick bite at one of the local tavernas. He hadn't contacted any of the locals to let them know he was coming, but the news would spread fast as it always did in the village.

As he walked along the road to Hieronero, there was the toot of a horn as a vehicle pulled up alongside him and came to a halt, its engine still running.

'Greetings, friend!' the man called from the driver's seat of the battered old pick-up truck.

Tom looked over, a smile on his face, 'Greetings, old friend – how are you? I'm off to Barboyannis's for a drink. Can you meet me there?' Tom asked in Greek.

'I'll see you there in a few minutes,' the man replied and accelerated slowly as he continued down the road.

Tom walked along the road, taking in the fresh country air and looking out at the landscape. Everything was so much greener than it was in the summer. He crossed the little bridge over a dried-up river that only flowed in the springtime and walked on to the little village of Hieronero. The proprietor of the raki hut, Kirios Barboyannis, was sitting inside at a central wooden table, chatting with a man who had come in to buy some cigarettes.

'*Ahhh, Palaikari, kalos orizete!*' Barboyannis's raspy voice boomed. It was a traditional Cretan welcome. The phrase '*kalos orizete*' means 'may you grow good roots and stay awhile'.

Tom took the old man's hand and shook it warmly before sitting down at the central table to wait his turn. The other fellow continued his conversation as Tom looked around the small room. It was a tiny place really, with a square floor plan. Besides the central table, there were even smaller tables in three corners and a small pot-bellied stove with a flat top for cooking against the back wall. The chairs were the classic traditional taverna type, with rush seats and slat backs of a light brown oiled hardwood. The tables had plain wooden tops and bright green legs that matched the lower walls. The upper walls and ceiling were painted a bright white like the exterior. A large refrigerator sat against one wall next to a door that led to Barboyannis and his wife Georgia's living quarters. Between the refrigerator and door was a public rotary telephone. When Tom had first come to Dikta in 1988 for a three-month excavation season from March through May that had been the only public phone in the village. In fact, it had served as the phone for most of the villagers since they did not have telephones in their own houses. Now that mobile phones were everywhere and another public telephone had been installed at the edge of town, the phone at the raki hut was not used so much any more. It was Barboyannis and Georgia's own personal line.

On the other side of the raki hut was a small kitchen where Barboyannis washed the glasses, poured the raki, and prepared the *meze*, snacks that he served with carafes of raki. The kitchen had a little window, the only one in the establishment, with a lace curtain so that Barboyannis could look outside while he was doing the dishes. Tucked in a corner on a high shelf was a television. Tom remembered how, when it had been installed in 1989, Georgia had had the remote covered with thick plastic to protect it from the fine red dust that got into everything at Dikta, especially in the summer months when the *meltemi*, or summer wind, was blowing. The toilet was outside and around the back of the building and it was the most primitive one that Tom had ever seen – built right into the rock of the landscape. The crevice could have doubled as an entrance to the underworld.

The man buying cigarettes finally left, and Barboyannis turned to Tom, slapping him on the back and addressing him in Greek.

'It is good to see you, Tom. What brings you here this time of year? We did not know you were coming.'

Tom responded, also in Greek, 'Just doing some research down at the site. I can't stay long. In fact, I'll only be here for a few days. I leave for Rome on Friday.'

'Well, what'll it be?' Barboyannis asked in his best bartender tone. 'I've got this year's raki, straight from the *kazani*. I think you are going to like it.' Barboyannis was famous for his raki and he kept his sources very close to his chest. This was the time of year when people made the home-brewed liquor at their stills, called *kazanis*, that were often set up in the hills.

Tom ordered a *carafachi*, or small bottle, and two glasses. Then he said, 'Achilles will be here any minute.'

A moment later Achilles walked through the door with a big smile on his face. Tom stood up and they embraced. Then they sat down together at the big square table to enjoy the raki, sit, talk and watch the evening light. Occasionally a car squeezed by along the narrow road in front of the little hole-in-the-wall bar. Otherwise it was a blissfully quiet evening with only the sounds of village life and birds singing in the olive trees that surrounded them.

'It's good to see you, Tom,' Achilles said as he raised his glass of raki and gave the traditional Cretan toast: '*Sti geia mas.*'

Tom tapped the bottom of his glass on the wooden tabletop, then raised his glass and repeated the toast, which meant 'to our health', and took a long sip of the refreshing alcohol that warmed his throat as it went down. He and Achilles continued to converse in Greek.

'What are you doing here this time of year? How long are you staying? If it's more than a few weeks we can get some good duck hunting in. I know the perfect place where they come in on their migration to Africa for the winter. As you know we only have a three-day season so it is hit or miss, but I've been doing some reconnaissance and a few birds have already been coming through. I think it is going to be a good year.'

Raki was served with *mezes*, the Greek version of the Spanish tapas. Barboyannis brought over a tray full of snacks, a small plate of soft cheese and crusty bread, a plate of olives, and a small dish with raw tomato and cucumber slices doused in sea salt. Alcohol was never served by itself in Greece. It was always accompanied by some kind of food.

'Unfortunately, I'm just here for a few days. I'd love to see the wild ducks coming in. You know, there are some representations in Minoan wall paintings of ducks. They probably followed the same migration routes back then. There's an especially beautiful Nilotic scene from Akrotiri on Santorini where the ducks are very naturalistically portrayed. I think that they must have been observed from real life.' Tom looked for a response in his friend's eyes but Achilles had a great poker face. Tom continued: 'I've brought some special equipment to examine the stele we discovered this past summer in front of the small temple to Alexander the Great. Part of the inscription is very worn and I'm hoping that the device I brought will help in restoring the areas that are not legible to the naked eye. I'm going down to the site tomorrow. I should have results quite quickly, though, so there's no need for me to stay too long. We are also finishing up the conservation of the Alexander statue. I guess I'll have to miss the duck hunting this year. How was the opening of the hare season? Did your new dog work out?'

Achilles had two fine hounds, both Cretan hunting dogs. The breed was one of the oldest in Europe. The Minoans used them over forty-five hundred years ago. In fact, a few of their Minoan ancestors had been excavated in a Late Bronze Age well at the site. They were wiry, compact dogs with a good nose and sharp eyes and they looked something like representations of Anubis, the dog-headed Egyptian god. They had a strong taste for the hunt and, not surprisingly, they also resembled Classical Greek hunting dogs.

'He's still young but he did fine. I got two nice hares. It's my favourite sport, you know. The dogs were amazing. I think they love it as much as I do. You should see them out there. They can pick up the scent of a hare and track it like one of those heat-seeking missiles you see in American war movies. Once they lock in on it, they seldom fail to find their target.'

'No problems with the other hunters?' Tom asked. Achilles was known to be an excellent animal breeder as well as a keen sportsman, and there were intense rivalries between him and some of the other hunters from neighbouring villages. On two previous occasions his dogs had been poisoned with tainted meat, a painful death for them and an effective end to his own hunting season.

'No. I'm much more careful these days. I don't let anyone near the dogs,' he replied.

'Any other news since I was here in August?' Tom asked as he poured them both another raki from the little bottle. Barboyannis brought over another small bottle and placed it next to the first.

'This one's on me,' Barboyannis said as he set down a plate of wedges of baked potato and another plate of hunter's sausage, a seasonal treat served only at this time of year.

'Well, as a matter of fact, there was something very strange and tragic not too long ago,' Achilles said, pausing for effect and to pour some more raki. 'An old shepherd woman from the village – Danaë, you may remember her – died tragically just a few weeks ago. She had led an unusual life. As a young girl of only six, she lost her entire family in a boating accident and was raised by her aunt and uncle. She tended their sheep and spent much of her life in the countryside with her flock.'

'Yes, of course I remember her,' Tom replied. It was an unusual profession for a woman in eastern Crete. Almost all the local shepherds were men.

'They said that she was quite beautiful when she was young, long before my time. But after spending so much time alone she had got a bit wild and no man was able to tame her. She never married. Some spread rumours that she was a pagan, because she seldom, if ever, went to church – a blatant lack of religious observance that is frowned upon in our small village. There were rumours too that she was a priestess of Zeus who performed strange rituals of animal sacrifice in the hills while she was out with her flock. Of course, as a part-time shepherd myself I did not believe this for a moment. I thought these were just the imaginings of superstitious villagers who liked to gossip about such things. It is true that she loved to wear bright blue dresses with gold trim and as she grew older she stood out from the other elderly women in the village who are widows and wear only black all the time.'

Tom had always thought that this was a severe cultural practice, especially since the women of Greece tended to live much longer than the men. It seemed unfair, in any case, that men were required to wear black for only three years after their spouse died.

'She never married and so she was not bound by the custom of wearing black. As in antiquity, it was considered great bad luck that she had never found a husband and never had children and the misfortune of her family life was doubly compounded by her strange and tragic death.' Achilles paused again, took a long sip of his raki and then refilled his and Tom's glasses.

'She had been out in the fields picking figs from a tree when she fell into an abandoned well. She survived the fall – she was a strong woman even at eighty years of age – and cried out for days. Some tourists later said that they had heard her cries. The well is not far from the old service road that leads to the beach behind Kastri, but the tourists did not know where the cries were coming from. Eventually she gave up and died. They found her body a week after she had disappeared. It was a bizarre and truly sad end.' Tom listened to this sad news, remembering the spirited woman.

'But something even stranger happened the following week, seven days after her body was discovered. There was a great electrical storm. We don't usually get torrential rains in the beginning of October so the farmers were happy. Then, shortly thereafter, a shepherd noticed that a large part of his flock had gone missing. Often in the bad weather the sheep will shelter in a cave. At first he suspected that his missing flock might have been stolen by a rival shepherd, as still goes on from time to time in these parts.' Achilles paused for a sip of raki and winked at Tom. Achilles had probably stolen his fair share of sheep in his day, Tom thought as he raised his own glass to drink.

'Well, the sheep were found in the strangest of

circumstances, up on the top of Petsophas by the remains of the Minoan peak sanctuary. They had been struck by lightning. I've never seen anything like it: eight ewes and two big rams. I went up there to see it for myself. People began to talk and said that it was Zeus's tithe in retribution for the loss of his priestess. You can imagine what our priest said when he heard that.' Achilles poured them another round and nodded towards the church whose little cupola was part of the view outside the door.

'He sees the devil in this pagan talk. You know how he felt about your plans for a pagan ceremony down at the site in 2004.'

'Yes, but that was perfectly harmless,' Tom replied. In the summer of 2004, just before the return of the Olympics to Greece for the first time since the modern games had been reinstated in 1896, the Olympic torch made its way across the island. The townspeople had been keen to have it come to Dikta but the Olympic committee had decided that it would only travel as far as the neighbouring town of Siteia. The runner they had picked to carry the torch to Siteia was a Cretan who had won a gold medal in 1948. He looked older than Methuselah and he ran at less than a snail's pace. He was a very touching choice but Tom could understand why the Olympic committee had not wanted him to go the extra distance to Dikta.

In any case, the archaeologists joined the townspeople

to create their own Olympic festivities. They had arranged to have a performance of the Hymn to Diktaian Zeus accompanied by music and followed by a big Minoan feast at the site. It was all set to be a jolly occasion – until the church heard about it. They boycotted the event and tried to dissuade people from attending. Tom thought they were overreacting, but then he started hearing more and more about present-day pagans practising their chosen religion in Greece and elsewhere. The religion was called *Ellinais* and members numbered in the tens if not hundreds of thousands. Last year *Ellinais* had even succeeded in gaining legal recognition as a cultural association in Greece. That had really got the Orthodox clerics' hackles up. Tom had begun to understand why the priests in the area were concerned.

'Well, people are still shaken up about Danaë, bless her soul – the mysterious circumstances of her death and the storm afterwards. It's been the talk of the village for the last month. Everyone crosses himself or herself when they pass her house, you know, the one built on the old cyclopean Minoan foundations down at the end of the street on the edge of the village.'

'What a terrible way to die and how sad to think that she could have been saved. I've never heard of Petsophas being struck by lightning. The sanctuary's not even at the very top of the hill. It's very strange.

Did you know that in Classical times the Greeks believed Neolithic stone axe heads were physical manifestations of lightning bolts lying in the earth? Many of these have been found at Dikta.'

'Yes, I found one myself a few years ago. Remember? I turned it in to the Ephoreia for antiquities at the archaeological museum,' Achilles replied.

'That's right, I'd forgotten about that. It was a nice one made of that distinctive light green stone that seems to have been popular. We still don't know the source of that green stone. The axe heads may be evidence of a Neolithic settlement in the area, but it also appears that they were dedicated to Zeus, the god of thunder, at the Diktaian sanctuary.'

The evening stretched on and after another bottle of raki and more little plates heaped with the delicious food that Barboyannis continued to prepare, Tom realised that he was not going to need to eat dinner after all. Eventually, he decided it was time to say goodnight.

'Well, gentlemen, I've got an early morning tomorrow. I have an appointment with the abbot at Toplou to see an old book in their collection. I'll be down at the site in the afternoon.'

'It is great to see you, Tom. Good luck with your research and give my regards to the abbot,' Achilles said, winking. He was not a particularly devout

Orthodox Greek although he believed in God and the many miracles of nature.

Tom settled up with Barboyannis and walked back to the dig house and his little room off the kitchen. It was a clear night and the stars, always amazing at Dikta, filled the sky. Tomorrow was a big day, Tom thought. He hoped that the device Arthur had given him would work properly and that more of the inscription on the stele would appear, perhaps revealing the location of Alexander's tomb. Before going to bed, he walked over to the little church of Agios Stephanos that was located next to the dig house. He went inside to light a candle and say a short prayer for good luck the next day.

16

THE FOLLOWING DAY dawned with one of those cool, lovely mornings that you can get on Crete in October. Tom had the windows of his car down to catch the breeze as he drove along the road towards Toplou Monastery. The road paralleled the coast but was set back inland so that you rarely saw the sea. Instead, the rolling hills of eastern Crete with their distinctive vegetation dominated the landscape. It was a rural area and most of the land once you left the plain of Dikta's fair haven was owned by the monastery. Soon Tom came to the fork in the road where a sharp left turn headed up to Toplou, nestled in a high plain, and a sharp right turn led to the beach at Vai. Tom took the right turn. He had some time before his meeting with the abbot and decided that a quick dip in the sea would refresh him.

Vai was an extraordinary place, the only naturally occurring palm grove in Europe. There were conflicting stories about how old the palm trees were and just how they had ended up there. For a long time people believed that the Romans or the Arabs had brought them to the island, but they were now recognised to be an endemic subspecies. They are tall and majestic and the place looked like a beach on an island in the tropics.

Vai would be gloriously empty on a day like today now that the tourist season was over, thought Tom. Soon he was driving alongside the palm grove, which stretched back from the beach several hundred metres, a veritable forest of palm trees. The grove was fenced off from the beach and had been left in its natural state. Many of the taller trees still shed their branches from years of growth, appearing quite shaggy. Suckers and small bushlike trees grew beneath the tall mature trees that provided a dense shade.

When Tom arrived at the large parking lot, the ticket booth was unmanned and the flat dirt space was empty. No one else was here this early in the morning. He parked at the entrance to the beach, grabbed his towel from the back of the car and walked onto a wooden promenade that ran the length of the beach. Tom slipped off his moccasins so that he could walk in the very fine white sand beside the water. When he reached the middle of the beach, he laid down his towel and stripped off his clothes. Looking down the length of beach, he saw that it was completely quiet. Not a soul was there. Tom ran into the water until it was up to his waist and then dived and swam further out until he was deep enough to float without his feet touching the bottom. The cool water was invigorating and amazingly refreshing.

The sea was completely calm, its surface smooth as olive oil as the Greeks say. Little fish swam around Tom as he floated belly up, looking at the cloudless sky. He swam two lengths of the beach, got out, towelled off, and got dressed again. It was the perfect start to the day. He was hungry now and thinking of the little cantina at Toplou where he would have a fresh yogurt and honey before his meeting with the abbot.

Continuing his drive, he turned up the winding road toward Toplou. The car was climbing into the mountains now. There was a point near the highest elevation when he was able to glance back towards the bay of Dikta and, looking the other way, he could make out the impressive silhouette of Dragonera island. Dragonera is a deserted island where a colony of falcons breed during the late summer.

Soon Tom drove past a small double-apsed church built of stone and beyond this to the upper edge of a wide mountain plain where the monastery was. Tom stopped the car at a spot with a breathtaking view before the road wound back down into the plain. 'Toplou' is an old Turkish word for cannon and it refers to the cannon that the monks installed in the seventeenth century to protect them from marauding visitors. The monastery was first established in the late fifteenth century when it was dedicated to the Virgin Mary of the Cape. A monk had come upon a miraculous icon of the Virgin Mary in a cave nearby and had decided to build a retreat there.

Tom looked at the fortress-like monastery picturesquely set amid miles of vineyards and olive groves. It followed a typical layout for the monasteries of the island, although Tom could not think of another that could be viewed so well from a distance. In the monastery's heyday there had been more than a dozen monks living there and tilling the fields. Now there were just a few friars, but they had secular assistance with their organic farming. Tom had visited the great monasteries on the holy peninsula of Mount Athos and the extraordinary monastic retreats built at Meteora in northern Greece. He had also been to the famous monastery of Saint John on Patmos. To his mind, Toplou, although its history was less well known, was every bit as impressive a testimony to this ascetic and deeply religious way of life.

Tom drove down into the plain and parked his car by the little stone church. He walked into the cantina for some breakfast. Tom ordered a delicious combination of thick Greek yogurt covered in thyme honey – both foodstuffs made by the monastery – a double Greek coffee with one sugar, and a freshly squeezed orange juice. He sat down at one of the low Ottomanstyle tables in the cool shade, where he ate and admired the purple bougainvillea cascading over the roof and the various potted succulents arranged artfully around the tables. When he was finished, he settled his bill and asked the woman about the abbot.

'Kiria, do you know where the abbot is? I have an appointment with him at nine o'clock.'

'No, sir, you must be mistaken. The abbot is not here today. He is travelling at the moment. You can see Brother Stelios, though. I'm sure that he can assist you. He is at morning prayer now. But you are welcome to wait here or in the church. He usually finishes around 9:15 a.m.'

'Oh, okay. I'll go and wait in the church. Perhaps it will do me some good.' Tom smiled and thanked the woman before turning and walking towards the main building of the monastery.

Entering through the double doors of the monastery forecourt, past the gift shop and the large meeting room that the abbot used to greet official visitors, Tom walked up to the old main door of the building, known as the Gate of the Wheel. It was heavy and designed to be opened with the assistance of a wheel. He paused to admire the craftsmanship. The stone above the lintel was carved to depict a cross and a dolphin, and high above that was the 'murder hole', where at one time the monks would pour boiling oil down onto unwelcome visitors. During the centuries of Venetian control, the monastery was attacked a number of times by Muslim corsairs and later by the Knights of Saint John. The monks learned to secure their place like a fortress. With good reason, too, Tom thought. Toplou was one of the only places in eastern Crete that, for the most part, had withstood such attacks. Many villages had been burned to the ground, never to be inhabited again.

Pirates had been fond of eastern Crete and the neighbouring island of Karpathos, since both places were on the main shipping routes from the western Mediterranean to the east. They were also far enough away from major cities to be able to plan their attacks and escapes without fear of imminent reprisals. According to local legend, there was an old pirates' cove along the coastline just past Dikta. As a young man, Tom had gone there to do cliff jumping when he'd first worked on the dig. The place was a deep and narrow cleft in the rock, big enough for the crew of a single large pirate ship to conceal themselves and their craft and still maintain the element of surprise when they pulled out to intercept their prey. Since the water was exceptionally deep, they could immediately start rowing at full speed for maximum ramming impact. Anyone with enough nerve could climb the sheer rock like the pirates used to do and look out along the coast of the island, and then, like Tom and his colleagues, hurl themself sixty feet into the water. It was a terrifying experience. Youth laughed in the face of death, Tom thought, or at least tempted fate, overcoming gut-wrenching fear by jumping into the abyss. He had learned a few things since those early days of his youth.

The Gate of the Wheel was open so Tom stepped inside through a small foyer into the open-air court-yard and onto a blue-and-white mosaic floor made of sea pebbles. In front of him on the right was the entrance to the church, the 'Katholikon' or central place of worship in the monastery. The old wooden door of the church was slightly ajar and Tom could hear the monk praying inside. Before he entered the church, he stopped to look at the ancient inscription carved on a marble slab built into the façade. Written in ancient Greek and dating to the year 138 or 132 BC, its carefully cut letters were neatly arranged on the stone. The letter forms were of an earlier type than the letters of the stele from the temple to Alexander the Great, which Tom intended to examine later that afternoon.

Tom walked into the church and crossed himself in front of the icon of the Virgin and Child that was set on a fine eighteenth-century wooden stand near the entrance. To his left a few thin beeswax candles had been placed upright in bowls of sand. Their flames flickered and provided a warm glow that cast shadows against the stone walls of the church. In front of Tom was the apse of the northern nave of the church, dedicated to the nativity of the Virgin Mary. It was the oldest part of the church and its elaborate silver iconostasis separated this holiest area and its richly decorated icons from the worshippers. Numerous votive plaques of silver and gold were attached with ribbons or wire to the front of the iconostasis and two silver lamps hung in front of the icons, their wicks fuelled by olive oil.

Adjacent to the northern nave was the slightly larger southern one, dedicated to Saint John the Divine. The monk stood at an elaborately carved wooden lectern with a sculpted eagle that supported on its back the large prayer book from which he was reading. Brother Stelios read the prayers in a steady rhythmic chant, almost as if he was reciting them from memory. Tom sat down at the rear of the nave on one of the tall-backed seats originally meant for the monks of the monastery. He had met Brother Stelios a few times before. A young man, probably in his late twenties, Brother Stelios had been living at the monastery for several years. He was tall, with a long full black beard and thick black hair that he wore in a ponytail. An industrious fellow, he had become the abbot's right-hand man. He had been born in Athens, grew up there, and attended the city's university. Afterwards he joined his family business but then had the calling and joined the Church. After some ecclesiastical training at one of the monasteries of the Holy See of Mount Athos, he was sent to Toplou. The solitude of the monastery appealed to him after the bustle of

Athens, but he had a keen business sense and a love of technology. He helped the abbot to develop an organic olive-oil and wine business that flourished and brought in significant revenue for the monastery. Then they added honey and mountain tea to their list of products, and were now thinking of expanding with raki. Brother Stelios established business connections with people in Athens where they exported their goods, as well as to cities on the island from Siteia to Herakleion.

Tom listened quietly to the prayers. Through a small window behind the lectern there came some natural light and a slight breeze. At one point he heard Byzantine chimes. He thought it was part of the service until he saw Brother Stelios pull a chiming and vibrating mobile phone out of his pocket with one hand, silence it, scroll through a text message, and continue his rhythmic chant without missing a beat. Aside from this slightly comic modern intrusion, the scene could have been taking place in the eighteenth century. Tom seated himself so that he could look at the monastery's greatest treasure, an icon entitled 'Great Art Thou, Oh Lord', hailed as one of the finest examples of Cretan religious painting. It hung on the central wall between the two apses of the church.

An inspirational work of art, the icon had four main scenes: the descent of Christ into hell, the Virgin Mary enthroned and holding the Christ Child, with

Adam on her right and Eve on her left, the Baptism of Christ in the Jordan River, and the Holy Trinity – God the Father, God the Son and God the Holy Spirit – surrounded by heavenly powers. Around these four central scenes were an additional fifty-seven scenes that followed the clauses of the Great Benediction. In the dim light of the church, Tom had to get really close to the painting to appreciate its richly detailed depictions. His favourite scene showed the Great Flood with Noah's ark sailing the vast sea. Next to this scene the ark was shown grounded on Mount Ararat beneath a rainbow as all the animals disembarked. Above this was Jonah being released from the whale, which looked like a giant fish, before the ancient Near Eastern city of Nineveh. Each vignette was intriguing – Moses leading the Jews through a dramatically parted Red Sea, the Last Supper – and the list went on and on, each subject with its own beautiful miniature painting.

Tom loved to look at this icon. The painting particularly inspired his interest this morning because the book that he had come to see was a late-eighteenth-century copy of the *Alexander Romance* made by the same monk – Ioannis Kornaros – who had painted the icon. The abbot had told him about the book during the summer, but there had not been time to see it then. Tom was eager to see what this master miniaturist painter had done with the *Alexander*

Romance. What was more, it was a work that was virtually unknown to scholars. The abbot had not shown it to anyone during his tenure at the monastery. They had a small but fine museum where they displayed many of their treasures but Kornaros's illustrated manuscript of the *Alexander Romance* was not one of the works on display. The abbot did not see it as central to the mission of the Church since it was not strictly a religious text.

Brother Stelios finished his prayers and started to close up the church. Tom came up to him in front of the great icon and introduced himself. 'Brother Stelios, I am Tom Carr. I work on the excavation of the Diktaian sanctuary. We met briefly this past summer and the summer before. I had an appointment this morning to see the abbot but Kiria told me he's away today. She suggested that I speak to you.'

'Mr Carr, of course I remember you. Welcome to Toplou. The abbot did mention to me that he was expecting you today. He sends his apologies and has asked me to assist you. He was called away on urgent Church business in Herakleion yesterday. But I have located the manuscript that you want to see and have set it out for you.'

'That's wonderful. I'm especially excited to see it since it was illustrated by Ioannis Kornaros, the artist who painted this amazing icon.'

'Yes. You are certainly in for a treat. I was looking

through the manuscript yesterday. The illustrations are especially fine. You know, Alexander may be represented in this painting as well. See the scene here where two kings kneel before Adam?' Brother Stelios moved closer to the icon, pointed to the scene, and continued. 'It represents the phrase, "And save, O Lord, Thy servants our faithful rulers and guard them under the protection of Thy peace; tread under their feet every enemy and foe; grant them every petition to salvation and eternal peace."' You will see that the king kneeling in front closely resembles the mature Alexander the Great as he is depicted by Kornaros in scenes in the *Alexander Romance*. I suppose Alexander the Great would have been a natural choice for Kornaros since he was representing all earthly rulers with just two figures. I am not sure who the other ruler is. It could be one of the Roman emperors, like Augustus or Constantine, or perhaps one of the Byzantine emperors.' Stelios turned to leave the church and motioned for Tom to follow him.

'The manuscript is upstairs in our library. Ordinarily we do not allow visitors in there since it is within the private quarters of the monastery but as the abbot is away and I am the only one here right now, I thought it would be best since it means less disturbance of the manuscript.'

Tom followed Brother Stelios up the open staircase that climbed one side of the courtyard to the second floor. From there they walked around to the entrance of the library. Brother Stelios took out an old skeleton key and unlocked the door. They walked into a small room full of old books on wooden bookshelves that were built into the walls. In the centre was a large reading table on which the manuscript was set up on a reading stand. Brother Stelios drew the curtains of two nearby windows, letting in natural light, and opened the windows as well to introduce some fresh air.

'Please make yourself comfortable. How much time do you expect you will need?' Brother Stelios asked Tom.

'Thank you, Brother Stelios. I greatly appreciate your taking the time to assist me. I expect that I will only need a couple of hours.'

'Very well. Take as much time as you need. I will check in on you in a while to see how you are doing.'

Brother Stelios walked out, leaving the door open, presumably to increase the air circulation. Taking a deep breath, Tom sat down in front of the manuscript and prepared to examine it. He took out his notebook and magnifying glass and put them on the table. The pages were held in a finely tooled leather binding. He began to leaf gingerly through them. Many of the scenes were familiar to Tom from other editions that he had seen. Kornaros must have been familiar with earlier versions of the *Alexander Romance* since many of the scenes followed the standard iconography. Tom thought that Kornaros might have studied these previous accounts when he was at the Monastery of Saint Catharine on Mount Sinai, or even while he was in Cyprus, where old Greek traditions were strong. The sheets of the manuscript were made of vellum and there was an illustration at the beginning of each chapter.

The first scene that caught Tom's eye was one that was particular to the *Alexander Romance*. It represented a myth created long after Alexander's death, one that portrayed Olympias, Alexander's mother, and the Egyptian pharaoh-magician Nectanebo II, coincidentally the same man whose sarcophagus had been brought to the British Museum and identified as that of Alexander before they were able to read its hieroglyphic inscription. According to the *Alexander Romance*, when the Persian king Artaxerxes invaded Egypt in 442 BC the reigning pharaoh Nectanebo foresaw that he was destined to lose his kingdom to the Persians and fled the country to Macedonia where he was received at the royal court of Philip II. Nectanebo fell in love there with Olympias, and devised a plan using the art of magic to seduce her.

Crafting wax images that he floated in a magic potion, Nectanebo was able to induce Olympias to dream that she was visited at night by Zeus Ammon who seduced her. Their union, the god told her, would produce a son who would rule the world. The story related Alexander to Egypt's royal line of pharaohs in much the same way that some versions of the *Alexander Romance* made Roxane a Persian princess, which brought Alexander into the Persian bloodline. It echoed the story of Alexander's fathering by Zeus, which was current in Alexander's lifetime and was spread by Olympias. The latter story sometimes described how she slept with Zeus in the form of a snake, and in another version Olympias dreamt of being possessed by a lightning bolt. The trickster tale of Nectanebo was perhaps more believable and made for a good story to boot.

In Kornaros's fine illustration, Olympias lay alluringly on a huge bed covered with soft cushions. Torches hung on the wall as Nectanebo approached in the guise of Zeus Ammon, a ram with long golden horns. A black fleece covered his back. From the front, his own curly black chest hair was visible. He held a golden sceptre in one hand as he walked gingerly towards the foot of Olympias's bed. As she raised her head, she looked at him approvingly. The artist cleverly conveyed the sense that she was not entirely deceived by the ruse but was a party to it. As in the icon, the colours were brilliant and the detail was remarkable even though the images were on a very small scale.

The next scene that caught Tom's eye was one that

he had not seen illustrated often. Alexander had been only twenty-two years old when he set out from Macedonia with his army in 334 BC to begin an unprecedented campaign of military conquest. Just after he had crossed the Dardanelles with his army from Europe into Asia, Alexander was the first to step off the boat. He hurled his spear into the ground and dramatically claimed all of Asia as spear-won. With this display, he intended to echo the Homeric hero Protesilaos, who had been the first to land at nearby Troy. Protesilaos was also the first Greek warrior killed, thus assuring himself immortal glory. Alexander, however, intended to garner his immortal fame like Achilles on the battlefield. Indeed, his favourite book was Homer's *Iliad* and it was said that he took a copy of it with him wherever he went. Legend had it that he kept under his pillow a copy that had been given to him by his tutor Aristotle. Thus Alexander was interested in visiting the ancient ruins of Troy and made it his first stop in Asia. He was especially interested in visiting the tomb of Achilles.

The illustration now in front of Tom represented this very moment in Alexander's life. Alexander and his best friend Hephaestion were racing each other around the great tumulus of Achilles set on the plain of Troy where he had died. Kornaros's simple but beautiful depiction captured a precious moment in the great hero's life. Jubilant at visiting for the first time the tomb of his childhood hero Achilles, Alexander put aside his kingly duties. In this scene he was competing with his best friend, two young men enjoying life and each other's company at a time when all Alexander's great accomplishments still lay before him. It was a poignant moment from his youth, one that Alexander would recall years later at the time of Hephaestion's death near Babylon when he built a great funeral pyre for his friend and organised lavish funeral games like those that Achilles arranged for Patroclus in the penultimate book of the *Iliad*.

Ancient literature provides some descriptions of the tomb of Achilles. In book XXIII of the *Iliad*, the ghost of Patroclus tells Achilles that he wishes their bones to be buried together in a golden two-handled urn provided by Achilles's mother Thetis. The *Iliad* ends before the death of Achilles but at the end of Homer's *Odyssey*, when Odysseus visits the underworld, the ghost of Agamemnon describes the burial of Achilles and the placement of the golden urn under a giant tumulus mound. There were many recorded visits to the tomb of Achilles in antiquity, including that made by the Persian king Xerxes and by many of the Roman emperors. It was a kind of pilgrimage site for hero worship but, like Alexander's tomb, its precise location was no longer known. In ancient art, the tomb was sometimes illustrated in scenes of the sacrifice of

Polyxena, the youngest daughter of Priam, king of Troy. Later European artists tended to depict it as a tomb near a temple. Kornaros's illustration followed the ancient tradition.

Tom was pleased to see another illustration of Roxane dancing before Alexander. In a tightly fitting veil, she twirled before the king and his entourage. In Kornaros's illustration, though, Roxane looked boldly at Alexander as she danced. Their gazes met, locked in a stare that foretold their future together. Tom thought again of Victoria Price, and the Baker Dancer's pose that closely resembled this illustration. Could that masterpiece of Hellenistic bronze sculpture actually represent Roxane dancing for Alexander? The comparison was striking but not close enough to be certain, given the vast chronological and geographical differences. Only Victoria Price's extraordinary vision made the identification compelling, but there was no way of confirming her wild tale.

Tom was intrigued to see an illustration of Alexander and Roxane on their wedding night. It clearly echoed a famous painting of that historic night completed by the painter Aetion during Alexander's lifetime. Roxane sat on a bridal couch and Alexander stood before her. Here she did not look directly at him but was turned slightly away, her eyes glancing downward in modesty. A cherubic Eros pulled back her wedding veil to reveal her beautiful face as another knelt at her feet to remove her sandals, preparing her for the nuptial bed. Alexander stood enraptured with Roxane, a garland in his hand. Other Erotes played with Alexander's armour in the far right corner of the scene. According to the ancient writer Lucian, Aetion's original painting, which hung at Olympia and was later brought as booty to Italy, called attention to Alexander's other love – war – and to the idea that he never forgot his weapons. Aetion's artwork had been lost, but it was believed to have inspired a Roman wall painting at Pompeii, which Tom had seen. Kornaros must have seen another ancient copy since the painting from Pompeii had not yet been excavated in the eighteenth century. In the scene before Tom, Alexander clearly did not seem to be thinking of his armour. The specific placement of the arms might have recalled another famous painting that represented Ares and Aphrodite with Erotes stripping the god of war of his armour as he prepared to make love to the goddess. The subliminal message was 'love disarms war'.

It was a stunning manuscript and Tom was eager to speak to the abbot to see if he would consider lending it for the Met's Alexander exhibition. But that negotiation would have to wait for another day since the abbot would probably not return before Tom had to leave. The abbot was a forward-thinking man, though, and Tom felt confident that he'd be willing to lend the manuscript as long as the curator ensured that it would receive the proper care. The difficulty would be in choosing which of the illustrations to exhibit since only one could be on view at a time. When Brother Stelios returned, Tom thanked him for the extraordinary opportunity. The monk accompanied him back downstairs and outside the walls of the monastery. It had been a very productive morning. Tom could only hope that the afternoon would turn out as well.

17

VICTORIA WAS STILL jet-lagged after her flight but a cup of strong coffee, some fresh melon, and a warm Italian pastry from her favourite bakery had gone a long way towards making her feel better. It was so good to be back in Rome. It really felt like home to her. She looked at her watch as she sat at the kitchen table. She only had half an hour before her appointment with her therapist. She'd been relieved when Dr Winter had texted her to say she could make time for her this morning. After placing the dishes in the sink, she checked herself in the mirror and then headed out. It was a beautiful autumn day and she had just enough time to walk there.

Dr Winter's office was in a small apartment building on the other side of Trastevere, the district in Rome where Victoria lived. Victoria walked up the steps and rang the buzzer. After a few moments, Dr Ilse Winter came to the door. She was a small woman, fine-boned, with birdlike features, short black hair and dark brown eyes.

Opening the door, she said, 'Victoria, you are right on time. Come in. Please make yourself comfortable. It seems that we have a lot to discuss.'

Dr Winter led Victoria into the room where she met with her patients. The walls were painted a neutral white colour and bookshelves lined three walls. A white orchid bloomed on a long side table beneath a large window behind the couch. Victoria took off her coat and sat down on the couch. Dr Winter sat opposite her in a wooden chair.

'Thank you so much for fitting me in like this, Dr Winter,' Victoria started. 'I would not have asked if it was not an emergency. It's just that I had two extraordinary channelling experiences in New York. I actually lost consciousness – and the visions . . . they were so real, as if they truly happened to me.'

'Please take a deep breath and continue,' Dr Winter replied.

Victoria began her story, speaking quickly as though she could not wait to start the next sentence. First she related the experience at the Metropolitan Museum.

'Before you go any further, let's discuss the first vision or dream,' Dr Winter interjected. 'I am struck by the antiquity of the setting. To be honest with you, I have not had any patients with such vivid early past-life recollections, although there are certainly documented cases. More common are the recollections of children, whose psyche is perhaps less formed, who at an early age, typically before they are eight or nine years old, recall memories of a previous life. I've had two such cases myself, children here in Rome. One child, she was only six years old, recollected the experiences of a man who had died as a teenager years before, also in Italy. There was no way that she could have known about this boy and his tragic end. Another child described in great detail the hill town in Sicily where he had lived as a young man even though his parents swore that he had never been to Sicily. He was able to describe his previous family in some detail. After some research it became clear that the family was still living in that small town and they had lost a son some twenty years before. They were completely spooked by this news and did not want to meet the boy.

'Your experience seems quite different,' Dr Winter continued. 'Your visions were set off by objects that triggered a memory – if that is what it was – from a previous life. It seems possible that the statuette you saw was in fact the very one that you had held centuries before in Alexander's tomb. Objects can be powerful memory aids and it is so rare to have the very object, a kind of time traveller, survive from such a distant age. There could be other explanations, however. You have to keep in mind that all of what I am saying remains in the realm of theory. There are no proofs. According to another theory, you could have been channelling energy from the object, which triggered the recollection. You acted merely as a conduit, like a medium at a seance. It's clear to me, though, that this is not how you felt. It felt as though it was a part of your own experience. Am I right?'

'Yes, utterly, and for me that is the disturbing part,' Victoria replied. 'But let me tell you the second vision so that you have the whole story.'

'Okay, continue,' Dr Winter replied.

Victoria related her second vision at the Morgan Library and how she had come so close to death while clutching the amulet of Nereida in her hands in the darkness of Alexander's tomb.

'What bothers me so much is to think that I was this horrible person in a previous life. Was that really me? How could I have done such a thing – desecrate someone's tomb trying to find an amulet that would give me immortality? How vain is that? What was especially chilling was how close to death I was during the vision. I felt as if I was dying and it was awful. At the very end, death was there with me, a physical presence, about to take me off to the underworld. It did not feel like I was going to heaven. If I had not woken up when I did, would I have slipped away again? The medic at the scene only arrived after I had woken up screaming. They monitored my heart rate after that and it was erratic. It scared the hell out of me.' Victoria was getting emotional and could feel herself on the brink of weeping. Then she really did burst into tears.

Dr Winter gave her a few minutes to calm down and then she spoke. 'Let me address your question about how could you have done such a horrible thing. Sigmund Freud had a theory – not much accepted by science, admittedly – that people could tap into the collective unconscious. We can look at this another way. Your interest in this amulet and immortality can be seen on a more generic level. Mortality is something we all face and thoughts about our own death crop up in our conscious and unconscious sooner or later. Carl Jung on the other hand saw dreams as relating to contemporary experiences, a way of expressing thoughts that have been suppressed at a conscious level. If we see everything in the vision as relating to you or stemming from an issue that you have, it could have been generated out of your own anxieties. You mentioned that you had spent the weekend with your friend on Long Island and how she seemed so much further along her own path, happily married and with children. Do you think this vision could have been an anxiety or panic attack brought on by this encounter and couched as a continuation of your vision of the previous week, which was no doubt also heavily on your mind since you were visiting an exhibition about Alexander the Great?'

Victoria was caught off guard by Dr Winter's question. Could the experience have been a vivid creation of her own imagination? Then she thought about her talk with Tom Carr and taking up his time. Did he think that she was just some narcissistic dreamer? It gave her an awful feeling in her stomach. She knew that she had to see Tom when he came to Rome later that week.

Victoria answered, 'It was just so real – the details of the vision were extraordinarily vivid, let alone the way it caused me to faint. I really don't think I was daydreaming. It is true that the sensation before I fainted each time was something like a panic attack and as you know I have had panic attacks before, especially with my fear of enclosed spaces. This feeling, though, was even more intense and it had a different quality, very distinct but hard to describe. But I recognised it as it was happening and I felt like I had experienced it before.'

They stopped to reflect on this and then Dr Winter spoke. 'Returning to your question, and for the moment accepting that what you saw was a memory of your own past-life experience, you should not feel guilty about it. It is hard to say if you bring that nature with you, if it is a part of your soul. It is tempting to think so. Still, you must remember that you have had a window into a very small part of that previous existence. You don't have the whole story to consider. Don't judge yourself on the basis of this single episode. I have spent a great deal of time working with you now over several years and

I see nothing of a hardened criminal nature in you, not even a trace. The important thing to remember is that you are living your life now, not in the past. Anything you learn from these channelling experiences should be used to help you grow and be strong for the present.'

'It has helped me with my claustrophobia. Our work together has improved that immensely, so that I can function like a normal human being. But this was a kind of breakthrough. I felt better getting into elevators and I even flew back to Rome without my usual medication.'

'See, this is what I am talking about. Knowing that your fear could stem from a past-life experience where you were essentially buried alive, you can recognise that your fear need not consume you. Your situation now is very different.'

18

IN THE EARLY afternoon, Tom gathered his equipment to go down to the site to get a digital reading of the stele and check the conservation of the cult statue of Alexander the Great. He was already tired from his morning at the monastery, and he had not slept well the night before. He had had vivid dreams of a large spider crawling over him and when he awoke startled and slightly disorientated in the middle of the night there *was* a large spider crawling on him. It gave him the chills just to think about it. He'd jumped out of bed and killed the spider with his shoe. It was as big as a tarantula but not really dangerous, although it could have given him a nasty bite. There was only one truly dangerous type of spider on Crete. It was much smaller and very compact, shaped like a futuristic tank and with incredible strength – and its bite was deadly. One bite could kill a full-grown man.

Tom had seen this spider in the wild but it was not very common. He had also seen it depicted in Minoan art so it must have been a long-time inhabitant of the island. Its power must have impressed the Minoans, too. The Met had a nice representation of the deadly spider on a Minoan sealstone from the Middle Bronze Age that was part of the collection bequeathed by the archaeologist Richard Seager, who had excavated in eastern Crete, at Mochlos, and elsewhere. Seager collected many sealstones pieces from local peasants who called them *gallopetres* or milk stones. Cretan farmers found them while tilling the fields and gave them to the women who wore them as talismans when they were of child-rearing age. They believed that the ancient stones ensured rich, healthy breast milk. The woman who wore the sealstone engraved with the spider probably also believed that it would protect her from the venom of such arachnids.

In truth, Tom did not like staying at the dig house. It was fine during the day but at night its aura was negative. There had even been reports of sightings of spirits of the dead. Tom had never seen anything himself but he could sometimes feel the lingering, sharply foreboding atmosphere. It was no wonder, either, since it was said that there had once been an Ottoman cemetery on the site. It was also said that the many bodies were of those who had been killed in a bloody massacre during a pirate raid on the village. One of the students working on the dig had come in late one evening and as she'd stepped down into the large common room had found herself standing face to face with a tall man wearing the turban, baggy shirt and trousers of an Ottoman subject. Blood had gushed forth from a terrible gash across his forehead. The young woman had run screaming from the room, waking up everyone else in the dig house.

Still, Tom had to shake off his weariness. He was excited to see the results of Evangelia's work on the statue of Alexander the Great and at the prospect of trying out the Red Phantom program. He had had a double Greek coffee at lunchtime to make sure that he was suitably caffeinated for the afternoon's work. On his way down to the archaeological site, he would stop at the guard's house to get the keys for the gate that led into the new excavations and for the shed that enclosed the stele and remains of the temple dedicated to Alexander the Great. The seated statue of Alexander Cosmocrator, King of the World, was still inside. The local museum had built a new gallery to display this important work, as well as the other new finds from the sanctuary of Diktaian Zeus. It would be transferred to the museum tomorrow if Tom approved the conservation work. The guard told Tom that Evangelia was already inside with the statue, waiting for him.

Tom drove through the main site gate and parked his car opposite the guard's house. He got out and surveyed the area of the sanctuary. They still were not sure of its limits. Usually these spaces were carefully delineated with a temenos wall or at least sacred boundary stones. The notion of distinguishing sacred space from the secular was very important to the ancient Greeks. Visitors to the sanctuary must never, in any way, desecrate it. When the Homeric hero Ajax raped Cassandra within the sanctuary of Athena at Troy, he brought about his own demise. He went mad with grief when he realised what he had done and this remorse led to him taking his own life by falling on his sword. Tom had a pretty good idea where the location of the propylon or entranceway into the Diktaian sanctuary was. He thought it lay in the eastern quadrant, but they would not be able to dig test trenches until next summer to confirm his hypothesis.

He opened the gate into the sanctuary area and walked up to the shed that enclosed the temple and the two stelae set up in front of it. As he slowly opened the shed door, he peered inside and saw Evangelia on a ladder, inspecting the statue. The stelae were standing firmly on their stone socles just as they had been when he had last seen them in August. Inside the cella of the temple the statue of Alexander towered behind them. Tom took a moment to admire the statue and to note the progress that had been made with its conservation. When the statue had first been discovered, much of Alexander's leonine hair had still been gilt and the pupils of his eyes were painted black with deep blue irises. Evangelia had written to him that

the eyelashes were also painted black. It was remarkable how well the paint had been preserved.

'I think it looks magnificent. You've done a
wonderful job. By all means, let's proceed with the
transfer to the museum tomorrow. It will be good for
the statue to move it into a more controlled environment. Can you arrange it?'

'Yes, they are just waiting for my call. I'll let them
know now. We can move it tomorrow morning. It
will probably take a couple of hours. We've worked
it all out. Please come on down to the site at eight-
thirty a.m. tomorrow if you'd like to watch.'

'Terrific. I am going to work on the stele here now
for a while. I've brought a device that may help me
to read it.'

'Okay, I'll leave you to your work. See you
tomorrow.' Evangelia smiled and walked off to the
guard's house to make the arrangements.

Tom walked back to his Land Rover, opened the
back and took out the bag that contained his computer
and the Red Phantom equipment. He put down the
bag in front of the stele and laid out a canvas sheet
on which he placed everything. There was a pretty
good breeze blowing so Tom decided that he would
get the reading and then download the information
to his computer inside the car so that he wouldn't
expose his laptop to the dust. The site was known as
Roussolakos or 'Red Pit' after the colour of the earth,

which turned into a fine red dust that had a way of creeping into everything. He'd had lots of electronic equipment malfunction after prolonged exposure to the Dikta dust, so now he always took precautions. In any case, he could always take a second reading if the first was not successful. It might take a few tries before he got the equipment working the way he wanted. Arthur had said to try a variety of settings if the default one did not produce satisfactory results.

Tom needed to keep the shed door open for the natural light it brought in. He attached the straps to the sides of the stele. They fitted perfectly. Then he took out the device and turned it on to make sure that it was working. Nothing happened. Tom took a deep breath and muttered, 'Here we go.' He turned it off and then turned it on again. No response. He took out the batteries and put in a new set. This time the power light came on and the lens opened. Tom wiped his brow and attached the camera to the customised frame, adjusting the straps so that the lens was aligned with the portion of the text that needed work. He pressed the activation button and the device moved systematically across the surface of the inscription like a scanner, gathering information from the worn stele. It really was a remarkably simple process, at least from a technician's point of view.

Tom still didn't completely understand the technology behind the device. But the principle of paint reacting with the stone over time to leave an impression, even if it was not visible to the naked eye, made sense to him. Using infrared light and other non-destructive scientific analyses that could detect traces of faded paint, a number of Early Bronze Age marble statuettes in the Met's Cycladic collection were discovered to have been brightly painted in antiquity. Likewise there were a number of Greek and Roman marble sculptures at the Met that retained traces of their original painted decoration. Although people tended to think of ancient sculptures as plain unpainted white marble, most sculptures in antiquity were, in fact, brightly painted.

Tom took the device back to his car to download the data and see the results. He opened up his laptop and powered it up. When the computer had booted he plugged in the digital scanner. The Red Phantom program automatically opened itself and started to download and then process the data that Tom had captured. The little red Casper-like ghost flew around the screen while the program worked. In a minute the image appeared. Tom was amazed to see that the text was much more legible on screen than it was on the stone. The letters were not as crisp – their edges looked slightly frayed on the screen – but all of them were distinct and the words were decipherable! He could hardly believe his eyes and what he was reading: '. . . the tomb of Alexander, which was located in

Alexandria and was moved through the divine sanction of the Emperor Trebonianus Gallus *to the Pantheon in Rome*.'

'*My God*,' Tom thought.

'The Pantheon, the temple to all the gods,' he said aloud. 'Is it possible? Could Alexander's remains still be there, buried within the Pantheon?' It was one of the very few temples in Rome still standing much as it was when it was first built in Roman times. By coincidence, Tom was on his way to Rome. When the significance of this new discovery sank in, he called his Greek travel agent from his mobile phone, still staring at the screen: '. . . the tomb of Alexander which was located in Alexandria and was moved through the divine sanction of the Emperor Trebonianus Gallus to the Pantheon in Rome.'

'Yannis? This is Tom Carr. How are you? Good. Listen, I need your help with a reservation. I'm scheduled to leave on Friday for Rome but I need to go tomorrow. Can you see if you can get me on the morning flight from Siteia and change my connecting flight from Athens to Rome? I have a reservation on Delta Airlines for a flight from Athens at one p.m. on Friday. I would need the same flight but for tomorrow. I'm sending you a copy of my e-ticket right now.' He paused. 'Got it? Great. Call me at this number if it works out. Thanks so much, my friend.'

Then Tom called the American Academy in Rome

and asked to speak to the secretary. 'Hi. This is Tom Carr from the Metropolitan Museum of Art in New York. I have a reservation to stay at the Academy for several nights beginning on Friday. I wonder if it would be possible for me to arrive a day early?'

'Just a minute, Mr Carr, let me check for you.' Tom waited on the line.

'Fortunately, you are in luck. Your room was vacated earlier today so we can have it ready for you. I'll leave your key in an envelope with the guard in the sentry booth at the entrance to the Academy. Safe travels. We look forward to seeing you tomorrow.'

'Thank you so much. I look forward to seeing you tomorrow as well.' Tom turned off his mobile phone and sat there, still staring at the inscription on the computer screen.

19

ALL FEELINGS OF exhaustion seemed to disappear from Tom's body after his success with the inscription. Adrenalin now rushed through his veins. He couldn't believe this new revelation. His Greek travel agent called back to confirm the new reservation. Tom would be in Rome tomorrow afternoon. He planned to go to the Pantheon as soon as he'd checked into his room at the American Academy. He was now up at the dig house gathering his things, but he was too excited. He needed to remain calm. He needed to work some of the excitement out of his system, so he decided to go for an afternoon run. That would help and the exercise would be good for him. After changing into some running gear, he did a long loop, running the length of the bay, up one of the dirt roads through the olive groves and behind Kastri towards the site. When he joined the old service road that headed down towards the sea and the archaeological site, he got a strange intuition and slowed down.

Suddenly, Tom realised where he was and stopped running. There, fifty feet from the road, was the abandoned well where Danaë had met her fate. As Tom approached slowly, he could almost hear the echo of her screams. Her presence was still very strong. The closer he got to the wellhead the louder the screams became. Dikta was a very spiritual place: like Olympia or Delphi, it was sacred to the gods. Tom didn't think of himself as a particularly religious person, but whenever he returned to the museum after a stay at Dikta he felt that his senses were heightened. Living here, even for a few days or weeks, close to the land and sea, was like a purification process. By the end of his stay he was always much more in tune with his own energy and the energies of those around him. It was a centring process, much like he imagined the ancient Greeks experienced when they made a pilgrimage to Delphi, which they believed to be the *omphalos*, the centre of their universe.

Now he was at the edge of the well, standing next to the old fig tree with its large green leaves. There was still plenty of ripe fruit ready to be picked. More lay rotting on the ground. Bees buzzed around the fallen fruit in their attempt to get at the sweet nectar. At this point the screams of Danaë were becoming deafening. Tom paused, afraid to look into the well for fear of what he would see. But he got on his knees, took hold of the cold stones that lined the wellhead, and peered over the edge. The energy of the place was overpoweringly sad and while the screams seemed to dissipate upon direct contact with the deadly spot, muffled echoes of Danaë's cries still reverberated around the stones that lined the old well. Tom looked into the shaft of darkness. He couldn't see the bottom, but he dropped a stone down, waiting to hear it land. Soon there was a sound of stone hitting stone. Tom said a prayer for Danaë's soul. Whatever her religious beliefs, she had been a kind woman and he remembered the many times he had seen her walking in the village. He recalled her dark skin and toothy smile, her piercing blue eyes and the strong bowed legs beneath her faded plain blue dress. She often wore a blue kerchief tied in her platinum-white hair like a country girl as she carried large buckets of fresh goats' milk in her strong arms.

Tom continued his run, heading toward the beach near the archaeological site. When he got to the sand just beyond the salt flats, where locals sometimes played soccer, he slowed to a walk again. He thought that if he splashed some seawater on his face he might feel better after his experience at the well. He walked down to the edge of the water, took off his shoes and waded a little way into the sea. It was cool and refreshing, and the beach was nearly empty. Three teenage girls, looking a bit like the three Graces, the personifications of beauty, mirth, and abundance, were writing in the sand with sticks at the edge of the surf. Tom walked past them but they barely noticed, they were so engrossed in what they were doing. It looked like they were writing the names of hoped-for boyfriends. Their lithe bodies were full of desire. The ritual seemed the opposite of the little curse tablets that people wrote in antiquity. Those were inscribed on small lead scrolls that were folded and sealed with a nail straight through the text and then buried in the earth. Tom turned back and watched as the girls stood in the shallow surf as their love missives were erased almost instantly by the gentle waves that rolled in from the sea.

He decided that he would run up to the top of Mount Petsophas to the Minoan peak sanctuary. There was a good trail that had been put in only a few years ago and the view from up there was spectacular. He also thought that he might see something of the remains of the sheep that had been struck by lightning. He followed a dirt road through the olive groves up past the archaeological site and then before reaching the village of Hieronero he turned off to the left and headed up towards the mountain.

The footpath traversed the mountainside. It was slightly more than a goat track and was lightly graded with fieldstones. The view got more and more beautiful the higher Tom climbed. After about twenty-five minutes he came around the far side of the mountain. Now he could see the summit and the truncated surveyor's cement pylon that marked the highest point. Just below the summit, protected in the lee of the mountain, lay the remains of the Minoan sanctuary. When he got there he was amazed to see the carnage left by the bolt of lightning still preserved. Lying against the wall of the sanctuary were no less than ten sheep carcasses, their bodies laid out like corpses in a crime scene. Tom imagined what had happened on that fateful night as eight ewes huddled close together against the outer wall. It was the most protected spot on the mountaintop. Tom had slept out under the stars in that very spot many times. On either side of the group of ewes was a great ram, protecting the two ends of the herd.

Tom stooped beside the ram at the north end. Its horns were huge, curved and shiny. It reminded him of the great ram under which Odysseus rode to escape from the cave of Polyphemus in Homer's *Odyssey*. The shepherd must have been devastated to lose two such rams and eight strong ewes. Tom touched the tip of the horn and ran his fingers along its ridged surface. While growing up in Montana, he had heard about certain Native American tribes that viewed lightning as a positive force of nature. Shamans, notably the witch doctors of the Crow tribe, sought out places where lightning had struck, looking for tokens, a powerful medicine that they believed was capable of inducing a fine harvest and giving strength to athletes. He carefully removed one of the great horns and held it in his hand. He could actually feel its energy.

Storms of this amazing force usually occurred here in the springtime. Tom remembered watching one such storm that had come in from the sea. Great streaks of lightning had stretched all the way from the heavens straight down to the water, lighting up the sea in eerie flashes and illuminating the billowing clouds that filled the night sky. Looking down at the sheep, he thought how the electric force of the lightning must have passed through their wet coats and killed all of them instantly. He'd never seen anything like this before. What an incredible force of nature. It was no wonder that the chosen attribute of Zeus was the thunderbolt.

After pausing there for a few more minutes, Tom started up toward the surveyor's pylon. He looked down the mountainside at the archaeological site and across the bay of Dikta. Cape Sidero stretched off in the distance and he could see Dragonera island beyond. It was a spectacular view, he thought once more, especially at this time of day when the light started to soften. Tom would be sorry to leave; he always hated to say goodbye to this place. At the same time, he could barely contain his excitement. He held up the ram's horn, energised by its inner force, and offered it as a gift to the gods for a safe journey. Tomorrow he would be in Rome – and one big step closer to Alexander's tomb.

20

STANDING ON THE bridge of the large luxury yacht, the captain of the ship, lean and clean-cut in his crisp officer whites, looked at his watch. It was just one a.m. They had motored in under cover of darkness and earlier that evening had moored at this remote spot, just off the coast of eastern Crete and not far from the bay of Dikta. The moon was not yet out and stars filled the dark night sky. The boat rocked gently. The sea was calm and everything seemed to be going according to plan. *Let it begin*, he thought.

The captain walked out to the deck, leaned on the railing and spoke to a hand-picked group of crewmen who were gathered and awaiting his command.

'It's time,' the captain said in German to his first mate, who was dressed all in black like the other men with him. 'Be careful – and remember, we don't want any human casualties. Keep it clean. Radio me as soon as you are ready. We'll be there within ten minutes to get you.'

The first mate responded, 'Aye aye, captain,' and the men climbed down into a waiting Zodiac. The boatman started the engine and motored purposefully along the shore. As soon as they neared the bay, the driver cut the engine and switched on the electric motor, which propelled the boat more slowly but made practically no noise. It was completely calm on the bay; there seemed to be no one about at this late hour. They headed straight towards the butte-like hill called Kastri, which loomed in the distance, its massive truncated cone eroding into the sea. Beyond it, past groves of olive trees and nestled much further inland, was a cluster of village street lights.

The boat pulled up to the beach by the dig site and three men got out. As soon as they were off the boat, the Zodiac's driver turned the boat around and headed back out into the bay to return to the yacht. The first mate checked the magazine of his 9mm Walther to make sure it was loaded and then screwed a silencer onto its muzzle. He pulled a black face mask down over his head and motioned to the other two men to do the same and to follow him silently. One man carried a bag containing some heavy equipment and the last man held at the ready a sniper rifle with an infrared scope and a fitted silencer. As they walked inland, a breeze started to pick up and the olive trees rustled gently in the wind.

When they arrived at the site, they could see a tent set up beside a large olive tree and outside it two Alsatian guard dogs were curled up together. The first mate turned to the others and motioned to the bag carrier to drop it. He lowered it to the ground carefully and took out a coil of rope and a large knife. As he did so, the dogs sat up.

The men leaped into action. The sniper dropped to one knee, eased the rifle's safety off and took aim at one of the dogs. His infrared laser sight put a red dot on the animal's forehead. A second later he squeezed the trigger and the dog dropped to the ground. The second dog started to run at them, growling as the sniper squeezed off a second shot that made the dog yelp softly and stopped it in its tracks. The first mate and the man with the rope moved quickly towards the tent where the people inside were starting to stir.

'Yannis, wake up.' Evangelia sat up and shook her companion's shoulder gently. 'Did you hear that? The dogs were alerted to something.'

'It's probably just a hare. Go back to sleep,' Yannis replied sleepily.

'No, I'm serious. Can you go outside and see if everything is all right? This is our last night here. Please . . .' she said.

The man with the rope approached the tent silently. Taking out his knife, he made a long cut through the rear of the tent. Inside Evangelia screamed. Before Yannis could react, the first mate levelled his gun at the excavator's head and said in English, 'Don't make a move or I'll shoot you dead. Do what I say and you will get through this alive.' The rifleman was standing behind him with his weapon pointed at Evangelia, the infrared dot twitching around her heart.

'Don't hurt us,' pleaded Evangelia. 'We'll do as you say.'

The third man knelt behind them and tied their hands behind their backs. When he had finished he clubbed them both, knocking them unconscious. Then he dragged them to a nearby olive tree where he tied them to its trunk.

The men turned towards the sanctuary. They had been briefed on the location of the shed where the statue was located. When they got to the shed door the first mate shot open the lock and the door swung open on its squeaky hinges. Inside, the magnificent statue of Alexander the Great looked down on them from the shadows.

'Mother of God!' exclaimed the first mate. In the darkness, the image of Alexander looked truly awe-inspiring.

'Are you sure we are just taking the head? It's so beautifully preserved,' asked the man with the rifle as the other man opened his satchel and took out a large masonry saw.

'We have our orders. There is no way we could move this whole statue. You'd need a forklift. It must weigh nearly a ton. Proceed, Manfred, as soon as you are ready.'

The man climbed up onto a ladder that the conservator had left there from her work earlier that day, put on a pair of goggles, primed the petrol-fuelled saw and then pulled the starter cord. On the second try, the motor caught. He held the saw up to the statue's throat and started cutting. The sharp-toothed carbon-tipped blade cut through the marble, shooting fine dust into the air. After several cuts from different sides, the deed was done and the man brought the head down from the mangled statue. The painted eyes of Alexander stared back at him impassively as the first mate looked at the severed head. The power that the figure had seemed to emanate when they'd first looked into the shed was dispelled. Before them now was a fine but incomplete inanimate object. 'It's a hell of a portrait. Let's get out of here.' The first mate took out his mobile phone and called the captain.

'It's done. Awaiting Phoenix.'

'Roger. It's on its way.' The first mate closed his phone and looked out across the bay.

'Okay, pack it up. They'll be here soon.'

They wrapped the head in a blanket, placed it in a small duffel bag and then packed up the saw. A few minutes later, a helicopter flew low across the bay and landed next to the temple. The men loaded the head, climbed aboard and flew back to the ship in minutes. By 2:30 a.m. the captain was a safe distance from Crete, cruising at full speed towards the coast of North Africa. He put in the call to Oskar Williams.

'Operation Salome complete.'

'Excellent. Bring it to me through the usual channels as soon as possible.'

Oskar sat back in the chair at his desk and smiled.

21

VICTORIA SAT IN her studio on a wooden chair in front of her easel, painting. The light was soft this morning and spilled in through the window, illuminating the complicated drapery of her subject. Victoria was dressed in her painter's clothes: an old soft sweatshirt, a comfortable pair of jeans, and espadrilles, her long blonde hair coiled up in a bun. She stared at the canvas as she applied the paint in thin strokes and then back at the little statuette of a veiled masked dancer. She had bought the reproduction in the Metropolitan Museum of Art's store before returning to Rome. She had not been ready to see the original statuette again when she'd returned to the Met after her incident at the Morgan Library but it had been on her mind.

She had woken up early this morning, still suffering from jet lag, and had gone straight to her studio before first light. She had spent the first part of the morning trying to give form to the Amulet of Nereida and capture its eerie glow in a painting. She had got most of the detail of the great ram's head: the curve of its horns with their thick ridges and the majestic look of its noble face. It was not quite right but close.

There was a symbol carved in shallow relief on its forehead, like a birthmark, stubby but symmetrical with elaborate prongs pointing out from the centre. She had not seen anything like it before. In a funny way, it reminded her of the white question mark on her palomino pony's forehead when she'd been a little girl growing up in the Midwest. That horse had been her first love and one of the sweetest creatures on Earth.

Victoria had been a little nervous about unpacking the statuette. She was not sure what effect if any it would have on her but after her conversation with Dr Winter yesterday and her success in envisioning the amulet, she gained confidence and thought she would try. So far, so good: she had not yet had any strange sensations or passed out. What surprised her was that as she looked at the figure and painted it from different angles, her natural urge was to give it colour – not just the garment, which she kept wanting to embroider with complex designs, and the slippers which she painted bright red, but in particular the woman's eyes, which she made a piercing blue.

Her thoughts kept drifting to her conversation with Dr Winter. She had left the therapist's office feeling much better. It had been good to clear her head and she felt as though she had direction now. She knew that Tom was expected in Rome sometime later that week, perhaps even tomorrow, and that he would be staying at the American Academy. More than ever, she thought it was important that she should see him. She knew some people at the American Academy. It was a celebrated place for the American expatriate community of artists in Rome. She often attended events there and sometimes went to the library to do her research on Bernini.

Victoria looked at her watch and thought that she would go to the Academy now and see if they could tell her when Tom was expected. She could also spend the afternoon reading in the library about Alexander the Great. The librarian was a friend and could undoubtedly help her find the best books from which she could learn more about this king who had figured so prominently in her former life and about the Amulet of Nereida.

She climbed the old steps up to the top of the Janiculum and walked along until she came to the impressive facade of the American Academy. She told the guard that she was there to use the library and, after showing some identification, she was allowed to enter. She walked briskly up the steps. She checked at the office but the Academy's secretary was not available. She decided to leave a note for Tom, which they promised to deliver to him upon his arrival. In it she welcomed him to Rome and asked him to call her at her home. Then she crossed the central court-yard and entered the library.

She signed in at the front desk with her library card and then peeked into the librarian's office. There, seated at the desk, was her friend, Virgil Chestnut.

'Victoria, long time no see! How are you, my dear?' Virgil asked as he got up from his desk.

'I've just returned from a trip to the States. I did the obligatory family visit to Michigan and then had some days in and around New York City. I went to see the Metropolitan Museum of Art and an interesting exhibition at the Morgan Library. It was . . . well, revelatory.'

'I'm glad to hear it. Travel can be a potent inspiration. You look well. Welcome back.' Virgil beamed. He was an older gentleman, dressed immaculately in tweed, and he had a soft spot in his heart for beautiful young ladies. Victoria was one of his favourites. 'Now, what can we do for you today? Are you doing some more research on Bernini or is it something for one of your paintings? How is your painting these days?'

'My work is taking a new direction; it is kind of a long story. We'll have to have lunch again sometime soon. I'm glad I've found you here. I wonder if you could help me choose some books on Alexander the Great. I am trying to do some background reading on his life and also on the legend of the Amulet of Nereida. I know the literature is immense so I really need some guidance. Can you help?'

'Of course. Alexander the Great, eh? He certainly

makes for interesting reading. We probably have hundreds of books on Alexander in our library alone. The Amulet of Nereida is a more special case. I'll have to look into it with you. Of course, I know the story, but the details of its own tangled history are beyond my ken. At my age, one can't help but think about our mortality but I'm not sure that I'd want to live forever; it could get awfully boring, especially if all your friends died. Follow me.' Virgil led Victoria into the main reading room of the library and a large empty table. 'Give me a few minutes and I'll bring some books out to you.'

Virgil returned ten minutes later with a stack of books. 'These ought to keep you occupied for a while,' he said as he placed books in front of Victoria. 'I think you'll find the eighteenth-century volume on famous amulets of particular interest for the Amulet of Nereida. It was the classic work of its day and I dare say has not been surpassed – at least, for the erudition of its scholarship even though plenty of new work has been done since then. Enjoy.'

'Thank you, Virgil. I've got more than enough to get me started here. I really appreciate your help and guidance.' Victoria smiled at him.

'I'll see you later. Happy hunting,' Virgil said and then turned to go back to his office.

Victoria settled into her chair and picked up the old book on amulets, admiring the tooled red Morrocan leather with its gilt lettering. She opened it to the title page: *Magic Amulets of Egypt, the Ancient Near East and the Classical World* by James Turnbull, printed privately in Florence in 1786. Well, this seems like a good place to start, Victoria thought. She glanced over at six more books about Alexander the Great that were piled to her right. She could see that she would have her work cut out for her.

22

WHEN TOM ARRIVED at the dig site early on Friday morning, he could tell as soon as he got out of his car that something was very wrong. There, lying on the ground not twenty feet away was one of Evangelia's Alsatians dead on the ground. It looked as though it had dropped in mid-sprint. By the tent, he saw the second dead dog, flies buzzing around its eyes and chest in which a hole from a large-calibre bullet had been made.

Tom looked inside the tent, fearing the worst, but no one was inside. The entrance was still zippered shut but the back wall had been cut straight through and was flapping gently in the breeze. At least Tom did not see any blood inside the tent. He wondered where Evangelia and Yannis could be. Then he saw them, limp and tied to an olive tree not far away. He ran over to them. They were alive if badly bruised. Taking out his pocketknife, he cut them free. He ran back to his car to get a bottle of water. Evangelia came to first.

She sat up and cradled Yannis's head in her lap, caressing his face. 'My God, Tom. It was horrible. These men came and threatened us with guns. They tied us up and then knocked us unconscious. I did not recognise them. They looked like foreigners. They were all dressed in black and were wearing ski masks. One man carried a rifle that had a huge silencer and an infrared scope. He killed my dogs.' She sobbed. 'He had the gun pointed right at my heart. Another man, who seemed to be the leader, held a pistol that also had a silencer. He spoke English to us with a heavy accent, perhaps German. There was a third man who carried a sack.' She paused and then asked, 'Is the statue okay?'

Tom's heart started to race. *The statue!* He had been so consumed with concern for his friends that he had forgotten about it. A terrible knot formed in his stomach as he answered. 'I have not looked. I was worried about you two. Stay here with Yannis. I'll go see.'

Tom walked over to the sanctuary and as he approached the shed, he whispered, 'Let it be there. Please, God, don't let them have taken it.'

Tom came to the entrance of the shed that enclosed the temple and the statue within. The doors were open, the broken lock lying on the dirt nearby. At first he thought, thank God, it's still there – and then he looked up to see that the head was gone. Tom stared in disbelief at the headless figure. He was dumbstruck. The brutal act of vandalism made him want to cry. He moved closer. As he approached the statue and saw the jagged edges of the neck, he started to get angry. Outside he heard the trucks of the workmen who had arrived to move the statue to the museum. That would not happen now; not right away, at any rate. They had to call the police. Representatives from the Greek Archaeological Service would need to be alerted, too. This would take hours if not days to sort out before they could disturb what was now a crime scene.

Whoever had done this was long gone, though. From the looks of it, they were professionals and they would not have waited around. Hours had passed since this had happened. The head was probably already off the island and on its way out of the country. Given Crete's position as the southernmost island in the Aegean, there were any number of places that they could have taken it: Turkey, Cyprus, Lebanon, Syria, somewhere in North Africa. Libya was less than 200 nautical miles due south. They could be there already. They could also have gone to any number of remote Greek islands instead, waiting for the right moment to get it out of the country. The possibilities were endless.

Tom looked at his watch. It was just about 8:30 a.m. He had to leave for his flight to Rome in an hour and a half. Tom sat down in front of the decapitated statue for a minute to think. It could not be coincidence that the thieves had struck the night before the archaeologists had planned to move the statue to the museum where the security would have been much tighter. Whoever had done this must have known their plans. The news must have leaked somehow. Of course, the statue had been sitting here for months now. It had been in the papers and everyone in the village knew about it. The plans to move it this week had only been finalised a few days ago. Whoever had done this had clearly been planning it for some time and they'd been ready to act.

Evangelia walked in and screamed when she saw the statue. She ran to Tom who held her as she cried on his shoulder. Tom spoke with more certainty than he really felt. 'We'll get it back, Evangelia. We have your excellent photographs. They cannot sell it on the open market. It will be posted with Interpol and IFAR. It will turn up and we'll get these criminals.'

'I hope you're right, Tom.'

23

THE BOEING 737 landed on the tarmac at Fiumacino Airport with a slight bump and slid to a halt before taxiing to the gate. Tom looked out of his window at the large cumulus clouds that dotted a bright blue sky. The temperature outside was 65 degrees Fahrenheit, fairly typical for this time of year. There was a chance of an afternoon shower, but he was prepared for rain. Thunderstorms in Rome tended to roll in violently, pour down briefly, and then clear up miraculously, leaving fresh clean air over the city. The airport was quite a way out of town. Tom had admired the lush green hills of Latium as they had flown in. Italy was such a beautiful country.

After collecting his bag at the luggage claim, Tom took a taxi straight to the American Academy. He felt glad to be back in Rome as his cab pulled up at the entrance of the fine neoclassical building perched high on the Janiculum hill overlooking Rome. The keys to his room were waiting for him with the guard as the secretary had promised. He went into the main building and upstairs to the south apartment where he would be staying. It had been years since he had last stayed at the Academy. It was a very congenial place for getting work done and extremely civilised. He wouldn't have to worry about waking up here with spiders crawling over him. He dropped his things on the couch in the sitting room and looked out the window to the magnificent umbrella-pine trees in the garden. It would have been nice to relax in the room but he couldn't wait to get to the Pantheon.

It had been a long morning. The police had questioned Tom at the site, keeping him there until he'd had to drive like a lunatic to get to the airport. He had just made his flight off the island on a puddle jumper to Athens, and had then taken a connecting flight to Rome. It almost felt like a bad dream. He still could not believe that someone had so brutally decapitated the statue of Alexander. He had to put it out of his mind, though. Otherwise he'd never be able to focus on his work. It was in the hands of the authorities now. Sooner or later the head would resurface. With any luck, they would track down the criminals and justice would be served.

Together with Tom's keys was an envelope addressed to him in a woman's handwriting. When he opened it, there was a note inside from Victoria Price. She had sent him a short e-mail earlier that week thanking him for seeing her and saying that she needed to speak with him again. He had not responded. There had been so much going on. Now she was asking again. He was surprised to learn that she lived in

Rome. She gave her telephone number. Tom looked at the phone in his room and thought for a moment about calling her. He wanted to make the most of his early start here in Rome, though. He'd have time to call her tomorrow. Now he had important business to attend to. He decided to walk to the Pantheon. It would do him good. Rome, after all, had to be one of the best walking cities in the world. With his camera and a small notebook tucked in the pocket of his jacket, he set out down the Janiculum hill.

Tom walked briskly through the narrow cobbled streets of Trastevere and across the Tiber river at the Ponte Sisto, upstream from the little island that had once been used as an infirmary.

He decided that he would have a cappuccino at the Sant' Eustachio cafe. It was one of the best places in the world to have a coffee and it was not far from the Pantheon. He paid for his coffee at the register and then gave his order to the *barista*. He watched as the man expertly prepared the coffee, foaming the milk to a light frothy consistency without scalding it. He never could understand why there was no place in the States, at least that he knew of, where you could order a cappuccino without worrying that you were going to burn your tongue. Tom savoured the aroma as a single spoonful of sugar sat on top of the froth for a moment before slowly sinking into the liquid. The *barista* stirred it briskly and then sprinkled some chocolate powder on top. Afterwards he tore Tom's receipt in half and left it on the counter by the cappuccino before turning to his next order. Tom nodded his thanks and took his coffee outside to sit down at one of the tables in front of the cafe.

From where he sat he could see the roof of the Pantheon looming in the distance. In antiquity, this area was known as the Campus Martius and lay outside the city's walls, at least until the reign of the emperor Aurelius in the third century AD. Originally, it had been land that belonged to the Tarquin kings but it became the property of the people during the Roman Republic. The area was named after an ancient altar to Mars, the god of war, and it was traditionally a place where the Roman army performed their military exercises. As he savoured the coffee, Tom picked up his cup and looked at the green embossed stag with a cross between its antlers that was the symbol of the cafe.

He looked across the piazza at the facade of the church, whose pediment was crowned with a similar stag's head with a large cross between its antlers. It was the Christian symbol of Saint Eustace, patron of hunters and those facing adversity. Tom finished his coffee, carefully scraping the cream from the sides with his spoon, and washing it down with a glass of water before getting up from the table.

It was a short walk to the Pantheon and soon he

was standing before the great temple in the Piazza Rotunda. He walked to the centre of the piazza, to the front of the sixteenth-century fountain surmounted by an Egyptian obelisk. It had been excavated at a nearby sanctuary to Isis and had been set up in the piazza in 1711. Tom wanted to get a good look at the facade of the Pantheon. From this vantage point, he couldn't see the building's dome and the impression was one of a traditional rectangular Roman temple. The large colonnaded porch, or *pronaos*, originally stood on a stepped podium, again a typical feature of Roman temples, but the ground level was higher now. The original effect would have concealed the dome from an even greater distance so that an approaching visitor would have had no idea of the incredible circular plan of the interior.

The building was remarkably well preserved although, like most ancient monuments, it had a long history of periodic pillaging, as well as renovations that had not always been true to its original design. The Byzantine emperor Phocas presented the Pantheon to Pope Boniface IV, who in turn reconsecrated it as a church dedicated to the Virgin Mary and the Martyrs in AD 609. In fact, it was said to have been the first pagan temple in Rome to be Christianised. The Pantheon was greatly admired during the Renaissance as a symbol of the Roman Empire.

Tom walked from the fountain in the Piazza Rotunda

to the front porch of the Pantheon. On either side of the main entrance there was an aisle bordered by two more massive columns that terminated in a tall niche where once had stood two monumental statues of the emperor Augustus and Agrippa, now lost. The sculptures had originally adorned the front of the earlier temple commissioned by Agrippa. Tom paused for a moment to appreciate the massive grey- and rose-coloured Egyptian granite columns. He ran his hand over the cool stone of one smooth unfluted drum. These columns stood over forty-four feet high, not the tallest from antiquity, but each was, incredibly, carved from a single piece of stone. The Corinthian capitals were made of marble and beautifully carved with intricate acanthus leaves and foliate designs. The total effect was grand and impressive.

Tom walked inside through the massive bronze doors, restored in 1560 by Pope Pius IV but amazingly mostly original, and into the circular space of the rotunda. It really was one of the great architectural wonders of all time. His gaze was immediately drawn to the oculus in the centre of the dome, which opened to the sky. Sunlight streamed through the great oculus, illuminating part of the upper dome like a spotlight. The dome, with its elaborate series of five rings of concentric coffers, was beautiful to behold. The height and diameter of the rotunda are the same, measuring 43.3 metres or nearly 143 feet, a perfect sphere within the building. The dome, the largest of its kind ever built, rested on a solid foundation of concrete over twenty-two feet thick that also supported a cylindrical wall nearly seventeen feet thick. The thickness of the walls decreased with the height of the dome and the dome itself was made of lightweight volcanic stone.

Tom marvelled at the space. It was Hadrian's greatest architectural achievement, a symbol of Rome as the centre of the ancient world. The Roman historian Cassius Dio, who wrote an eighty-volume history of Rome in the early third century AD, mentioned the Pantheon by name and stated that the temple contained many effigies of the gods, including Mars and Venus. Presumably these statues were set up in the seven niches around the interior. Each niche could have held more than one statue since the number did not correspond to the canonical pantheon of twelve gods. Between the main niches are eight evenly spaced smaller niches. The entire space itself had a mystical, cosmic quality that, Tom thought, derived from its perfect geometry oriented on the four cardinal directions – north, south, east and west. The floor paved with coloured marble added to this effect, as it was composed of alternating squares and circles, perfect forms that re-enforced the geometrical precision of the building itself.

Tom walked slowly into the centre of the Pantheon and looked systematically around him to see where

Emperor Trebonianus Gallus might have entombed Alexander's remains in the middle of the third century AD. He thought that one of the niches or an access point in the floor was the most likely place for the entrance to the tomb. He noted that some of the niches had been turned into chapels, and that a number of others now housed Christian tombs.

After going over every square foot, Tom could find no sign of Alexander's tomb. What was more, it became clear to him that the floor had been extensively restored. He looked again and again but there was nothing to indicate Alexander's final resting place.

As Tom stood there thinking, the sky darkened and it started to rain. It was one of those sudden violent storms, and water poured through the oculus onto the marble pavement. Periodic flashes of lightning illuminated the great space and rolling thunder echoed off the walls of the giant dome. Tom realised that he might be on a wild-goose chase. What did he expect to find? The Pantheon had been in use continuously since antiquity. How could he possibly expect to walk in and discover Alexander's tomb when no one had done so for the past seventeen centuries? Or had they? He needed to learn more about the post-antiquity history of the building and its restorations. If Alexander's remains were not here, then someone must have found them, and there ought to be a good reason why they had never made public such a spectacular discovery.

Tom knew that archaeologists had made systematic investigations of the building in test trenches in the nineteenth century, and that some of the restorations of the floor had been done at that time. Their work had revealed the rectangular plan of the original building erected through the patronage of Agrippa. But, out of necessity, those early investigations had been made only on patches of the floor. If they had found anything to do with Alexander the Great, it would have been announced as a major find. Any secret discovery must have occurred at an earlier time. The marble commemorative plaques inside the Pantheon described considerable renovations undertaken in the seventeenth century under the auspices of Pope Urban VIII, and later under Pope Alexander VII during his urban renewal of Rome.

Tom looked at his watch. The rain had stopped and the sky was clearing. It was time to head back to the American Academy. He needed to do more research in the Academy's library after a shower and some dinner. He couldn't shake off his feeling of disappointment, but it was not time to quit, not yet. He had to continue to follow every lead. He walked outside into the piazza and headed towards the nearby Largo Argentina where he knew that he would be able to catch a cab back to the Academy.

As he stood there waiting at the taxi stand, he looked across at the fenced-off remains of four

Republican Roman temples nearby. The theatre of Pompey was located behind them. From where Tom stood, he could see the spot where Julius Caesar was murdered. There was no marker or plaque and, in fact, it was now just another pavement in front of a video-game arcade. Time changes a lot of things, Tom thought, but sometimes history records the facts for posterity. Modern-day Romans still honoured Caesar's memory on the anniversary of that fateful day, the Ides of March, by leaving roses for him by his temple in the Imperial Roman Forum where he was cremated. Time and chance had yielded a new lead on the location of Alexander's tomb. Now Tom needed more information about the later history of the Pantheon in order to determine its location – if, indeed, it was still there.

24

WHEN TOM RETURNED to his little apartment at the American Academy he found an envelope with his name written on it sitting on the mahogany Queen Anne slipper-foot side table by the door. Inside was a short note written in elegant handwriting on heavy cream-coloured stationery.

> You are in grave danger.
> We need to talk tonight.
> Go to Pasquino. He will
> tell you where to meet me.
>   A Friend

Next to the word 'Friend' was drawn a Roman-style thunderbolt, stubby but ornate and with prongs emanating from either side of the handle grip – Zeus's signature weapon. Tom sat down on the couch and looked out the window at the Academy's garden where the tall umbrella pines swayed gently in the breeze and towered over an immaculate green lawn bordered by hedges. It was now late afternoon and the light was already beginning to soften. Wisps of clouds dotted the bright blue sky. What was this all about? No one should have known that he was here in Rome already, except the secretary of the Academy who had helped arrange his early arrival. Originally, he had not been expected until tomorrow and even then he had not contacted anyone about this trip other than the librarian at the Vatican. And how had someone got into his room? He had locked the door, but there was no sign of forced entry. He quickly checked his bag and his computer to make sure that everything was in order. It was – or, at least, it appeared to be.

What possible danger was he in? Tom thought back to the break-in at his home in Carroll Gardens and the man who had followed him in Athens. His stomach turned when he thought about the vandalism committed against the statue of Alexander at Dikta and the theft of its head. Was that related too? Maybe there was even more going on here than he realised. And who the hell was Pasquino? Tom thought hard. He had spent a couple of years in Rome as a student, but that had been long ago. He had also been a visiting curator at the Academy more recently. But did he know anyone named Pasquino? Perhaps it was someone who worked at the Academy. Right then it dawned on him. He smiled. He *did* know a Pasquino and he was sure to be at his usual haunt.

Tom looked at his watch and decided that he had better follow up on this curious new development.

What did he have to lose? He would indulge in a little Roman intrigue. He changed into some casual evening clothes and headed back outside. The guard in the booth at the front of the Academy called Tom a cab and Tom directed the driver to take him to Piazza Navona. The driver sped down the Janiculum hill and made his way through Trastevere and across the Tiber, along its far banks and towards the heart of the city. Soon he screeched to a halt at the end of Via Zanardelli just off the Piazza Navona. Tom paid the driver and stepped out onto the cobbled street.

Piazza Navona was one of Tom's favourite squares in Rome. It had a long oblong shape since it had been built directly upon the foundations of a Roman stadium erected by the emperor Domitian. The driver let Tom off near the one place where an observer could still see part of the Roman foundations of the arcade that once surrounded the playing field. He walked over to a railing that overlooked the ancient foundations and had a quick peek at the old travertine blocks that extended well below the present-day ground level. Then he turned and walked down the narrow pedestrian street into the square.

It was a beautiful early evening in autumn and everything smelled fresh after the rain. The sun's rays still reflected off the tops of the buildings, accenting the fine details of a Baroque church that faced onto the centre of the square. Tom ambled towards the great

Fountain of the Four Rivers by Bernini that stood in front of the church.

There was a crispness to the air and one vendor was selling roast chestnuts. Reaching into an old canvas sack hanging from his vendor cart, he cut open the shiny polished shells with a short broad curved knife, and then roasted them over open coals on a traditional pan with holes that allowed occasional direct contact with the fire. The smell was delightful and Tom stopped to buy a small bag to munch on while he strolled around the piazza. Cafés were positioned at various points around the square, each with its own gaggle of outdoor tables shaded by big round canvas umbrellas. Large gas heaters were carefully placed around the tables, ensuring that as the coolness of the evening set in it was still pleasant to sit outside and enjoy an aperitif or a coffee. As always the people-watching was amazing. An accordion player strolled along the square playing his own version of 'That's Amore' and a number of painters stood beside their easels, their paintings displayed for sale. Some were drawing portraits or caricatures for tourists. A number of West Africans, probably from Nigeria, hawked various pieces of African art or knock-off designer handbags spread out on blankets on the street. Piazza Navona was a big square and there were lots of people wandering about, some purposefully, others just enjoying the evening. Pigeons walked and fluttered about, looking for scraps and hoping for handouts from the tourists.

Tom walked up to the fountain in the centre of the square and admired the dramatic statues that symbolised the four great rivers: the Danube, the Ganges, the Nile and the Plate, representing Europe, Asia, Africa and America. He sat for a few minutes on the edge of the fountain and took in the scene before moving across the square to his destination. He took a small side street that angled off the curved arcade of the piazza. All the streets in this part of the city followed ancient routes and so frequently turned this way and that. Just around the corner he came to a convergence of three side streets that created a small triangular space, hardly a piazza, that was nonetheless known as the Piazza di Pasquino. There, standing against the Palazzo Braschi on a tall travertine pedestal, was the so-called talking statue Pasquino. The marble statue had been discovered nearby in 1501 during excavations of the Orsini Palace and had been set up at this very spot over five hundred years ago. It was an ancient sculpture, probably an Imperial Roman copy of a famous Hellenistic statue group, and might have originally decorated Domitian's stadium. According to one interpretation it represented Ajax holding the body of Achilles. But more probably it depicted the Spartan king Menelaos holding the dead body of Patroklos, Achilles's great friend who was slain by the Trojan prince Hector on the plain of Troy. The statue was badly damaged but still retained some of its original drama.

Looking at it, Tom could understand why it was greatly admired by Bernini, who thought it was one of the finest ancient statues in Rome. Tom took a moment to reappraise the statue. The bearded hero Menelaos knelt as he cradled the body of Patroklos in his right arm and over his left knee. A baldric was draped across his semi-bare chest, and his scabbard and sword were bound close to his body. Menelaos turned his head sharply to the right, looking away from Patroklos's limp body. His helmet was pushed back on his head. The marble of the Roman Pasquino group was badly weathered but one could still imagine the original Hellenistic statue in gleaming bronze.

When the Pasquino group was first displayed in the early sixteenth century, a cardinal by the name of Oliviero Carafa initiated an annual Latin poetry contest. Each year on the twenty-fifth of April, people hung poems near the statue or on its base for all to enjoy. Soon other kinds of missives appeared on the statue throughout the year. The ancient sculpture became a place where people posted critical commentary or mocking satirical notes often aimed at the government or prominent political figures, including the popes. The statue eventually came to be known as 'Pasquino' after an infamous anonymous agitator

believed to have been a local barber or tailor with a
particularly biting wit. According to legend, Pasquino's
prolific notes were especially potent disseminators of
gossip during the enclaves when the new popes were
elected. By the middle of the sixteenth century,
Pasquino's tirades had become so caustic that the
religious authorities considered dumping the statue
in the Tiber river, but in the end relented for fear of
being ridiculed for punishing a statue. Laws were
introduced that forbade the display of notes and
guards were posted to enforce this draconian measure.
That only led to the genesis of other talking statues
around Rome, such as the colossal sculpture of a river
god, named Marforio, that stood at the foot of the
Capitoline Hill and now resided in the Capitoline
Museum. Pasquino still spoke in modern times and
the word 'pasquinade', which meant a satirical piece
of writing posted in a public space, could be found
in most serious dictionaries.

Tom looked at the dozens of notes that were fixed
to the base of the statue and the walls of the Palazzo
Braschi. Many of them had clearly been there a long
time. Some were typed, others computer-printed, and
some were handwritten. There were complaints about
the prime minister and rousing calls for increases in
wages for union workers. There was one that questioned American foreign policy and its presumed
imperial goals. There was even a love poem addressed

to Rome. Each was very different, but all were boldly signed 'Pasquino'. Then Tom noticed on the right side of Pasquino's base a small posting in bold block letters, written on the same heavy cream-coloured stationery as the note that he had found in his room. It read:

Quod non fecerunt Barbari fecerunt Barberini.
(What the Barbarians did not do, the Barberini did.)

After Pasquino's signature was a depiction of the same Roman thunderbolt of Zeus that had been drawn on the earlier note. The quote in Latin was one of the most famous of Pasquino's early statements and had been posted sometime in the first part of the sixteenth century. It had originally been addressed to Pope Urban VIII, of the Barberini family, whose relentless quest for antiquities was likened to the medieval barbarian invasions of Rome that had left the city's artistic heritage in a shambles. That note had referred particularly to the pope's destruction of the bronze ceiling of the front porch of the Pantheon, an interesting factor given Tom's interest in the temple. Tom carefully removed the paper from the statue's base. On the other side were written in the same elegant handwriting as the note in his room the instructions: 'Meet me at Atalante at 7:30.' Atalante was a little restaurant in Trastevere that specialised in grilled meats and hunters' dishes; Tom knew it well. He looked at his watch. It was 7:15 p.m. He had just enough time to walk there now. Although he was still not certain whom he was meeting, he had a hunch.

When Tom arrived at the restaurant it was just after 7:30 p.m. He opened the door and walked inside.

'Good evening, sir. Do you have a reservation?' the maître d' greeted him.

'I'm meeting a friend. I expect that they've made a reservation.'

'And what is the name?'

'Well, I'm not sure. Is there anyone here who is waiting for someone to join their party?' Tom replied rather awkwardly.

'Oh, yes, of course.' The maître d's expression turned more friendly and he smiled. 'You are Mr Carr? We have been expecting you. Right this way.' He led Tom into the back room where a man was seated at a table studying a menu that hid his face from view. As Tom approached he finally saw who it was as the man, with his big blue eyes topped by large white slightly wild bushy eyebrows, peered sheepishly up.

'My goodness, Virgil, I should have known it was you!' Tom exclaimed. He shook Virgil's hand warmly as he stood up to greet him.

Virgil Chestnut had written the standard Latin textbooks used all over the United States for twenty years when Latin had still been a requirement in American high-school curricula. The royalties from the sales of his books and a small fortune that he'd inherited from his father meant that he was able to retire early from his work as a distinguished high-school Latin teacher. He spent half the year in Rome pursuing his own interests and the other half as a teacher at a small boarding school in Massachusetts. He was a distinguished-looking older gentleman, almost a caricature of himself. If he were a character in a child's book, he would have resembled Toad of Toad Hall in *The Wind in the Willows*.

'It's good to see you, Tom,' Virgil said. 'I apologise for the cloak-and-dagger messages.'

'How did you know I was here?' Tom asked.

'Oh, the secretary of the Academy told me. News travels fast in this town, as you well know.'

'Well, how did you get into my room to leave that note? The door was locked,' Tom persisted.

'Maria, the maid, let me in. She and I go way back. But listen.' Virgil held up his finger, calling for silence. 'There's something that I urgently need to talk to you about. I'm writing a "secret history" of the antiquities trade here in Italy. Mind you, I am a collector myself, in the ancient Roman tradition, but I see myself as a steward preserving some important works that I enjoy having around me and that I shall one day give to a museum.' Virgil looked up and then realised that he was preaching to the choir. He continued. 'What I find unconscionable are the clandestine excavations that are destroying Italy's cultural patrimony. God's teeth, those ruffians are everywhere. The countryside is rampant with them. Why the government does nothing about it is beyond me – the mystery of the Egyptians to tell you the truth.'

'So listen to this.' Virgil leaned over the table closer to Tom and continued. 'I was down in Lucania the other week staying at a B&B. During my morning constitutional, I came across this fellow at the side of the road. He was selling Parma hams out of the trunk of his BMW sedan. Fell off the back of a truck, I suppose. He was probably in his fifties, a real *paisano*, but with flair. He wore a red and gold silk ascot and a rumpled tan linen suit. His hair, jet black with grey streaks, was slicked back, of course, and he wore gold-rimmed sunglasses that were propped back on his head. I'll tell you, he really thought he was the cat's pyjamas.'

Virgil paused for a sip of water. 'After I told him that I was a classics professor, he stated proudly that he was the local tomb robber! He told me about his historically rich country, going on and on about the Romans and the Greek colonists before them. He seemed quite knowledgeable. I was amused at first, but then he began to describe some of the tombs in the surrounding foothills. He claimed that it was his right to plunder them. It was his cultural patrimony, he said. Can you imagine? Since the police don't cotton on to tomb robbing these days, he does his at night. He takes a long thin metal pole that he uses to find the tombs, jabbing it in the ground. When he hits one,' Virgil pounded the table with his fist for emphasis, 'he gets out his spade and starts digging. And listen to this. This is the most unbelievable part. He said that what he loves most, what he's almost addicted to, like a drug, is seeing the tomb paintings when he first opens a tomb. He described their remarkable freshness and how it fades within minutes, as the air reacts with the natural pigments that for so many centuries have been sealed away from the atmosphere. He told me how he quickly takes out any vases or jewellery in the tomb and then sits right on the remains of the deceased, and examines the paintings with his flashlight. That first bloom, he said, when they look just like the day they were painted, is truly something special to behold. He said that he almost feels guilty that he is the only one who gets to appreciate these paintings before they fade to a dull shade of their former self, much like the waxen pallor of human flesh that has lost its vitality after death.'

'The world is what it is,' Virgil continued. 'God

knows, a person has to make a living. And, to tell the truth, I almost envied the man. Almost, but not quite. I mean, I understand the thrill of discovery but, by Jove, the price is too great!' Virgil thumped the table again with his fist.

Then he apologised. 'Sorry, Tom. I work myself up sometimes.'

Tom and Virgil ordered a Florentine steak for two, a superb cut of beef grilled to perfection on an open flame. Tom asked the waiter to uncork a *fiasco*, a two-litre bottle, wrapped in wicker, of house red wine. Diners only paid for what they drank in this restaurant, and the waiter made the assessment at the end of the meal. He divided the bottle roughly into quarters and if two people managed to drink an entire bottle they'd really be in their cups. Tom and Virgil drank moderately.

'I've gotten off track.' Virgil resumed talking. 'You'll remember that's a rather persistent habit of mine. What I wanted to say was that while researching this project I've come to know a rather strange cast of characters, like the fellow I just described. All sorts of information has come my way. I was surprised to hear your name come up in a casual conversation with one of my informants. Of course, I can't reveal my sources – the journalist's code of honour and all that – but I was surprised to learn that your activities were on the radar of such a rough lot. I don't have any specifics but I thought that you'd want to know.' Virgil paused to look at Tom and then continued.

'You know that I am still a part-time librarian at the American Academy, a duty I have undertaken for many years. I love being around the books all day but it is a bit like working at a bowling alley. I get everything set up properly and people come in and knock it all down again. They pull out books and I have to start all over again – like Sisyphus with a book cart, if you will.' Virgil took another sip of his wine.

'Is there any reason why *tombaroli* would be interested in your research? Look, I'm talking too much. Tell me about your trip. I'm eager to hear about your research. By the way, you shouldn't put so much information in your e-mails. These people are technologically savvy. They can hack into anyone's account.'

Tom thought Virgil was being a bit melodramatic but he was also alarmed at what he was hearing. His computer had been stolen just before his trip and the most important find from his site, the cult statue of Alexander the Great, had just had its head sawn off and stolen by antiquities thieves. Could the two events be related? Maybe Virgil was not being absurd after all. Tom responded, 'Virgil, they have already struck! Antiquities thieves visited the site at Dikta just last night and cut off the head of our cult statue of Alexander the Great.'

'*Porco Dio*! Those unconscionable sons of bitches,' Virgil exclaimed.

'We had just finished the conservation and were going to move it to the museum. Their timing was impeccable. They must have had some kind of inside information to have been able to strike at the last possible moment. I did not put that information in my e-mails, though. I am heartbroken about the theft and vandalism. It made me sick to my stomach to see the statue this morning with its head gone, like a freakish execution. But I have something else that I need to tell you and you have to promise that it does not go beyond this table.'

Virgil nodded his head and leaned in closer as Tom told him about the new reading of the inscription and its identification of the Pantheon as the more recent resting place of Alexander the Great. Virgil gave a low whistle, took another bite of his steak, and let Tom continue.

'I went to the Pantheon this afternoon, thinking that the location would be somewhat obvious. But the building, despite being one of the best-preserved Roman temples in existence, has undergone extensive restoration over the years. In particular, I expected some kind of sign, maybe on the floor or elsewhere, but the renovations in the seventeenth century, especially those of the popes Urban VIII and Alexander VII, seem to have completely precluded that possibility.'

Virgil pointed to another table where a man who looked like a satyr, with black woolly hair over his pointed ears, was eating. The man laughed merrily as he talked quickly in Italian to a woman across the table from him. Virgil said, 'Do you remember that marvellous passage in D.H. Lawrence's *Etruscan Places* when he's up in Tuscany and he remarks that you just don't see satyrs so much any more after the war? Of course, he's referring to the First World War.'

Tom replied, 'Do you think he meant that they were all killed off in the trenches or that they just could no longer put up with mankind's folly?'

'Hard to say,' Virgil responded, 'but I think he meant the latter. Of course, woodland folk, like satyrs and maenads, are not like you and me. They're much more in tune with nature and the natural order of things. Warfare is mankind's unique contribution. It is not a product of nature and its destructive aftermath would be difficult for a satyr to comprehend. The Etruscans might have had a little satyr blood in their lineage. Their funerary art, in any case, seems to draw deeply from the undercurrents of the natural world. I think old D.H. Lawrence would have agreed.'

'You know,' Tom reminisced as he took a draught of his wine, 'I once saw Pan. It was on the island of

Thasos about fifteen years ago. I was just a graduate student on a trip with the American School of Classical Studies and we had the afternoon off. It was early October, one of those halcyon days that sometimes occur in Greece in October, warm and beautiful like an Indian summer. The tourist season was over, though they don't have many tourists anyway since the island's rather out of the way. Anyway, it seemed deserted. That afternoon, I rented a moped and drove up into the country. I only had the bike for a half-day and I was supposed to be back before dark. I got way out on a country road and the sun was beginning to set. I was up in the hills and came upon a large field of wheat bordered by olive trees. It was a real rustic spot. There at the far end of the field, in broad daylight, was a giant lumbering Pan, with shaggy goat legs and the upper body of a man, his tall curling goat horns reflecting the evening light. He was slightly hunched over and he was moving slowly in the opposite direction. I could not believe my eyes. I slammed on the brakes and cut the engine of the moped. He was about a hundred yards away from me and he actually looked back when I cut the engine. Then he just continued slowly and purposefully on his way. There was a sadness about him but also a real sense of power. I mean, I could've run after him, but something inside me or perhaps something emanating from him kept me from doing so. A minute later he was at the other end of the field and then he disappeared into the olive groves.

'The Greek gods may be all but forgotten to most people today but as immortals I suppose they live on. Think how vast and great was Pan's domain in antiquity. All of the woodlands, the kingdom of nature, belonged to him. Today the world's wild places are becoming increasingly fragmented and more and more they are just disappearing altogether. It's no wonder that Pan looked so weary. When will we realise the damage we're wreaking on nature and the irreparable losses that are being incurred?'

'I am not surprised though that Pan appeared to you, Tom. You've always had a strong love of nature,' Virgil replied. 'After all, you grew up in Montana, didn't you? That's God's country. You spent some time in southern Africa too, right? Come to think of it, I'm not sure how you ever ended up as a classical archaeologist.'

'Well, there were the seven years of graduate school at Bryn Mawr College,' Tom said, smiling.

Virgil continued. 'Now, about the Pantheon. I know a person who might be able to help you discover what happened to Alexander's remains. Her name is Victoria Price. She's an American scholar who specialises in Baroque Rome. She knows everything there is to know about the patronage of the popes in the seventeenth century and I know that she has worked on the history of the Pantheon as well. She's a friend of mine – a beautiful lady too, I may add. I've helped her many times over the years to locate books at the American Academy. She comes from a long line of distinguished Warsaw art historians, on her mother's side. Her family emigrated to America before the Second World War. She moved to Italy about seven years ago to pursue her doctoral work here for the University of Michigan, which she finished a few years ago. Now she devotes more time to her painting. If anyone can answer your questions about renovations of the Pantheon and Alexander's tomb it's sure to be her. Shall I give her a ring and try to arrange a meeting? She lives here in Rome. And what's more she is completely discreet. You can trust her.'

Tom could barely believe his ears, 'Did you say Victoria Price? Is she a tall attractive blonde lady?' A blonde lady who seemed to keep surprising him.

'Yes, do you know her? I saw her yesterday and she said that she had been to New York recently and visited the Metropolitan Museum of Art. You old scallywag, Tom.' Virgil winked.

'We met quite by coincidence. She came to a gallery talk I gave and, well, we had coffee afterwards. I found a note from her when I arrived, asking me to call.' Tom did not want to get into all the details here. He continued, 'Do you think it's too late to contact her tonight?'

'Absolutely not, I'll call her as soon as we're done here. She's a woman of means, so to speak – I won't say lady of leisure – and she often comes to the library at the Academy in the mornings, in any case, to do her research. But Tom, I have to ask you. What do you hope to accomplish in this quest? After all that the remains of Alexander the Great have been through over the centuries, moved from here to there like holy relics, I don't imagine that there's going to be much left, even if you do locate his final resting place – a few bones at most. These characters who seem to be following your every move, well, they're dangerous types. I've had only the most cursory dealings with them and I can tell you that I wouldn't want them on my tail. Personally, I would recommend walking away from the whole thing. You don't want to find yourself on the wrong end of a loaded gun or razor-sharp knife. They live in a different world from us. To them, human life is expendable.'

'I appreciate your candour and concern, Virgil. And I will be careful. I can take care of myself,' Tom replied. The *fiasco*'s contents were starting to kick in. 'I can't give up on this now. It's too important to me. In truth, I don't know what I'll find and you're right that there may not be much, if anything, left in Alexander's tomb. It is almost too much to hope for. Yet don't you want to know? My God, just think how close we are! People have sought to answer the question for centuries and, with this new discovery at Dikta, it suddenly seems that the answer may be within our grasp. It's the last chapter in the history of one of the greatest men who ever lived. I've got to pursue it – at least, as far as I can. Who knows, the story may end with the Pantheon. But we'll have to see.'

25

AFTER SETTLING THE restaurant bill, Tom and Virgil walked out into the evening air. It was not late by Roman standards and there were still many people walking about. They made their way to a nearby piazza and Virgil took out his mobile phone to call Victoria while Tom stood nearby.

'Hello, Victoria? Good evening, my dear. Sorry to call so late. It's Virgil. Can you talk? I hope I'm not calling at a bad time.'

'Hello, Virgil. What a nice surprise! Is everything all right? It's not like you to call at this hour.'

'Yes, yes, everything's fine. Right as rain. But I'll get right to the point. I have a friend visiting from out of town. His name is Tom Carr. I believe you know him?'

Victoria's heart raced. 'Tom Carr is with you now?'

'Yes, he's an old friend. As I think you are aware, he's researching a rather extraordinary subject. What you may not know is that he is in need of some expert advice on Baroque Rome, and the Pantheon in particular. I immediately thought of you and, well, I wonder if you would be willing to meet with us briefly? This is a confidential matter.' Virgil looked over at Tom and winked as if to say not to worry.

Victoria had been waiting for some kind of response from Tom but this was not what she had expected. The shoe was on the other foot. He needed her help.

'Well, Virgil, you are one for surprises. Where are you now? Do you want to meet this evening, or sometime tomorrow?'

'This evening would be perfect,' Virgil replied. 'You're so kind to accommodate us. I promise that we won't take up a great deal of your time. As I remember, you live in Trastevere and, as it happens, we're just around the corner from your apartment building.' Virgil winked at Tom again.

'Well, if it was not you, Virgil, I would be taken aback at the suggestion of a gentleman caller at this hour. But I know I can depend on your honour.' Victoria had sensed the jocular tone in Virgil's voice. He liked to play the pretend rake with her at times and Victoria found it more endearing than off-putting. Virgil was about as sexually threatening as a puppy dog. 'Give me fifteen minutes to collect myself. You can call on me at my apartment. It'll be more private than meeting out somewhere. I look forward to seeing you both soon.' Victoria hung up the phone.

Virgil closed his own phone and turned to Tom. 'We're in. She'll see us in fifteen minutes. I knew she would. She's a doll. She lives just around the corner

so we have time for a quick *digestif*. Do you like
Fernet Branca?' Virgil asked Tom as he led him to a
nearby cafe. Fernet Branca was about the most nasty
drink Tom could imagine, like a spoonful of medicine
from the doctor. The Italians loved it but Tom could
not tell if Virgil was pulling his leg or not. This was
great news, though. He could not believe that Victoria
Price was an expert in Baroque restorations of the
Pantheon. That could save him days – maybe weeks
or even months – of research since it wasn't an area
that Tom specialised in at all.

Virgil and Tom stood at the bar. Virgil ordered a
Fernet Branca and Tom decided to opt for an
amaretto. They sipped their drinks and watched the
people go by.

As they waited, Tom told Virgil the full story of
how he and Victoria had met, including her vivid
dream about robbing the tomb of Alexander the
Great.

'Well, now I am the one to be surprised. I never
pegged Victoria as an old soul. She's so young and
beautiful.' Virgil smiled and then continued, 'Come
to think of it, she was researching the subject of
Alexander the Great at the library yesterday. I helped
her with some books. In fact, of all things, she was
particularly interested in the Amulet of Nereida.'

'Really? I wonder what that is about,' Tom replied,
looking a little confused.

'Did you tell her about your research on the Tomb of Alexander? I think you'll need to share the latest spectacular development. She is trustworthy.'

'Are you sure that you're not letting a little crush cloud your judgement?' Tom chided.

'Oh, I admit I have a soft spot for the ladies but you should know, Tom, that in serious matters as this I always keep my head clear. Victoria is a beautiful woman, all right, and smart as a whip. But I was only teasing her. My judgement is sound. She won't tell anyone, I can assure you of that. It's time to go. Shall we?' Virgil finished his drink and put the glass down on the bar before turning for the door. Tom followed him back out into the square.

As Virgil had said, Victoria Price's apartment block was just around the corner. It was a pleasant old structure and reminded Tom of the best of the Imperial Roman apartment buildings in Ostia, the ancient port of Rome. Virgil walked through the entrance of the building and approached the attendant who was sitting at a large desk in the lobby. 'Good evening, my fine young man. We are calling on Ms Victoria Price in apartment 5C. She's expecting us. My name is Virgil Chestnut.'

'Just a moment, sir. I'll see if she's there.' The attendant picked up an old rotary telephone and called up to the apartment.

'Ms Price? A Mr Chestnut and friend are here to

see you. They said that you are expecting them. May I send them up? Very well.' The young man turned to Virgil, 'You may go on up. Take the lift on the right.'

'Thank you,' replied Virgil and they walked to the lift. Just beyond was a large communal indoor garden that also allowed light into the interior of the building.

As they rode the lift up to the fifth floor, Tom turned to Virgil. 'It is amazing how similar these old Roman apartment buildings are to the ancient Imperial Roman equivalents, with their stucco brick facades, light wells and interior gardens.'

'Yes, in some ways things haven't changed much since antiquity. It's nice to ride an elevator to the fifth floor, though!' Virgil replied. When they got out of the lift, Virgil knocked on the door of apartment 5C. A few moments later, the door opened and there was Victoria elegantly dressed and fresh-faced, her large blue eyes sparkling as she greeted them.

'Virgil, what an unexpected pleasure to see you this evening. Tom, I had hoped to be hearing from you but I did not expect to see you tonight!' Victoria stepped aside so that they could enter the apartment.

After kissing her softly on both cheeks, Virgil replied, 'Victoria, it is so kind of you to receive us at this late hour. You'll appreciate the urgency once Tom has had a chance to explain.'

Tom took Victoria's hand and kissed it gently. 'How nice to see you again.'

'Likewise, I'm sure,' Victoria replied coquettishly, gazing at Tom with her deep blue eyes.

'Could we sit down and talk for a minute?' Virgil asked Victoria. 'We're in need of your counsel on a matter of the utmost delicacy.'

'Of course – let's go into the living room. It's a bit too cold this evening to sit on the veranda.' Victoria led them from the foyer into her living room. Tom looked around the well-appointed space. A large gilt mirror, stretching nearly from floor to ceiling, had the effect of making the room seem twice as large as it was. Oil paintings hung on two walls and wooden bookcases lined another. A fine terracotta bust in the Baroque style of a young woman graced the top of a table placed against the overstuffed sofa where Victoria suggested they should sit down. Flowering plants seemed to greet Tom wherever he looked. A large orchid bloomed on the table in front of the couch.

'Would you like something to drink?' Victoria asked, fingering the heavy amber necklace that she was wearing.

'No, thank you. We just had a nightcap at the little bar around the corner,' Virgil replied.

'Very well, then, gentlemen – what is it that I can do for you?'

Virgil looked to Tom who turned to speak to Victoria. 'I've just come from eastern Crete – from the sanctuary of Diktaian Zeus where I work. I made a remarkable discovery. I was able to decipher a worn inscription about Alexander's tomb. It states that the tomb, the Soma, was moved from Alexandria in the middle of the third century AD to the Pantheon in Rome during the reign of the Roman emperor Trebonianus Gallus. The inscription gives no indication of where the tomb was set up within the temple, though.' Tom had a troubled look on his face as he continued. 'When I went to the Pantheon today I could find no trace of its location.' Tom paused, looking deep into Victoria's eyes before he continued. 'I was wondering if you could help me understand the post-antiquity history of the building so that I might be able to locate the tomb, if in fact it is there, or determine if it was removed at some time.'

'My word! The tomb of Alexander the Great in the Pantheon? That was what your inscription at Dikta revealed? How remarkable!' Victoria paused for a few seconds to reflect and then continued. 'This is news to me – and I have done quite a bit of research on the building. As Virgil probably told you, the Pantheon is one of my particular areas of interest. It's a magnificent structure. Still, there are many gaps in the building's history. It's strange that there's no other record of such an important fact. As you probably know, it's said that when the building was turned into a church consecrated to the Virgin Mary and the Martyrs in AD 609, some twenty-eight wagonloads of bones belonging to Christian martyrs were brought into the Pantheon and must have been reburied within the building.'

Tom interjected, 'Given Alexander's prominence as a historical figure and his acceptance by the Church – the Bible mentions his doing the work of the Lord by keeping at bay the unclean nations at the ends of the earth – it's not likely that they would have desecrated his remains in the temple. It's more likely that they left them with the bones of the martyrs.'

'That does make sense,' Victoria replied. 'I know of hardly any references to the building in the ensuing centuries, although it remained in use. Most of our sources refer to various restorations. After the gilt-bronze roof tiles were removed in AD 679, lead sheets were installed to repair the roof during the papacy of Pope Gregory III in the first half of the eighth century. Repairs to the roof, as you might expect, are recorded several times, in the early fifteenth century under Pope Martin V and again in the early sixteenth century under Pope Clement VII. Around 1560, Pope Pius IV made significant repairs to the massive bronze doors.'

Tom said, 'I was looking at them earlier today. They are truly amazing, especially when you think of all the other bronze work that no longer survives.'

'Yes, and they work perfectly, too,' Victoria

continued, looking across at Virgil, who was sitting comfortably and watching her intently with his puppy-dog eyes. 'There was a great flood in the late sixteenth century, the worst in Rome's history. The overflow from the Tiber seeped into the temple, causing extensive damage to the floor. But major repairs to the floor were not done until the nineteenth century.'

Tom raised his eyebrows. The flooding might have exposed or damaged the area of Alexander's tomb, necessitating immediate repairs – or its removal.

Virgil spoke up. 'The great flood of 1598 was certainly the worst in Rome since that of 54 BC, vividly described by Cicero in one of his letters. It rained for five days straight, not quite as much as in the Bible with Noah's ark but enough to cause general alarm. Damage to the city was significant. The flooding of the Tiber was a recurring problem in antiquity.'

Victoria nodded in agreement and continued. 'Certainly, though, the most extensive repairs and renovations to the Pantheon were done during the seventeenth century under Popes Urban VIII and Alexander VII. It seems to me that if the tomb of Alexander were discovered, it would have been during this time. However, I've studied the existing papal documents extensively for this period and I can tell you that I've not come across anything to suggest that any major relics – much less the tomb of Alexander the Great – were discovered in the

Pantheon.' Victoria paused for a moment and seemed to be lost in thought.

Tom and Virgil looked admiringly at her sitting there opposite them. She was indeed a beautiful woman and, as Virgil liked to say, there was nothing sexier than an intelligent woman. They were both captivated by her.

Victoria pulled herself back to the conversation and looked up. 'Still, there's something that is bothering me. What you've said about Alexander's tomb reminds me of a cryptic passage in Pope Alexander VII's private diary, now in the Vatican Library. Alexander VII was born Fabio Chigi in Siena in 1599. The conclave at which he was elected pope was famous for its duration of eighty days. It came as a surprise when he took the name of Alexander VII. Ostensibly, it was in tribute to Pope Alexander III, but Pope Alexander VII was a serious student of antiquity and clearly an ardent admirer of Alexander the Great. He might have identified more with Alexander the sage as promulgated in the *Alexander Romance*, but I don't suppose I need to tell you about that.' Victoria smiled at Tom. 'Alexander VII often suffered from poor health as a young man and was more of an intellectual than he was a world leader like Alexander the Great. He had great ambitions for Rome, though, and was interested in the Pantheon from the very beginning of his papacy in 1655 up to his death in 1667. This particular passage in his personal diary refers to a tomb of Alexander, and not of Pope Alexander. As I recall, it refers to another monument in Rome, near the Pantheon, the sculpture of an elephant carrying an obelisk that Pope Alexander VII commissioned from Gianlorenzo Bernini. Tom, I think that you and I should go to the Vatican Library tomorrow morning and take a look at the diary. I know the librarian so I think that he'll be able to arrange it for us. I'm a regular visitor there.'

'I have an appointment to go there early next week to look at some manuscripts of the *Alexander Romance*. My letter of permission and Vatican Library reader's ticket were waiting for me when I got to the Academy earlier today so at least they'll know who I am,' Tom said.

'Excellent. Shall we meet by the obelisk in the centre of Saint Peter's Square tomorrow morning at ten a.m.? I'll e-mail my colleague tonight in preparation.'

'That sounds perfect. Thank you, Victoria, for helping me at such short notice and for seeing us at this late hour.'

Virgil chirped in, 'Yes, Victoria, I knew you were the person to go to. You're an absolute angel.'

'It's been my pleasure. You were kind enough to give me some of your time when I was at the Metropolitan. As you know, I too have an interest in Alexander's tomb.' Victoria winked at Tom. 'You've certainly piqued my interest. And don't worry – I won't mention anything to the librarian about Alexander's tomb. I'll just say that I've got to check something for an article, and I'm up against a deadline. He'll understand. I've consulted that diary literally hundreds of times.'

Victoria got up and walked them to the door. 'Take care, *carissimo* Virgil.' She kissed him lightly on the cheek. 'Tom, I look forward to seeing you tomorrow morning.'

'Thank you, Victoria. You have surprised me once again and I am grateful.'

When Victoria closed the door, she leaned against it and thought to herself out loud. Her heart was racing.

'If you only knew, Tom . . . Still, I've got to tell him tomorrow before we go into the Vatican Library.'

26

Oskar Williams sat at his desk, admiring a bronze statuette of a dancing faun and a marble head of Hermes that he had just unpacked from a box. The package had arrived earlier that day from Japan. What was it that the Roman poet Horace once said? If you have seen a thousand works of art you have known a thousand frauds. He chuckled to himself.

Oskar picked up the bronze and turned it in the light, appraising the patina. Its surface was a deep green colour with tinges of blue and red in places. Next he assessed the sculptural form. The features were carefully modelled. It was a distant cousin to the famous dancing faun from Pompeii. He just hoped that the buyer would not realise how distant since Oskar had commissioned it from a forger he knew in Kyoto. The pose was lively, the legs muscular, the faun prancing with arms held aloft in an ecstatic dance. The spritely tail shook to a Dionysian revel. It seemed to Oskar to capture something of the Hellenistic baroque style that, he found, enjoyed a brisk market these days among some of his wealthiest clientele. The patina looked convincing to him even though it was very difficult to replicate an ancient bronze surface successfully. The best forger could not reproduce the ageing process.

This patina had been enhanced by being buried in the earth for a year, with regular doses of urine poured onto it to help the fake sheen look right and get the earth to adhere in a convincing fashion. If the statuette was examined scientifically it would be clear that this patina had been chemically induced and was much too thin to be ancient but you would need to sample it to do that, which was a destructive process, and most buyers were rightly loath to damage the work in any way. Part of the trick was to produce a piece that did not have a surface that could be easily sampled. Oskar's forger had become expert at this.

Oskar turned to look at the marble Hermes head. It was an attractive piece, the sort of thing that collectors loved to display in their homes. The messenger god – also the god of thieves, as Oskar liked to recall – looked serenely forward with the full-fleshed face of the Classical Greek style prevalent in the middle of the fifth century BC. If a buyer questioned its date, Oskar could grudgingly concede that it might be a very fine Roman copy. The break at the neck was natural-looking, as was a break on one ear. He could have that repaired here, which would add another layer of complexity. He would live with the piece for a little while and then make his decision. The surface was well done, too. It had signs of wear but not everywhere as it would if it had been dumped in a vat of acid. There were even artificial root marks at the back of the neck, usually a telltale sign of authenticity that suggested the piece had been buried in the earth for centuries. His man had become very adept at replicating root marks, though. To the naked eye, it looked ancient.

Another wonderful thing about marble was that unlike terracotta, which could be dated by thermo-luminescence techniques, sampling the marble only gave you the age of the material, which was of course very old indeed. One could also test for the type of marble. This was Parian marble, the finest available in antiquity and the preferred type of many ancient Greek sculptors. The determination of a marble sculpture's authenticity often came down to a judgement call based on connoisseurship – essentially an expert opinion – and Oskar knew that one could always get experts in the field to disagree.

Oskar had found out early on that the antiquities market was full of forgeries. He had himself been burned a number of times. His remedy was to learn as much as possible about the craft and then he began to commission his own forgeries. If you could not beat them, then join them, Oskar thought. He learned to spot the questionable pieces but the trade just continued to get better and better at making them. There were people who bought things they liked and did not question or examine too closely. He realised that from time to time he was able to augment his income significantly by unloading a forgery and since the buyer was not aware that they were not getting the real thing, everyone was happy.

The telephone rang and Oskar called to his assistant to get it. 'Nestor, please get the telephone,' he said through the intercom. 'I don't wish to be disturbed. Thank you.'

A minute later, his assistant came in and said, 'Boss, I think you'll want to take this. It is Luigi, calling from Rome. He said you would want to speak with him.'

'Okay, yes, thank you. Put him through. I'll pick up in here.'

The red light of the phone on his desk began to blink and Oskar picked up the receiver.

'Hello, Luigi. What news?'

'Carr checked in a day early. He is staying at the American Academy, as we expected. He is out now. I was able to get into his room but could not find anything of interest.'

'Was there a personal laptop computer?' Oskar asked.

'He has one but he takes it with him everywhere.'

'Well, if you get access to it, copy the files for me. Only new files within the last week. *Capiche*?'

'*Va bene*,' Luigi responded.

'Tail Carr everywhere. I want a full report with regular updates.'

27

IN THE MORNING, Tom was waiting by the obelisk in the centre of Saint Peter's Square at ten o'clock sharp. He looked around the magnificent key-shaped square that is oriented towards Saint Peter's Basilica, the largest and most beautiful church in the world. The Basilica was the culmination of efforts by some of the world's greatest artists and architects over the course of more than 150 years, and the work had been carried out under some twenty-two popes. If Tom had time later he'd stop in to pay a visit, as he always did when he was in Rome. Saint Peter's Square was a masterpiece in and of itself. It was designed by Bernini, appropriately enough under Pope Alexander VII. Tom was smiling at Victoria's choice for the meeting place just as she strolled up to greet him.

'Tom, good morning. I take it you are not a stranger to Rome?'

'You're right – I love it. The city's so full of history. I've been many times but there are still many parts that I haven't seen. I've never been to the Vatican Library, for instance.'

'Before we go there, I've got something I have to tell you.' Victoria had a troubled look on her face.

'It's been on my mind and it was the reason that I e-mailed you. Do you mind if we stop at a cafe and talk over a cappuccino?'

Tom sensed the tension in Victoria's voice. 'Of course,' he replied, giving her a reassuring look.

'I know the perfect place. It's on the way. I did not make our appointment until ten-thirty so we have time.' Victoria could feel her anxiety lifting as she started to walk briskly across the square.

With Tom at her side, she continued, 'We have to walk around the Vatican's walls to the main entrance.'

Tom could see a long line of people moving slowly towards the entrance to the Vatican museums.

'Thankfully, we don't have to join that queue. Those people are waiting to see the Sistine Chapel and the Museum's collections.' They walked past the throngs of tourists. 'The library is housed in a sixteenth-century building near the Belvidere Court. The cafe I am thinking of is just down the block from here,' Victoria said as she turned down a little side street. 'Afterwards, we'll go straight to the manuscript room where the diary should be waiting for us.'

They ordered coffee at the bar and sat down in the back of the cafe at a small round table. There were people at the other tables having coffee and light breakfasts but it was not crowded. Victoria leaned in towards Tom and said eagerly, 'Tom, I had another vision at the Morgan Library. It was at the exhibition that you had recommended I go see.' She locked stares with Tom. 'I was looking at a manuscript page of the *Alexander Romance* illustrated with a scene of Alexander receiving the Amulet of Nereida from his daughter. It meant nothing to me. I had never heard the story but as I looked closer and saw the amulet, the scene triggered a channelling episode. I fainted. The next thing I knew I was back in Alexander's tomb. It was as though I was continuing the dream that I had at the Met. I realised the amulet was the reason that I had broken into the tomb in the first place. I thought that it would bring me immortality, that it was made from the water of the Fountain of Youth. I was looking at it when my accomplices hit me from behind and left me to die. I took it from around Alexander's neck and clutched it for ages even after the torch died and I was alone in the dark. It was made of a clear stone like diamond and was cut in the form of a ram's head. It was exquisitely crafted and on the forehead of the ram was carved an unusual symbol.'

'What did the symbol look like?' Tom asked.

Victoria started to describe it. 'It was long with symmetrical prongs that curled out from its centre. I made a painting of it yesterday.' She drew the symbol on her paper napkin on the table and Tom was amazed to see the thunderbolt of Zeus with the fiery lightning charges emanating from its centre.

'The amulet had an eerie glow in the dark as though it was emitting its own special power. I don't know how long I sat there with it – hours, days, weeks. It seemed like an eternity in my dream. When I knew I was close to death, I woke up screaming.'

Victoria looked to Tom for a response.

Tom replied hesitantly. He could see that she was visibly upset and he did not want to make her more so. 'Victoria, I don't know what to say. The Amulet of Nereida is a myth. There is no evidence that Alexander the Great even had a daughter. It is part of the later fantastical tradition, part of Alexander's transformation from a historical leader to a legendary hero and god.'

Tom looked into Victoria's eyes tenderly. 'I have to admit to you that I find these visions hard to believe. I don't mean that you did not have them and that they are not meaningful to you. Clearly they are but are they really based on historical events, your own past life? They go against my scientific training.'

Victoria said, 'Tom, you must keep an open mind. I was more closed to these things before my own revelations about reincarnation. I was brought up Catholic, after all. I see things differently now. How can you explain my detailed knowledge of items in the tomb – like the veiled masked dancer that I had never heard of or seen before I had my vision?'

Tom held her gaze. 'I recognise that energy forces

exist. I've felt them myself on Crete at Dikta and at Delphi, at the great sanctuary of Apollo, along the Great Rift of Africa and at holy Christian places like the grotto of Saint Francis of Assisi.' He took a sip of his cappuccino and continued. 'There is another way of approaching this. Most likely, the amulet you saw in your dream was made of rock crystal. Rock-crystal amulets were a popular luxury item in the time of Alexander. The Roman writer Pliny described rock crystal as a rare form of ice, therefore a form of the purest water. The ram's head is a natural shape for Alexander because of his association with the god Ammon, who according to Egyptian religion took the form of a ram. Alexander was even represented on the coinage of his successors with ram's horns. The symbol you saw on the forehead of the ram is a Greek lightning bolt, one, it seems, of exceptionally lively character. Accepting your vision as an image of events that actually happened, it is possible that the myth of the Amulet of Nereida developed from the existence of an amulet that Alexander wore, the one that you saw in your vision. It clearly did not give immortality to Alexander, though, and it did not give immortality to you in your former life.'

'And what about how it glowed in the dark?' Victoria asked.

'I can't explain that,' Tom replied.

Victoria nodded her head and looked at her watch.

'I have to admit to you that I've been thinking about the veiled masked dancer and wondering about what it would mean if your vision were true. I've found some remarkable illustrations from the *Alexander Romance* that represent Roxane, Alexander's wife, dancing for him on the day when they first met and fell in love. The images are much later, of course, and there is no proof, but they resonate strongly with the statuette.'

'Roxane. That would explain its presence in the tomb and its personal association with Alexander much better than a prostitute accompanying him to the next world!' Victoria said. 'I'm so glad to hear that you've been giving what I said some serious consideration.' She looked up at the clock on the wall. 'Well, it's time for us to go to the library. The diary of Pope Alexander VII awaits and my friend is expecting us.'

As they stood up, Victoria took Tom's hand and, squeezing it, said, 'Thanks for talking this through with me, Tom. It may not have any bearing on your search for the tomb of Alexander but it is something to think about . . .'

28

Tom followed Victoria into Vatican City and through a labyrinth of buildings until they finally reached the library. He had to show his papers and museum identification a couple of times but there were no problems. In the manuscript room, they were led to a table in the back and Victoria's colleague brought out the volume of Pope Alexander VII's diary that she had requested.

Victoria pored over the book for a couple of minutes until she found the section she'd been seeking. 'Here it is, Tom,' she said, pointing to a passage in the book that was written in the pope's own hand.

'This is the final volume of the pope's private diary. It covers the last years of his life. It's a remarkable resource. We don't have anything like it for the other popes. Alexander VII was a true scholar and he liked to keep a record of everything. The diary refers to the commission of the elephant and the obelisk in front of the Santa Maria *sopra* Minerva church. Then it describes a related building project involving the tomb of Alexander. Scholars have always assumed that it is a reference to a tomb for Pope Alexander VII himself that never got beyond the project stage, one different from the tomb that was built for him by Bernini much later in Saint Peter's. Yet it seems clear to me that he's referring to the tomb of another Alexander. If he did find the tomb of Alexander the Great during his renovations of the Pantheon this passage may well refer to the Macedonian king's tomb and would mean that the pope probably moved it to another location. The pope provides a rather cryptic clue where he writes: *Disregard the sacred letters of the obelisk but look to the elephant, wisest of beasts, for writing of a different nature. Seek and you shall find.*'

It wasn't a lot to go on, Tom thought, and he wondered if they were grasping at straws here. The diary did not explicitly refer to Alexander the Great although, if Victoria was right, what she said made sense. It seemed like a big 'if' to Tom and his archae-ological training gave him too much pause to be optimistic. The last sentence certainly was intriguing, but who knew what it meant?

Victoria could see that Tom was not overly enthu-siastic. Still she persisted. She had spent years studying the pope's life and something about this passage had always bothered her. When Tom had told her about Alexander the Great's tomb being moved to the Pantheon, something had clicked. It all seemed to make sense. She wrote the phrase down in her note-book.

'I know that the passage does not explicitly mention Alexander the Great but I think it's worth going to the monument with the text to hand to see if we can learn anything more from it. The elephant and the obelisk have puzzled scholars for generations. Perhaps we should go early tomorrow morning when there are not so many people around. Since it stands on a high pedestal, we'll probably need to climb up onto the sculpture to see if there are any inscriptions, and that would best be done when there are not a lot of people watching.'

'Okay, let's meet tomorrow morning at first light in front of the Church of Santa Maria *sopra* Minerva,' Tom said. 'I'm sorry, Victoria – I don't have much of a poker face. I thought that the reference to Alexander's tomb would be more explicit than this. But you're right. Let's have a look tomorrow. I really appreciate your help.'

Victoria smiled back at Tom and said, 'I've got some other work I can do while I'm here. I'm going to stay on. Don't lose that power of positive thinking that led you to my apartment last night, Tom Carr. I'll see you tomorrow morning. As Virgil has often said to me, Don Quixote didn't slay the dragon without faith.'

29

TOM ROSE THE next morning before first light. Getting up this early reminded him of the summer he had spent as a safari guide in the South Luangwa Valley in Zambia. It had been a kind of last fling with alternative careers before he had started work at the Harvard Art Museum and it had been a wonderful experience. In Africa, he had always got up before the clients, about an hour before daylight. Walking from his grass hut to the main camp, he would look with his lantern for tracks on the path to see what animals had passed through during the night. Sometimes there would be lion spoor or even elephant tracks. Occasionally he would spook a hippo that was still out night grazing and had not yet returned to the nearby river. Sitting at the campfire, perched on the edge of an oxbow with a view of the wild African landscape, he would have a cup of strong coffee and listen to the sounds of the night before preparing the Land Rover for the early-morning game viewing.

This morning in Rome, however, Tom had a very different agenda but one no less exciting. After preparing some coffee in the mini-kitchenette in his apartment, he walked over to the tall window that faced the gardens of the Academy and opened it to let in the fresh air. He stood there thinking as he sipped his coffee. All was quiet and stars shone brightly over the tall umbrella pines.

Tom was well aware of how all-consuming the field of archaeology was for its practitioners. It was like a religion. It made him laugh to think of Agatha Christie's murder mystery *They Came to Baghdad*, in which Christie accurately and comically portrays an archaeologist at work. Agatha Christie's real-life husband, Max Mallowan, was a famous British archaeologist of Ancient Near Eastern culture. In Christie's book, murders take place on an archaeological dig and the archaeologist, who is loosely based on Mallowan, is oblivious to the real-life mayhem around him because he is so focused on his work.

Tom thought about his own predicament. It was clear that someone wanted to find the tomb of Alexander before he got to it. There was also no doubt in his mind that this person was not interested in the scientific value of the discovery. This was no malicious colleague trying to beat him to the finish line. This person, whoever they were, probably believed that the discovery would yield valuable antiquities that could be sold on the black market. Tom had to be careful. If the tomb still existed, he could not let someone plunder it. He would not let anyone destroy whatever remained of Alexander and the answers to an important piece of history. There was too much at stake.

He started to think about the many people who had tried in vain to find the tomb of Alexander before him. Sometime following Caracalla's visit to the tomb in the early third century AD, it had slipped into oblivion. People had been trying to locate it for centuries. Even after Alexandria fell from prominence and became a backwater in the Late Roman period, the legend of Alexander lived on. When the city was taken over by the Muslims in the seventh century AD, Alexander remained a prominent figure in folklore and even in religion – tales of his accomplishments were included in the Koran where he was called Zulqarnein, 'the Two-Horned One'. This epithet was probably a reference to the many ancient images of him with the ram's horns of Zeus Ammon or when he was shown wearing elephant tusks as part of an elaborate headdress that signified him as ruler of Africa.

Although the precise location of the tomb seemed to have slipped from memory by the ninth and tenth centuries AD, Arab historians mention a mosque of Zulqarnein in Alexandria, and the tomb of the prophet and king Iskender. Such stories fired the imaginations of visitors to the city and divergent traditions developed. The tomb was linked to at least two different mosques in the city, the Attarine mosque where an impressive ancient sarcophagus was still located and the Nebi Daniel mosque whose subterranean vaults were said to contain Alexander the Great's mummified remains and other treasures. In 1517, the Ottoman sultan Selim the First invaded Mamluk Egypt and claimed it as the latest part of his empire. He re-established trade relations with Egypt and the West at a time when Renaissance Europe was rediscovering its Classical heritage. It was only a matter of time before European interest in the location of the tomb, among the most famous monuments of antiquity, would resurface.

The tomb of Alexander became a political prize during the clash between the French and British colonial empires in the late eighteenth century. As Alexander had done before him, Napoleon envisioned a vast empire for his nation, beginning with his invasion of Egypt in 1798, which incited a holy war with the Ottoman sultan and his armies. In the tradition of Alexander and the ancient Roman emperors, Napoleon brought with him a large retinue of scientists, artists and scholars to record the ancient ruins of Egypt. This grand expedition led to a monumental publication, *Description of Egypt*, and to the collecting of ancient treasures that were crated and shipped back to France for the Imperial National Museum, which would later become the Louvre.

Napoleon envisioned making Alexandria his capital of Egypt, but his plans were thwarted by the Ottomans with the aid of the British. In 1799 he was defeated at the battle of Acre and returned to France shortly thereafter. While Napoleon's return turned out to be in his interest since he was able to arrange a *coup d'état* and proclaim himself emperor in 1804, it meant the loss for France of some of its newly found Egyptian antiquities. The British seized many of the crates of valuables that were intended for France, including two great prizes – a monumental sarcophagus of green stone covered in the ancient sacred writing of the Egyptians, and the Rosetta Stone, a Hellenistic trilingual inscription which would in time provide the means to translate hieroglyphics.

The green sarcophagus, according to local legend, had belonged to Alexander the Great and was the one that had been located at the Attarine Mosque. A British scholar called Clarke wrote a book laying out the argument that the sarcophagus was Alexander's tomb and it became a centrepiece of the British Museum's antiquities collection in the early nineteenth century. However, with the decipherment of hieroglyphics in 1822 by the French scholar Champollion, it became clear from the sacred text on the sarcophagus that it did not belong to Alexander but to the pharaoh Nectanebo II, who reigned from 360 to 342 BC. This reopened the question of the whereabouts of the tomb.

Stories resurfaced locating Alexander's tomb beneath the Nebi Daniel mosque but they could not be confirmed.

The discovery at Sidon by the Ottoman archaeologist Osman Hamdi Bay of a spectacular sarcophagus, which featured outstanding sculptural friezes of Alexander the Great fighting Persians, probably at the Battle of Issus, and hunting with Persians was misidentified as Alexander's sarcophagus but, in actuality, belonged to a local king named Abdalonymus who knew Alexander and owed his sovereignty to him. The sarcophagus was brought to Constantinople in 1887 and became the centrepiece of the new archaeological museum, where it remains to this day. Interestingly, the Alexander Sarcophagus's ornate mouldings and elaborate decoration might have echoed the funerary cart that brought Alexander's remains from Babylon to Egypt and which would have passed through Sidon on its long solemn journey.

Indeed, numerous archaeologists had tried to locate the tomb in Alexandria from Heinrich Schliemann in 1888 on down to the present day. Tom wondered, if he finally came upon any concrete evidence, would there even be anything left of the tomb itself? Or was all of this a grand goose chase, folly – even arrogance, given how many people had failed before him? Still, he had been dealt more cards than the others. It was remarkable, he thought, how Alexander's body had been moved so many times during the course of history. First it had been brought from Babylon, where he had died, to Memphis-Saqqara. Then it was moved from Memphis-Saqqara to Alexandria, probably in the late fourth century BC by Ptolemy I or by his successor Philadelphus when Ptolemy I died in 282 BC. In the latter part of the third century BC, during the reign of Ptolemy IV, it was moved a third time in Alexandria to a new royal cemetery honouring his ancestors. Finally, according to the stele at Dikta, it was moved a fourth time during the reign of Trebonianus Gallus in the middle of the third century AD to the Pantheon. With the deification of Alexander and the establishment of his cult, his body became a holy relic. It remained a potent symbol and destination for pilgrims according to the accounts of some its most illustrious visitors, the Roman emperors. Could it have been moved again, from the Pantheon, under Pope Alexander VII?

Tom hoped that Victoria's intuition was right about the entry in Pope Alexander VII's diary. They would know soon enough. Tom wanted to be prepared so he made a list of things he should bring. When he finished his coffee, he packed a small torch, his note-book, his camera, and his laptop and the digital scanner that Arthur had given him, in case they did find an inscription. Then he set out.

Tom arrived at the square in front of the church

of Santa Maria *sopra* Minerva as dawn was just beginning to bring light to the sky. He had seen the occasional passer-by on his way but for the most part Rome was still sleeping. Victoria was not there yet, so Tom decided to have a closer look at the sculpture on his own. He walked slowly around it. It certainly was a curious and inventive design. The elephant stood squarely on a narrow plinth that was supported by a tall rectangular base, which was itself raised on a stepped podium. On the beast's back, supported by a saddle with an elaborate blanket, was an Egyptian obelisk made of granite and carved with hieroglyphs. The elephant turned his head to the right and his trunk stretched jauntily back behind him almost as if he was checking his monumental load or, perhaps, paying homage to it.

As Tom looked at the statue, his jaw dropped. There, just beneath the elephant's head, was the star of Macedonia prominently carved right on the saddle blanket. It was also depicted rising above a mountain range on the two hanging folds of the blanket. What was more, it appeared again in three-dimensional form at the top of the obelisk, just below the Christian cross that surmounted the entire monument. The Macedonian star was all over the place. Tom was beside himself. It could not be a coincidence, and yet the star was not widely known in the seventeenth century. Tom could barely contain his excitement.

He didn't even notice Victoria until she was standing right next to him. 'It's a fine monument, isn't it? It's always been one of my favourite works by Bernini.'

'Victoria, good morning. I was just standing in awe of it. I'm beginning to think that your intuition is right. But please tell me first about the sculpture and then we can discuss it together,' Tom said, smiling at her.

Victoria looked up at the monument and began to speak. 'Salvador Dali thought the elephant and obelisk symbolised time travel, and I rather like that idea. The obelisk is, after all, a device for telling time and here the elephant is moving it. Bernini's work inspired a number of Dali's paintings, such as *The Torment of Saint Anthony*. However, as I mentioned to you yesterday, its true significance has long puzzled scholars. The inscriptions on the long sides record the official dedication. Here on the west side it says that Pope Alexander VII dedicated this obelisk, which is sacred to Egyptian Pallas Athena, to divine wisdom.'

Pointing to the hieroglyphs, Victoria said, 'Of course, in the seventeenth century they could not read hieroglyphs. As you well know, it was not until after the discovery of the Rosetta Stone that they cracked the code. Consequently, Pope Alexander VII didn't know that the hieroglyphs identify the obelisk as sacred to Isis and that it was carved in the first part of the sixth century BC, during the reign of the pharaoh Apries in the twenty-sixth dynasty.'

Walking round to the eastern side, Victoria continued, 'Pope Alexander VII's dedication continues on this side. It asks everyone who looks on these engraved images made by the wise Egyptians and borne by the elephant, the strongest of beasts, to remember to be of strong mind and to uphold solid wisdom.'

Victoria turned back to look at Tom. 'The question remains why Pope Alexander VII chose to dedicate a monument to divine wisdom in this form in this square. Certainly, the monument might have been meant to convey more than one message. On one level it is a monument to the pope himself, as elements from his coat of arms are placed all over the sculpture, especially the Chigi star. It was the very last commission that Bernini finished for Alexander VII, and it was dedicated in the year of the pope's death. The obelisk, as I'm sure you know, was excavated nearby in the garden of the Dominican monastery and probably comes from a sanctuary to Isis and not, as is intimated in the dedicatory inscription, from a sanctuary to Minerva, the remains of which were found underneath the church behind us.'

'The obelisk might well have been brought to Rome in the late third century AD during the reign of the emperor Diocletian,' Tom added.

Victoria turned around to point to the facade of Santa Maria *sopra* Minerva and then, turning back towards the monument, she continued. 'Interestingly, we know that Bernini was contemplating a sculpture portraying an elephant carrying an obelisk as early as 1630, long before Alexander VII became pope. There are preparatory sketches for a similar monument that might have been intended for the gardens of the Villa Borghese but was never executed. It is even recorded that an elephant was brought to Rome in 1625. Seeing an elephant in the flesh might well have inspired Bernini. He certainly did a better job than other artists in rendering its features, although they are not completely proportionate. Another source of inspiration for Bernini could have been a book called the *Hyperotomachia Poliphili* or *Poliphilo's Dream of the Strife of Love*, a romance published in 1499. It features an illustration of an elephant carrying an obelisk. Bernini's design, however, is much more dynamic.' Victoria paused to look at the statue and then continued.

'A popular nickname for the elephant is "Pulcino", which means "little chick" in Italian. The name might originally have referred to the small scale of the elephant in proportion to the obelisk. Or, according to another theory, it may be an obscure reference to a charity run by the Dominicans that raised money for young women in need of marriage dowries. There are other stories that describe how Bernini gave the elephant a smile and carved his head to show it turning back, suggesting that the animal is defecating to taunt a local official whose office stood opposite the elephant's behind. In my opinion, all these stories are utter nonsense, gossip that became legend. In fact, it's apparent from Bernini's preparatory sketches and a small-scale clay model that the sculptor deliberately moved away from a more whimsical garden creation to this bold and quixotic monument. The serene expression on the elephant's face is really marvellous, though. It's almost as if he's keeping a secret to himself. Could that secret be the location of Alexander the Great's tomb?'

Tom pointed to the stars on the elephant's saddle. 'You mentioned that these stars are identified with Pope Alexander VII. As soon as I saw them I immediately thought they represented the star of Macedonia, Alexander the Great's royal insignium, which may in fact represent a sunburst like the one on the top of the obelisk. The resemblance is uncanny. What I do not understand is how Alexander VII would have known about this symbol. It was only with the excavation of the royal Macedonian tombs at Vergina in 1972 that it became widely recognised.' Tom paused for a moment and then continued.

'The choice of an elephant and obelisk would be ingeniously appropriate for a monument linked to

Alexander the Great's tomb. Alexander the Great was the one who first introduced elephants to the western world. After his epic battle with the Indian king Porus, who used elephants for warfare against the great conqueror and still lost, Alexander adopted them himself as part of his royal entourage. It is said that Alexander dedicated Porus's greatest elephant to Helios the sun god and named him after the Homeric hero Ajax because of his strength.'

Victoria listened to Tom as he continued to build his argument.

'Alexander rode into Babylon triumphantly in a chariot pulled by elephants. The victory procession with elephants that became popular in Roman times stems from Alexander's triumphs, as well as those of the god Dionysos who, according to legend, conquered the East before Alexander. Alexander used the legend of Dionysos in his propaganda. The wild satyr-like faces and the ivy that decorate Bernini's elephant saddle and saddlecloth seem to me to be recalling this association. Otherwise, they would seem quite out of place.

'The obelisk, as well, seems equally appropriate to Alexander the Great, who was associated with the sun god Helios because of the vast kingdoms under his domain. The obelisk also refers to Egypt where Alexander was first buried and where he had set up his most important city, Alexandria. The notion of divine wisdom, which links the legendary Alexander, one of the seven sages of antiquity, with the intellectual Pope Alexander VII, would be a perfect way to bring these two otherwise rather different men of history together.'

Victoria took out her notebook and said, 'Shall we consider the statement from Pope Alexander VII's diary now? It reads: *Disregard the sacred letters of the obelisk but look to the elephant, wisest of beasts, for writing of a different nature. Seek and you shall find.*'

Tom looked up. 'Let's look closely at the surface of the sculpture. Perhaps there's an inscription that's not readily visible.'

As they looked it became clear that there were not many places on the elephant where an inscription could be placed that would escape notice. They carefully examined the animal's legs and trunk but found nothing. The only other place would have been the top of the elephant's head, which was not readily visible from the ground. It would be necessary to climb up to get a good look at that. For just a moment, Tom considered what the Italian laws might be regarding climbing on sculptures carved by Gianlorenzo Bernini. He didn't know of any, but he imagined there probably was some statute that forbade it.

'Well, I suppose I've got to climb up and have a quick look at the top of the head.'

Victoria looked around. The coast seemed clear. 'Go for it.'

Tom grabbed his digital camera and Arthur's scanning device, slipped off his shoes, and climbed up to the top of the pedestal. From there, with a slight jump, he was able to grab one of the volutes at the corner of the base of the obelisk and hoist himself up to the neck of the elephant. Sitting astride it, like an Indian mahout out on safari, Tom looked down on the top of the pachyderm's head. He could see that there was an inscription, at least the remains of one, carved into the elephant's skin. He turned on his camera and took a couple of quick pictures. Then he powered up the scanning device and ran it over the inscription. As he was doing this a man came running across the square, screaming at Tom in Italian to get off the elephant. Tom looked up for a second. At least it was not a policeman. Victoria walked towards the man and tried to calm him down with a story about official research, while Tom finished the job and got down as quickly as possible.

Victoria approached Tom. 'I think we should leave now. I tried to pacify that man but he's still hanging around and we don't want to attract any further attention. Let's go down the street to Tazza D'Oro's for a cappuccino. We can talk there.'

Tom couldn't contain his excitement and yelled,

'The inscription is there! I got some images of it. We can look at it together. Let's go.'

Sipping on a cappuccino at Tazza D'Oro's, Tom zoomed in on the inscription. He studied it intently and then handed the camera to Victoria.

'There's definitely an inscription there but the letters are almost completely worn away. The morning light was pretty good, too. I doubt that I could've gotten a better picture. I'm sorry that I didn't have time to take a squeeze, but given its condition I doubt that it would've done any good. I also scanned the letters with this new device I brought from the museum. It may help us to read it. I'm going to download it to my laptop and see what we get.'

After a few minutes, Tom had the Red Phantom program up and running and the inscription appeared on the screen. It was not much better.

Tom spoke to Victoria as he studied the inscription on his laptop. 'This program was designed to restore ancient inscriptions that were painted but it seems that this inscription was only carved, not painted as well. I suppose the damage could have been the result of acid rain or an over-cleaning of the statue. But it looks rather as though it was intentionally obliterated. The letters have been all but erased. Victoria, it seems that your hunch proved right. Pope Alexander VII must have rediscovered the Tomb of Alexander and reburied his remains. This inscription probably would have told us where. It seems that we have come to a dead end again.' Tom paused to sip his cappuccino. Then an idea came to him in a flash of inspiration.

'Victoria, this is going to sound crazy. I've just had an idea that might enable us to solve this mystery, but I need your help. Will you come with me to New York?'

Victoria's blue eyes sparkled as she returned his slightly desperate gaze. 'Why not?'

30

Luigi waited on the line as Nestor got Oskar Williams to the telephone. He knew that Oskar would not be happy with the information he was about to impart.

'He's gone. I just saw him get on a plane to New York with a young woman. She had blonde hair – tall, attractive. I am sending you a picture of them now. It was Delta Flight 376 to JFK.'

'You're kidding. He's on his way to New York now?' Oskar said. His first thought was why should Tom Carr have left Rome? Oskar turned to his computer and opened the attachment from Luigi. There was an image of Tom and the blonde. Oskar immediately recognised her as the woman he had seen at the Morgan Library. 'Did he know you were following him?'

'No, I'm sure that they did not see me. I am discreet,' Luigi said emphatically. 'It's strange, though. He did not even check out of his room at the American Academy. I've followed him all day. Early this morning he met the woman near the Pantheon and they were looking at a Bernini sculpture in front of the church of Santa Maria *sopra* Minerva. It was the elephant and the obelisk.'

'Yes, I know the sculpture,' Oskar replied and then listened.

'He even climbed up onto the statue and took some pictures of the elephant's head. Afterwards they had a coffee together nearby and then went straight out to the airport. I went back to the sculpture to look at the head but there was nothing there that I could see.'

'Okay, you've done good work. Thanks for alerting me. I'll let you know when I need you again. Goodbye.' Oskar hung up the phone. *Why was Carr returning to New York so soon? Something was going on. He could not know about me*, Oskar thought. There must be a new development. It was time for more drastic measures. It was not enough to follow Carr around. Oskar needed answers. He needed a plan that would bring Carr to him.

As he sat at his desk, he heard the fax register a call and begin to print out a message. He walked over to the elegant maple three-legged table and pulled the piece of paper from the machine. On it was a rough sketch of a crown made of oak leaves and a kylix with a scene on the tondo. The names of the figures were inscribed. It was the centaur Nessos, an arrow in his chest, clutching Deianeira, the beautiful wife of Herakles.

The phone rang. Oskar looked at the caller ID although he knew who it was. He picked up the telephone and answered in Turkish.

'I just received it. What is the material?'

'The one is made of gold with some enamel decoration. The other gilt silver.'

'And the quality?' Oskar asked.

'First quality. I immediately thought of you when they were brought to me.'

'I'll take them. Send them right away. We can discuss the price when I see them.'

'You won't be disappointed.'

Oskar hung up the phone. The wealth of the ancient Greeks never ceased to amaze him. Just when he thought there were no more tombs to be plundered, a new one would be discovered that contained exquisite works of art. He glanced down at the piece of paper in his hand. The myth of Herakles and Deianeira: it was a classic tale. Herakles and his wife were travelling when they came to a river. A centaur named Nessos offered to help Deianeira across. While Nessos was carrying her he tried to take advantage of her and Herakles shot him with an arrow from his famous bow. As the centaur lay dying he told Deianeira to collect some of his blood and use it as dye for a coat for Herakles. With his last dying breath, the centaur told Deianeira to give the coat to Herakles should she ever suspect he was being unfaithful to her and the coat would magically make him true again.

Deianeira made the coat as the centaur suggested and, eventually, Herakles was unfaithful. She knew the signs, as wives do. Deianeira gave him the coat, not knowing that the centaur's blood was deadly poison. Herakles could not get the coat off and was in such pain that he climbed to a mountain top, built a pyre, and killed himself on it in a dramatic act of self-immolation. Ironically, Herakles had saved his wife's honour by killing the centaur whose blood would eventually kill him for the same disgraceful act. And the whole story hinged on a lie cleverly told by the wily old centaur. It gave Oskar an idea. Suddenly, he knew how he could get Carr to come to him – and Carr's own actions would be his undoing.

31

BY THE TIME Tom and Victoria arrived at John F. Kennedy Airport, got through security and Customs, and got Tom's car out of long-term parking, it was nearly ten p.m. Tom drove straight from the airport to the museum. When he pulled up to the museum's service entrance, the guard in the outside security booth checked Tom's identification and then waved them through. Driving down the long ramp, they entered a huge hangar-like space and Tom parked the car near a massive loading dock.

As he was parking, Victoria suppressed a yawn and stretched her arms. She said groggily, 'What are we doing here? Isn't the museum closed?'

'I need to check something. Just wait in the car and I'll be back soon. Trust me,' said Tom.

'Okay, but don't be long.' She looked at him with a quizzical expression.

The museum was like a fortress at night. No one went in or out without proper identification. Tom had to go through two more security checkpoints. After verifying his fingerprints and a laser scan of his eyes, the guard buzzed him in and he passed through the thick steel doors of the sentry office. Once he was inside the building, he headed towards the Greek and Roman Department. He walked purposefully through the long series of Egyptian galleries with their massive granite sculptures of pharaohs and gods that cast dramatic shadows in the dim light. Tom felt the familiar sense of awe and privilege at the fact that he was allowed to work at this great institution; it was good to be back.

When he reached the Greek and Roman Department, he went immediately to the departmental library. Searching the stacks, he found the book that he was looking for and brought it to the wide wooden reading table. He sat down in front of the old book and began to scan it systematically.

'Now we'll see if I'm right,' he thought aloud as he ran his finger down the catalogue list. After several pages, his eyes lit up. 'Eureka! I've found it! I knew it was here, and there's no time to lose.'

Tom got up, tucked the book under his arm, closed up the library and walked to the end of the hall. He unlocked the door to his colleague's office and turned on the light. The mahogany-panelled office was lined with books on one side. Two huge bay windows looked out onto Central Park. The park was dark and still, the tops of the trees forming a canopy that stretched across to the west side. Inside the office, Tom crossed the room and reached behind a monumental head of the god Apollo, a one-to-one plaster cast taken from the famous statue of the god on the west pediment of the temple of Zeus at Olympia. He grabbed two skeleton keys on a brass ring that hung from a wooden peg. After touching Apollo lightly on the nose for good luck, he extinguished the lights and headed out of the building.

Victoria barely opened her eyes as Tom slipped into the driver's seat and started up the car.

'I found what I was looking for. We need to make one more stop before we go to my place. It shouldn't take too much time. It's not too far from here. Feel free to sleep if you like. I'll wake you when we get there.'

Tom pulled out of the museum car park, turned north onto Madison Avenue and headed uptown. Soon they reached the Madison Avenue bridge and crossed over into the Bronx. It was just after eleven p.m. and there were very few people on the street. Victoria woke up, rubbed her eyes, and said, 'Where on Earth are we going?'

'You'll see. It's not much further. We're almost there.'

A few minutes later Tom pulled into a parking lot next to a massive warehouse and drove into a space designated for Metropolitan Museum staff parking.

'What is this place?'

'It's off-site storage for the museum. I want to look at something that's stored here. It's a plaster cast.'

'Tom, is this why you have brought me back to New York? What are you talking about? What could you possibly be thinking?' Victoria asked.

'It may be a red herring but let's give it a try – don't judge yet.' Tom got out of the car and Victoria followed him. 'At one time, plaster casts were the very core of the Met's collections. The catalogue of these casts was a compendium of art history from prehistoric times through the eighteenth century. Most of the casts came from Europe and, later on, they were made at the Caproni cast factory in Boston. They were displayed in what are now the Medieval galleries at the museum – that is, at the heart of the museum's architectural plan.' Tom kept up a fast pace and Victoria walked swiftly beside him. 'Many of the casts remained on display until the 1940s. But with increasing demands for exhibition space for new acquisitions they were eventually relegated to storage. This massive warehouse is where they sit, mostly in the dark, collecting dust. It's a kind of plaster-cast purgatory. Shall we go in?'

They entered the building and took an old lift to the top floor. Tom unlocked the large padlock on the heavy metal door that opened into the storage area.

Standing in the vast space by a window in the moonlight, Tom turned to Victoria and said, 'When I was a boy in Montana one of my favourite things to do in the summertime after a storm was to look for rainbows. The sky in Montana is as big as the ocean. It seems to go on forever. It was amazing. I'd be out driving with my dad. Montana is such a big state that you have to drive everywhere. As soon as the rain stopped and that beautiful sky revealed itself again through the clouds, their white billowing edges lined with silver light, I would look for a rainbow while my father drove. After I spotted one, my dad would step on the gas and chase it. Even going fifty miles an hour on a graded dirt road, it seemed like we would gain on it but we never could reach it in the end. It always seemed to be just a little further away. This journey has been a bit similar. We get close and then the end of the rainbow seems to move away again.' Tom flipped the main light switch for the huge storage area and light flooded the place, illuminating thousands of statues.

'Welcome to the museum's cast warehouse.'

Victoria's blue eyes widened as she took in the extraordinary landscape of statuary and architectural elements revealed before her. The statues just stood one next to the other in rows. It was a huge space, the size of a football field. There were slabs from the Parthenon frieze and the Pergamon altar, statues of Egyptian pharaohs, monumental Assyrian reliefs from Persepolis, the relief from the Lion Gate at Mycenae, tomb markers of medieval knights, gargoyles from the cathedral of Notre Dame and the doorways of the cathedral at Chartres, Islamic sculptures and famous works of the Renaissance. The list that Tom had consulted earlier went on and on. There were nearly three thousand catalogued casts.

'I have not been up here in years. The pieces are not arranged chronologically, as you can see. I'm not sure exactly where it is but I've got an idea. Follow me.' Tom held a torch in his hand and proceeded into the forest of plaster casts.

Victoria no longer felt tired. The strange scene around her was like an art-history exam in 3-D. She paused for a minute to take it all in.

'Hey, Tom, look – Michelangelo's *Pieta* is sitting here right next to the Barberini *Faun*. Is that someone's idea of a joke? And there's the Terme Boxer looking like he's waiting for the bus. My God, it's like a surreal vision of the end of art history, all the greatest works of art from around the world brought together and locked away to gather dust. Imagine what Salvador Dali could have done with this place.' Victoria paused and then said almost to herself, 'It's really kind of sad . . .'

Tom abruptly interrupted her train of thought, 'Victoria, come over here. I've found it!'

Victoria walked around the end of a row of life-size casts and the space opened up slightly. There in front of her was Tom standing next to a full-size plaster copy of Bernini's *Elephant and Obelisk*.

'Oh my God, Tom – do you think the inscription is there? When was this cast made? It's amazing.'

'It was done in the 1890s. The museum negotiated with many different institutions in Italy, Greece and elsewhere to commission new casts of major works. I thought that I remembered this one and I was thrilled when I saw it in the inventory.'

Victoria walked up to the elephant and stood next to Tom.

'It's awfully dirty.'

'There's a dust bellows and a ladder near the entrance. Stay here. I'll be right back.' Tom was about to walk back the way they had come when in the distance there was a loud noise and a sound like the flutter of wings.

Victoria grabbed Tom's arm and whispered to him, 'Did you hear that?'

'It's just some pigeons at the far end of the room. They must've gotten in through an open window. Don't pay them any attention. There's no one else here. I'll be right back.'

In a couple of minutes Tom returned with a ladder and the dust bellows. He climbed up onto the elephant's head while Victoria held the ladder in place. Several blasts of air from the bellows blew dust from the surface of the sculpture. 'The inscription here is legible! It's in Latin.'

Tom got out his camera and took a couple of

photos. Then he took out his notebook and transcribed the inscription into it.

He climbed down the ladder and stood next to Victoria. The excitement on his face was clear as he translated. 'It says: "In the temple of Athena is a mermaid. The correct response to her question will lead you to the great sage and the path to divine wisdom." The temple of Athena must refer to the temple of Minerva, the remains of which are beneath the church opposite the statue of the elephant and obelisk. To think we were right there!' Tom could barely contain himself.

Victoria looked at him excitedly. 'The ruins of the temple are closed to the public but the access point is from the crypt of the church. I know the priest who runs that church. I spent a lot of time in the little museum there. They have an important sculpture by Bernini that I worked on. I'm sure that I can get the priest to let us into the ruins.'

'I knew I wouldn't be able to do this without you, Victoria.' Tom looked into her eyes. His heart was beating fast. 'The rest of the inscription is a bit puzzling but "the great sage" must refer to Alexander the Great. As you know, in the Middle Ages Alexander was considered one of the seven sages of antiquity and the use of the word "great" must clearly be an oblique reference to his epithet. We have to get back to Santa Maria *sopra* Minerva as soon as possible.

I'm sure the meaning of the inscription will become clear once we're there. I'll look into flights back to Rome first thing tomorrow morning. For now let's go back to my place in Brooklyn. I know you must be exhausted. A good night's sleep will do us both good.'

32

TOM WOKE AT nine the next morning feeling refreshed and exhilarated by their discovery at the warehouse. Victoria was still sleeping, so he thought he would step out and get some things for breakfast. It was a crisp and clear morning, and strong sunlight brightened the cobbled streets, giving everything a certain sense of clarity. Tom loved these days in the city when everything was in focus much more than when the frequent hazy pollution fouled the urban air. Such days had once had an unqualified splendour for Tom. But since the tragedies of 9/11, which had happened on a similar autumn day, Tom always wondered what the next hours might bring. He stroked the rabbit's foot in his pocket for good luck as he walked through the small park that formed the centre of the neighbourhood.

First he stopped at a little Italian bakery on Court Street. It was still early and the bread was piled high in baskets on the back wall and in a glass display case that faced the front window. The glass was slightly steamy from the heat of the fresh bread against the window that faced the cool autumn air outside the shop. The door to the back room was open and the baker was already starting the next batch, kneading balls of dough on a marble surface opposite the large ovens. As the young woman at the counter helped another customer, Tom turned to the big glass doors of the old chrome refrigerator, took out a quart of milk, and plunked it down on the counter. For a moment, he took in the amazing assortment of breads and baked goods – doughnuts, cookies, biscotti and colourful cakes. He settled on a loaf of seeded Sicilian bread, braided like a gypsy's bracelet and with a thick chewy crust.

He continued down the street to the local coffee shop. He could smell the strong aroma of roasting beans long before he got to the door. Once inside, it was almost intoxicating. Tom wouldn't be able to get a cappuccino as good as anything in Rome but the shop had an excellent selection. Besides, Tom had become quite adept at making his own at home. He selected two different types of bean, one for making espresso and another for drip coffee, and set the packets on the counter before settling up.

Tom's last stop was at the French bakery further down the street where he got two almond croissants and a brioche loaf. That ought to take care of things, he thought. He made his way back to the apartment, stopping only at the florist to get some fresh-cut flowers. Victoria was still sleeping, so he ground the fresh beans, made a pot of coffee and then, with a steaming cup in his hand, went upstairs to his office on the top floor to check his work messages.

Sitting at his desk, Tom called into the museum's answering service. There were quite a few messages but nothing urgent, except for a call from a dealer who claimed to have an important object related to Alexander the Great. The dealer said that he wanted to show it to Tom before offering it to anyone else. He asked him to call back as soon as possible. 'Now that's a peculiar coincidence,' Tom mumbled to himself. He knew that in all likelihood the object would not be something that the museum would want to acquire but he would not know for sure unless he saw it. If it *was* something exceptional, it would be worth looking into, and he knew that if it was really special the dealer wouldn't wait long before turning to other prospective buyers.

Tom called his travel agent to see if she'd be able to arrange reservations for a flight back to Rome that evening. With reservations confirmed for a nine p.m. flight, he went to the kitchen to get breakfast ready. Victoria came in just as he was preparing the finishing touches.

'Doesn't this look beautiful? Is that coffee? I'm dying for some. What a glorious sleep. Did you sleep well?' Victoria asked as Tom handed her a cup.

'Yes. I always do at home. I'm glad you did, too.' Victoria sat down at the table with her knees

334

pulled up in front of her and asked, 'So, what's the plan?'

'Well, I've been able to get us on a flight back to Rome this evening. So we have the day to ourselves.'

'You must take me to the museum. I cannot leave New York without returning to the Met. I want to see *your* favourite pieces in the Greek and Roman collection.' Victoria looked at Tom with those sparkling blue eyes as she twirled her long blonde hair around her finger and sipped the steaming coffee.

'Okay. Of course – it's the least I can do. We'll go after breakfast. I also had an intriguing call from a dealer in the city. He said that he has an important object relating to Alexander the Great that he wants to show me. His gallery isn't too far from the museum. Would that interest you? If not, I'll go by myself. It won't take long.'

'Yes, that sounds like fun. I've never even been to an antiquities gallery in Rome. It will be interesting to see one in New York City.'

After breakfast, Tom called the dealer to see if he could receive them.

'Hello, is this Mr Oskar Williams? This is Tom Carr from the Metropolitan Museum of Art.'

'Mr Carr, what an unexpected pleasure.' Oskar had to curb his giveaway keenness. 'I understood from your secretary that you were out of town.'

'Yes, well, I'm back and I got your message. You

said that you have something that would be of interest to the museum?' Tom didn't want to sound too eager.

'Yes, it's an exceptional piece. As soon as I saw it, I knew that the Met would be interested in it. In fact, I wanted to show it to you first because of your expertise on the subject of Alexander the Great. It really is a dream come true. The find of a lifetime.' Oskar baited the hook.

'Could I arrange to come and see it?'

'Yes, of course. When were you thinking?'

'My schedule is rather busy over the next week.' Tom didn't want to let on that he'd be leaving the city again. 'But I do have some time this afternoon if that works for you.'

'This afternoon is perfect. Shall we say three o'clock?' Oskar wanted a little time to prepare for the visit.

'Yes, that'll be fine. Oh, by the way, I have a friend visiting from out of town. Would it be all right if she came along?'

'But of course. I look forward to seeing you both then. You know where I am?'

'Yes, of course. Thank you.'

'Terrific. You really are in for a treat. It is the most exquisite object and of such historical importance. It is the signet ring of Alexander the Great.' Oskar hung up the phone, leaving Tom somewhat wide-eyed, his mouth agape.

Tom turned to Victoria and said. 'I don't know what to make of that. He just told me that he wants to show us the signet ring of Alexander the Great. My God! What are the chances of *that*?'

Victoria stood up and walked over to Tom. 'Who did you say this guy was?'

'He's one of the old-time dealers in New York. The museum has bought things from him in the past, but not recently. We buy very few antiquities these days. There are so many rules and regulations that need to be followed and the costs of antiquities with secure provenance have skyrocketed in recent years. Suitable pieces rarely come on the market. In any case I guess we'll see soon enough. He's expecting us at three p.m.'

'Great. Give me a little time to collect myself and then I am all yours,' Victoria replied.

About an hour later, with all their things packed for the return trip to Rome, they set out in Tom's Carmen Gia across the Brooklyn Bridge and up the east side of Manhattan towards the museum.

Tom took Victoria straight to the new Greek and Roman Galleries. As they stood looking down the long central gallery for Greek Art, the bright afternoon sun highlighted the sculptured masterpieces. Victoria gasped. 'How beautiful! I know we don't have too much time but I'd love to see some of your favourite pieces.'

Tom led her through the galleries. It was always

fun looking at art with other people and Victoria was the perfect companion. She took everything in so carefully and fully. Nothing escaped her notice and she was genuinely interested and deeply moved by a number of the pieces. When they got to the Treasury, Victoria turned to Tom and said, 'I am not sure I am ready to see the veiled masked dancer again.'

Tom took her by the shoulders and looked straight into her eyes. 'You'll be fine, Victoria. I am right here with you if you have another episode. The only way you are going to know is to try. Take control. You can do it.'

Victoria was nervous but after a moment she steeled herself and said, 'You're right, Tom. There is nothing to fear but fear itself.'

They walked in and Tom took Victoria's hand as they looked together at the bronze statuette of the veiled and masked dancer. Victoria's pulse was racing but the warmth and strength of Tom's hand grasping her own gave her an inner strength and she knew that she was going to be okay.

'The scale is so intimate. It's as though she's dancing for us. It really is a fabulous piece,' Victoria said as she stood there mesmerised by the small sculpture.

'People who have seen it in books are always surprised by the scale. They think it is going to be much bigger because of the fine detail. See, you are doing well: no blackouts.' Tom looked at her reassuringly.

Tom went on to tell Victoria about the illustrations that he had seen in some versions of the *Alexander Romance*. 'Imagine if it did represent Roxane dancing for Alexander on that night when they first met and fell in love . . . I find it interesting that there are other, albeit less fine, copies of the type, which suggests that it was popular and possibly a famous work. Leaving aside your own vision of it being in Alexander's tomb, which unfortunately we cannot verify, it could be a later representation of the scene, too – kind of an imagined history. Hellenistic artists were fond of such subjects, which they could make seem very real. That could also explain the resemblance to the scenes from the *Alexander Romance*. Maybe this dancer is a "quotation" from a famous lost painting or sculptural group. The problem is that we'll probably never know for sure.'

Tom led Victoria into the next gallery. He showed her the frescoes from Boscoreale, pausing at the central panel with the bride who looked out hauntingly into the distance.

'This painting is one of my favourites. Doesn't the way she looks out from the painting just give you chills? It's amazingly effective. All of these paintings come from the same reception room of a large aristocratic villa not far from Pompeii. They're probably copies of a famous lost Hellenistic cycle. If you are right that the original Hellenistic paintings decorated the tomb of Alexander the Great, we could be looking at Roxane staring out at us from the past. It's a very different representation from the bronze dancer, much more sombre and serious.'

'It's certainly not the portrait that I would have chosen to remember my wedding day by,' Victoria said. 'But you're right, though: she appears to be a woman with a good head on her shoulders. Is she reflecting on the future or the past? It's impossible to say.'

'The woman represented in the panel on the right has been identified as a soothsayer who saw a reflection of a young king on her shield that was the prophecy of a male heir who would be born from the marriage. In a perfect world the conception of a boy would happen on the wedding night, like the one that would follow the celebration depicted in this painting. For Roxane and Alexander, their conceiving a male heir did not happen until years later. In fact, judging by the date of his birth, it's likely that their son was conceived shortly after Alexander's best friend and companion Hephaestion died at what was one of the most difficult times of Alexander's short life. Roxane must have been a great consolation to him.' Tom paused for a moment. 'Alexander died unexpectedly only months later and the boy, named Alexander VIII, was born shortly after the Macedonian king's death. Alexander's tomb, of course, was not built until much later because of the controversy over the location of his final resting place. When the tomb was built, Roxane's role and that of her young son, the legitimate heir to the throne, was precarious – to say the least. If this painting represents the royal wedding, the artist who painted the original might have been trying to capture some of that uncertainty in Roxane's future in this haunting image.'

Tom ended the tour in the gallery for Late Roman art. He pointed out the very fine marble portrait of the emperor Caracalla. 'The sculptor really captured the sense that he was *not* a nice man.'

'That's something of an understatement. But you feel that he was a person of great strength and determination.'

'We have this bronze portrait of Caracalla as well.' Tom pointed to a bronze head in a nearby display case. 'This head would have been a more expensive commission than the one in marble, but there's no comparison in quality. This bronze is a much cruder work, which just goes to show that expensive materials are not always the makings of fine sculpture. As they say, you do not always get what you pay for.' Tom smiled at Victoria. 'Caracalla was obsessed with Alexander the Great. In fact, he was the last recorded visitor to Alexander's tomb. If the inscription at Dikta, stating that the tomb of Alexander had been moved to the Pantheon, had not come to light, my first guess for who could have moved it would have been Caracalla.'

Tom walked over to a large-scale bronze statue of a Roman emperor represented in heroic nudity. 'So I thought I'd end our little tour with this bronze statue. It's not our finest artwork. In fact, he's affectionately known as 'pinhead' in the department since his head is so small in proportion to his body. Nonetheless, it surely represents Trebonianus Gallus, the emperor mentioned in the inscription at Dikta as the person who moved the tomb of Alexander from Alexandria to the Pantheon. It's one of the very few large-scale portraits of him to have survived mostly intact. The body is quite battered so the original pose is not faithfully represented today. He's portrayed in heroic nudity and probably held a lance in his raised right hand. The original pose consciously imitated a famous statue by the court sculptor Lysippos of Alexander holding a lance. It seems that the emperor wanted to promote the comparison between himself and Alexander the Great to the people of Rome. The statue was excavated in Rome in the early nineteenth century and was probably originally set up in a public space somewhere in the city. Trebonianus was no great military leader, though. He only ruled for two years and was killed by his own army. The statue must date to the time of his reign and most likely to the year when he brought Alexander's remains to the Pantheon.' Tom paused to look at Victoria and he could tell she was ready for a break.

'Shall we have some lunch before heading over to Mr Williams's place? The Trustees Dining Room has excellent fare, even by Roman standards.'

'That was lovely, Tom. Thank you so much. Lead the way. I'm famished.'

33

AFTER LUNCH, TOM and Victoria hopped into a taxi and drove over to Oskar Williams's gallery. It was not one of those galleries that you could just walk into off the street. It was located in a small apartment building between Park Avenue and Lexington on 62nd Street and was really just a converted apartment. Oskar liked the building because it was discreet and was about half way between Christies and Sotheby's, a convenient location for him and those of his clients who came into town during the antiquities auctions that were held each year in June and December. The taxi pulled up in front of the building and a doorman came out to assist them.

As they walked into the lobby, Tom said to him, 'We're here to see Oskar Williams. My name is Tom Carr. He's expecting us.'

'Yes, of course, Mr Carr. He told me you were coming. I'll just let him know that you've arrived.' After calling up, the doorman looked at Tom and said, 'It's apartment 4B. The elevator is on your right.'

Tom gestured to Victoria to follow him and they got into the lift where the button was already set for the fourth floor. The lift door opened onto a small foyer with a maple floor and richly moulded plaster walls painted a dark evergreen. Between two apartment doors a flowering orchid sat on an elegant mahogany side table, behind which hung an antique gilt-framed oval mirror. Victoria looked at herself in the mirror, casually appraising her hair and adjusting a few tresses as Tom walked up to press the bell of apartment 4B. When Victoria turned to join Tom at the door she noticed that the umbrella stand next to the door was a bronze leg from a Roman statue of an emperor broken just above the knee.

'Is that ancient?' Victoria asked Tom just as he was about to ring the bell.

'I think so,' Tom replied.

'Well, he has a sense of humour.' Victoria smiled. 'I like that.'

Tom rang the bell.

Oskar came to the door and opened it. 'Good afternoon. Welcome, please come in.' He had a look on his face like that of the cat who swallowed the canary. Oskar could barely contain his excitement. He was keen to get whatever information he could from Thomas Carr, but he didn't want to blow his cover. Take your time, Oskar, he thought. Remain calm.

Oskar shook Tom's hand and said, 'It's been a long time since I've seen you at my little private gallery.' He made a gesture of welcome with his hands.

'Yes, it has been a number of years. Thank you for the invitation.'

'And who, may I ask, is your beautiful friend?' Oskar turned to Victoria. 'My name is Oskar Williams. I am enchanted to make your acquaintance.' He took her hand and kissed it softly. Victoria wanted to recoil from his kiss but she didn't want to seem rude.

Tom replied, 'This is Victoria Price. She is in New York for a few days, visiting with me.'

'Where are you visiting from, Ms Price?' Oskar asked as he led them into the apartment.

'Rome. I am a painter,' Victoria replied as she looked around.

'I lived in Rome myself for many years, long ago, but I still go back from time to time on business. Please come in and sit down.'

Oskar brought Victoria and Tom into the living room and sat them down on a large overstuffed sofa. Before them on the table he had laid out an array of objects, displayed seemingly at random. These pieces were intended to whet their appetite. Oskar never knew what might be of interest to people so he liked to offer a wide selection. Judging the reactions of clients to these initial objects helped him decide what to bring out next, and he was going to wait as long as possible to bring out the ring that Carr had come to see. Oskar knew that his story about the ring belonging to Alexander the

Great was a shabby ruse and that Carr would see through it once he saw the item for himself so he wanted to milk the opportunity for all that he could first.

Tom's attention was immediately drawn to the objects. There was a Greek Geometric bronze fibula with giant concentric spirals and a lovely grey-green patina. Its long pin at the back was still sharp and lodged securely in the catch. There was also a Neolithic stone idol, a terracotta figurine of Pan sitting on a rock and holding his musical pipes, a Chinese jade piece, an Egyptian wooden statuette of a standing male figure with some of its paint still preserved, and a small core-formed glass amphora on a little modern conical stand. Tom was amazed to see that sitting on the table amidst all of these objects was a silver cup, a kylix of the fifth or early fourth century BC, with a scene chased in gold on its tondo.

'Dread-yelping Scylla,' Tom said as he picked up the cup and looked more closely at it. In the centre of the tondo was Scylla, a monster in Homer's *Odyssey* who was infamous for attacking passing ships and snatching their sailors. Scylla was holding a rudder menacingly as though she had just ripped it from a ship. The workmanship was exceptionally fine. Victoria peered over Tom's shoulder, admiring the silver cup.

'Is that Scylla? What a strange rendering of the monster – a beautiful woman with all those dogs and snaky monsters bursting from her hips.'

'It's actually a fairly typical rendering of her,' Tom replied.

'Those Greeks – a fetching face and bare breasts, and then it's all scary monsters from the waist down. They ought to get their heads examined. You can tell that this was a man's vision of feminine power.' Victoria was indignant.

'Imagine how a Greek symposiast must have felt when he finished his wine and came face to face with Scylla!' said Oskar. 'It must have been quite the conversation piece at drinking parties – and a surprise for the unlucky guest.'

'It certainly is a different kind of scene from the one that Exekias depicted on that marvellous black-figure cup: Dionysos sailing the wine-dark sea in his skiff, a grapevine for a mast, and Tyrrhenian pirates turned into dolphins all around.' Tom looked at the cup in his hands and then continued. 'But the Greeks loved to have such surprises in their drinking cups. This one is very fine.'

'Thank you,' said Oskar. 'Speaking of drinking, have a look at this.' He walked into the next room and returned with a Greek black-figure amphora, which he placed before Tom and Victoria in the centre of the table. It rested squarely on a lazy Susan that could be turned easily without anyone having to handle the vase.

'It has been attributed by Sir John Beazley to the circle of Lydos, one of the best of the early Athenian black-figure painters. The main scene on the obverse represents satyrs pressing grapes with their feet in a vat, set up on a low table so that the wine pours out into this amphora.' Oskar pointed to the vessel represented on the vase, which quite happily recalled the shape of the vase itself, and then continued. 'I particularly like the satyr playing pipes on the right. The rest of them stomp the grapes to the accompaniment of his music. On the other side are revellers at a symposium.' Oskar paused to rotate the vase so that Tom and Victoria would not have to get up to see the scene he was describing.

'The men sit on couches accompanied by beautiful *hetairai* or courtesans. Look, this one has golden hair like Aphrodite.' Oskar paused again and pointed to the scantily clad woman seated on a dining couch, one of her breasts spilling out of her chiton. 'Look at the cup that she's holding.'

Victoria leaned forward and said, 'Oh my goodness – the handle is in the form an erect phallus!'

Oskar smiled. 'It *is* rather naughty, isn't it? And look at this reveller over here, pausing to vomit into a nearby bucket set up right next to his dining couch.' Vomit rendered in a dilute glaze streamed from the symposiast's mouth.

'It seems to have the complete cycle represented on the vase,' said Tom. 'It's in remarkably fine condition, and it sounds like the provenance is okay if Sir John Beazley knew of it. On the other hand, I don't think that I could get the trustees to approve its acquisition.'

Oskar frowned. 'Yes, of course. Sadly, this is not the 1970s. Such decadence is no longer in fashion. But I do have something that is right up your alley. Wait just one minute, if you would.' Oskar disappeared again into the next room and returned moments later with two gilt-silver *skyphoi*, Roman drinking cups. In deep relief on their sides were depicted scenes of the sea nymph Thetis bearing the armour of her son Achilles. She rides across the sea on a hippocamp. Each cup was similar but with slight variations.

As Victoria held one of the cups up and examined it, she joked, 'You have amazing things, Mr Williams. Your back room must be something like Ali Baba's cave.'

'Yes, but remember Ali Baba was an honest man even if his treasure came from the labours of forty thieves,' Oskar responded cheerily. 'I always loved the *Tales of the Arabian Nights* as a boy. Those Arabs could certainly tell a story.'

Tom passed one cup to Victoria in exchange for

the other and remarked, 'How interesting it is that these cups are often found in pairs. They seem to have been made that way. A few years ago, a pair was excavated outside Pompeii, not far from Stabiae. The original owner had placed them in a wicker rucksack along with the rest of his silver service and had stashed it in an unfinished bath house, most likely hoping to return for it. But he never did.'

'Now let me show you something truly extraordinary,' said Oskar. 'Just one more minute.'

Oskar disappeared again, taking the two gilt-silver cups with him, and returned with a battered sculpture of a bird. One of its wings was missing and inside it was possible to see corroded gears of some sort. The head was dented but intact. The beak was hinged, suggesting that it had once moved, although its gilt-bronze fitting was now corroded shut. Clearly, it had once been a very fine object.

'It's an automaton. I'd date it somewhere in the Hellenistic period. As I am sure you know, Hieron of Alexandria described them in the first century AD. It probably once strutted about and sang sweetly for its owner, possibly a king or a wealthy aristocrat. Perhaps your conservation department could get it up and running again?' Oskar mused.

'Now that is interesting,' said Victoria, as she leaned forward to look at the piece more closely. 'What do you think, Tom?'

'It's certainly a rare thing. I have to say that I've never seen anything quite like it – although, as Mr Williams says, they were made by the ancient Greeks as early as the Classical period. Automatons became more common in the Hellenistic period when such clever inventions were certainly in vogue.' Tom didn't voice his suspicions but something about the shape of the bird's head looked wrong to him. It was a subtle thing but, having looked at thousands of representations of ancient birds, it had hit him immediately. It literally made him feel lightly sick to his stomach and he wondered if it was a fake.

'There is a long history of automatons,' Tom continued as he studied the piece. 'They were popular in the Far East among the emperors of Byzantium and the sultans of the Ottoman period. Interest was also revived in Europe during the Renaissance. I love the passage at the end of Yeats's poem 'Sailing to Byzantium' where he described a golden automaton as an expensive amusement singing for a drowsy Byzantine emperor. I wonder if this bird is not later in date.' Tom tried to conceal his distaste for the object. 'Maybe you should show it to one of my colleagues in the Islamic or Medieval Departments at the museum.' Looking across at the dealer, Tom saw that he was not entirely pleased with his appraisal.

Tom looked at his watch and said, 'This has been quite delightful, Mr Williams, but we don't want to take up too much of your time. You said that you had an important ring that you wanted to show me. Actually, you said it was the signet ring of Alexander, which I must admit quite piqued my interest.'

'Yes, yes, of course. You are going to be thrilled when you see it. But first I must offer you some apricot tart and coffee. There's no rush. I ordered out from the French patisserie around the corner especially for you. Victoria, your visit to New York would not be complete without tasting it. Their confections are to die for. I'll bring it right in. And anyway, Mr Carr, I want to hear about your excavations on Crete. Did you know that I visited your site this summer?' Oskar disappeared into the kitchen and returned swiftly with a silver tray on which were cups of coffee and an apricot tart.

'You were at Dikta this summer? You should've come by the dig house.' Tom was surprised at this news.

'Yes, I was vacationing in the Aegean islands with my family when I saw the brief article in the *Herald Tribune* about your thrilling discovery. We weren't too far away so we sailed in for the afternoon before heading on to Santorini. The setting of the site is quite beautiful and the remains of the Minoan town and Greek sanctuary to Zeus are fascinating but I must confess we did not get to see what you had found. There was something in the *Tribune* piece about a new sculpture of Alexander and a stele with some sort of reference to his tomb. It sounds very exciting.'

'Yes. I'm sorry you missed the statue,' Tom replied, his heart sinking as he thought of the headless statue. 'It's impressive but still in need of considerable conservation. Much of the original paint is still preserved. We have the sculpture under lock and key.' Tom could not bring himself to mention the terrible vandalism of last week.

'Quite understandably, I'm sure. I'll have to wait for the academic publication of your findings,' Oskar said dryly. 'What about the inscription? The article said it contains a clue to the location of Alexander the Great's tomb. That *is* news.'

'Yes. Unfortunately, the inscription is very worn and not entirely legible. We're still working on deciphering it.' Tom looked across to Victoria to signal that he did not want to pursue this line of conversation.

'I see. Any developments?' Oskar pressed.

'No, not yet,' Tom said tiredly. 'Now, what about this ring? I'm curious to see it and, unfortunately much as we would like to stay, we don't have much more time.'

'What is the hurry?' Oskar asked.

'We return to Rome this evening,' Victoria replied. 'This tart is delicious,' she said before putting the last forkful into her mouth.

Tom shot her a look and she realised too late that she had said the wrong thing.

'This evening? You are *both* flying to Rome? But, Mr Carr, you've just come back from that city. No wonder the rest of your week is busy.' Oskar took a moment to process this new development and then continued. 'I didn't realise that you were under such time constraints. I'm sorry to have kept you so long. It was good of you to fit me in.'

Oskar disappeared again into his back room and returned with a small wooden box with a blue velvet-lined cover framed in gold brocade. Sitting down opposite Tom and Victoria, he opened the box and held it up for them to see. Inside was a gold ring in which was set a carnelian gemstone cut with a fine portrait head of Alexander the Great.

'The signet ring of Alexander the Great,' Oskar said with a flourish, trying his best to keep up the act.

'May I?' said Tom as he picked the ring up gingerly in his hands and looked carefully at the engraved image. 'It's very fine but why do you think that it was Alexander the Great's signet ring?' he asked.

'Well, it has his image right on it,' replied Oskar.

'There were many rings with Alexander the Great's image on it. We know for example that the emperor Augustus used a ring with Alexander's portrait as his personal signet ring. I don't think we know for certain what image was on Alexander's own signet ring, although he most certainly used one. In fact, we know that he used more than one. It's said that he took the signet ring of the Persian King Darius and used it as his own for affairs of state in the East.' Tom looked across at Oskar Williams but the dealer said nothing.

'What is the provenance?' Tom asked.

'Well, it belonged to Alexander the Great. You cannot get much better than that,' Oskar replied smugly.

'I mean what is its subsequent history? Where has it been since then?' Tom asked, surprised at Williams's cavalier response.

In the old days people would not even ask such questions about provenance, if they cared at all, unless they were certain that they wanted to buy a piece. But things were different now. In 1970, Unesco had passed a convention, ratified by the United States in 1983, that proposed that institutions should not acquire antiquities that did not have clear histories or which could not be proven to have been exported from their country of origin before 1970. Many countries had strict national cultural patrimony laws that declared all antiquities found in the ground the property of the state and forbade their removal from the country of origin unless a permit was secured. The Metropolitan Museum of Art had its own strict guidelines and it was necessary to conduct due diligence and know as much as possible about an object before acquiring it. There was even a highly publicised trial going on in Italy where a dealer and an American curator were being tried for selling and buying looted antiquities. Oskar did not care about all that, though. For him all these rules and regulations just got in the way of his doing business. As far as he was concerned, his competitor had become sloppy, which was too bad for him. Oskar thought that he would get what he deserved.

He continued, with a serious expression on his face. 'Ancient authors tell us that Alexander the Great gave his signet ring to Perdiccas while Alexander was on his deathbed. It was a clear sign that he knew the end was at hand and was also a nod towards Perdiccas's future role. After that we have no records. I am representing a European gentleman who inherited the ring from his father and he believes it has been in his family for several generations.'

From the look on Carr's face, Oskar knew that the game was up so he finished on a lighter note. 'That is to say, it's from an old Swiss collection.' He winked mischievously at Victoria. In any case, Oskar thought, he had obtained some significant information, information that he could act on.

Tom considered pressing Oskar Williams for more information about the ring's provenance but decided to drop it. He saw the dealer now with new eyes. This was a man of the old guard. He would not change his ways. Tom was looking at a dinosaur and not some lumbering leaf-eating brontosaurus but a dangerous carnivore. Tom needed to be careful with him. He could see this now. Oskar Williams had invited him here for a reason – but that reason was not to see the signet ring of Alexander the Great.

'Well, Mr Williams, it's a fascinating piece. I'll certainly give it serious consideration. Thank you for making the time to see us. We really must go. I'll be in touch.' With that, Tom motioned to Victoria that their visit was over, and they followed Oskar Williams to the door.

Just before they left, Oskar took Victoria's hand and held it to his lips, kissing it gently. 'Until we meet again.'

34

Tom and Victoria did not waste any time when they landed in Rome the following morning. After dropping their things at Victoria's apartment they went straight to the Piazza Minerva. As they stood by Bernini's *Elephant and Obelisk* in front of the church of Santa Maria *sopra* Minerva, Victoria told Tom the church's history.

'As far as we know, a small Christian basilica was first built here sometime before AD 800 on the remains of the Imperial Roman temple of Minerva.'

'The temple of Minerva itself may date from as early as the middle of the first century AD,' interjected Tom.

Victoria continued. 'The church was rebuilt around AD 1280 by the Dominicans, who sought to emulate their church in Florence, Santa Maria Novella, which the writer Vasari tells us was built by the same architects. The facade you see today dates from the fifteenth century and shares some of the austerity of its thirteenth-century predecessor. However, the interior was completely remodelled in the Gothic style in the latter part of the nineteenth century. In fact, it is the only such church in Rome. In contrast, the facade and the square we are standing in are essentially unchanged since Bernini's *Elephant and Obelisk* was installed as part of Pope Alexander VII's urban renewal of Rome.'

Tom was amazed to think that a soaring Gothic building now sat behind this austere facade. He had visited Santa Maria Novella in Florence and remembered its elegant but minimal design based closely on the ancient Roman basilica, the first true form of the Christian church to be developed.

'I wouldn't be surprised if the original basilica dated from even earlier than the eighth century,' Tom replied. 'It wasn't uncommon for the Church to build their places of worship directly on top of pagan temples, maintaining a sense of continuity of sacred space. Given that the emperor Theodosius outlawed the worship of pagan gods in the early fifth century, either the temple of Minerva had long been abandoned or the transition to a Christian church had taken place much earlier.'

As they approached the rectory next to the church, Victoria explained to Tom that the sub-basement of the church still preserved parts of the foundations of the Dominican plan. The nineteenth-century renovators had been careful not to disturb the crypt, where elements of the Roman temple to Minerva could still be seen. This area was almost always closed to the public, but Victoria was friendly with the priest, who was the caretaker of the church, and she knew that he would be able to get them in. She rang the bell and they waited for a few minutes. An elderly woman came to the door.

'Can I help you?' she said automatically and then, looking up, she recognised Victoria and smiled.

'My child, how nice to see you. It has been some time. How have you been? Have you come to see Father Bepino? Let me get him for you. He's in his study. It'll be just a minute. Please come in and make yourselves comfortable. I'll be right back.' The woman shuffled off down the corridor and disappeared around a corner.

Victoria led Tom into the reception room of the rectory where they sat down and waited.

'I spent a lot of time in the little museum that belongs to this church. I was studying a statue by Bernini in their collection and the priest, Father Bepino, was very helpful to me. We became good friends,' Victoria explained to Tom.

Soon they heard footsteps and Father Bepino appeared, a warm smile on his face. He was an old priest with white hair and he wore a white collar and the traditional vestments of the Dominican order.

'Victoria, what a pleasant surprise! What brings you to Santa Maria *sopra* Minerva again? I thought you were finished with your work in the museum on Bernini's statue.'

'Father, this is a friend of mine, Tom Carr, visiting from New York.'

Tom extended his hand to the priest. 'Very pleased to meet you.'

'Tom is a curator of Greek and Roman art at the Metropolitan Museum of Art, and we have a favour to ask of you. He very much wants to see the remains of the temple of Minerva in the crypt. Could you possibly help us?'

'Well, as you know, that area's generally closed to the public, but I'd be happy to let you in. The ruins are surprisingly extensive. The archaeological service has been talking of making them more suitable for tourist visits, but nothing has come of it yet. I suppose it's not high on their list compared with all the other antiquities in Rome. There is a little light, but not much. Did you bring torches?'

'Yes, we did,' Victoria answered. 'I cannot thank you enough, Father.'

'I have to say I've not been down there in years. It's rather dusty, too. Try not to dirty your beautiful clothes, Victoria.'

Father Bepino always admired how well Victoria dressed.

'The terrain is rather treacherous, at least for someone of my age, what with all the uneven surfaces and partial walls. If you'll forgive me, I'll just let you in to have a look by yourselves. You can come by the rectory when you're finished.'

'Of course, that would be perfect,' Victoria said.

'Let me get the keys and we can walk over together.'

The priest left them for a few minutes and returned with a set of old keys on an iron ring. Victoria and Tom followed him over to the church. They entered through a side door. Tom was amazed to see the soaring Gothic-revival interior. Father Bepino led them towards the front of the church. Just before the sacristy, where the priest usually prepared for Mass, there was a stairway leading down to the crypt.

Father Bepino turned to Victoria and Tom and motioned for them to follow him down the stairs. At the bottom, he unlocked the door and turned on the lights. Arches supported the floor of the church above and there were numerous tombs with marble markers laid in the ground. Primarily for Dominican brothers, the tombs dated back hundreds of years. The lights were situated along the main arches and cast a soft glow over the entire place.

'The ruins of the temple actually are not in the crypt but adjacent to it, back towards the front of the church. There's another door at the back of the crypt that leads into the temple ruins. Please follow me and get your torches ready.'

Tom and Victoria got out their torches and turned them on. They walked through the crypt and came to a doorway at the far end. Father Bepino opened the door and turned on the single light that only partially illuminated a large space receding into the distance.

The church's supporting walls transected the space and, in places, were built right on the foundations of the Roman temple. It was an incredible sight.

'Feel free to look around as long as you like. Most of the ancient temple is only preserved to the foundation level, but there are a couple of places where you can see a bit of the superstructure, including steps, part of the cella wall, and the lowest part of a few columns. Some of the architectural elements from the roof and upper part of the temple are lying about as well. You just have to look around. So, then, I'll leave you to it. Come and get me when you're finished and I'll lock everything up. In any case, the church is closed today so you won't be disturbed.'

'Father, thank you so much. This is so kind of you. We will probably need a couple of hours, but I'll come and see you as soon as we are done,' Victoria said.

As soon as the priest left, Tom turned to Victoria and said, 'I think we should split up and walk the perimeter first. We're looking for a mermaid that may be carved into a wall.'

Victoria walked in one direction and Tom went the opposite way. After some minutes Tom reached the far end of the church near the entrance to the building. He called out, 'I've found it!'

'Are you sure?' Victoria called back.

'There's no mistaking this mermaid! It's carved right into the wall. Come and see,' Tom said excitedly.

Soon Victoria appeared, walking carefully through the ruins with her torch in her hand. There in front of Tom was a mermaid carved in shallow relief into the wall. She was facing forward and had long flowing hair and a bare chest. Her lower torso transformed artfully and naturally into a scaly body, which divided into a forked tail whose ends she held in her outstretched hands. Above each hand was carved the Macedonian star and above each of these stars was a one-word inscription in Greek: 'lives' above one and 'reigns' above the other.

Tom looked at Victoria and said, 'It is the legendary mermaid of Alexander. Do you know the story?' he asked.

'I was reading about it the other day at the library but with specific reference to the Amulet of Nereida. Tell me the story from the beginning,' said Victoria, staring in wonder at the mermaid before her.

'According to some legends, as you know, she is a daughter of Alexander named Nereida. She drank from the Fountain of Eternal Youth and, out of jealousy, Alexander banished her to the sea. According to another version she is Alexander's sister. In any case, she appears to sailors during storms and asks, "Have you seen Alexander the Great?" If the captain answers her correctly – "Alexander lives and reigns and keeps peace over the world" – then the storm subsides, the waters become calm, and the mermaid returns happily to the deep. If the sailor answers incorrectly, the mermaid capsizes his ship, sending it and the crew to the bottom of the sea.' Tom looked at the mermaid. 'Look at the stars of Macedonia above her hands. They are just like the ones on the *Elephant and Obelisk*. There's no mistaking it. There must be a secret door here somewhere.'

'Open sesame,' joked Victoria.

'It may well function like the magical door to Ali Baba's cave,' responded Tom, thinking hard as he looked at the mermaid. 'But I am sure that it does not work by magic. There must be a trick to opening it.'

Tom looked more closely at the carving. He carefully and systematically examined every detail, looking for some clue to how the door worked. When he came to the stars, he noticed that their centres were slightly raised from the surface of the wall. The rest of the carving was set back into the stone as one would expect. That's odd, Tom thought. He tried pressing one of the stars. There was no response. Then he tried to press both stars at the same time, while standing face to face with the mermaid. As he did, the stars receded into the stone and a doorway opened before them.

'Lives and reigns,' Tom said. 'It is the response the

mermaid requires. That's the clue. You have to press the stars at the same time otherwise it does not work. Remember what the inscription on the elephant's head said: "In the temple of Athena is a mermaid. The correct response to her question will lead you to the great sage and the path to divine wisdom."'

Beyond the doorway a stone-lined passage, about six feet high and four feet wide, receded into the distance. Victoria grabbed Tom's hand and squeezed it with excitement. 'We may have just come to the end of your rainbow.'

'Let's find out. Follow me.' Tom walked in front while still holding Victoria's hand. 'If I've got my bearings correct, this corridor is taking us out under the piazza in front of the church.'

After about twenty feet the corridor appeared to open into a small room. As they approached the end of the corridor, Victoria pulled Tom back against the wall and looked up into his eyes, a look of fear on her stricken face.

'Tom, I don't think that I can go in there. I am terrified.' The feeling had been welling up in her ever since Tom had called to her and said that he had found the mermaid.

The look of surprise and concern on Tom's face showed that he did not understand the reason for her terror. Victoria continued, 'If the tomb of Alexander is in that room and I look again on his mummified

remains and see the Amulet of Nereida, I am afraid
that it will trigger another vision and send me back
to that time. I don't know if I can relive that terrible
and terrifying death. I felt like I almost died when I
re-experienced the end of my past life during the last
channelling episode. I woke up just before death.
What if I return to that moment? I don't want to die,
Tom.' Tears were welling in Victoria's eyes now.

Tom took her in his arms and hugged her. Gently,
he held her in front of him by her shoulders and
gazed into her eyes tenderly as he spoke.

'Victoria, nothing is going to happen to you. I
promise. Whatever you might have experienced in a
past life is just that: it's in the past. The tomb you
were in, that you recalled in your visions, no longer
exists. It was emptied long ago. It may be a part of
your consciousness but it can't hurt you. It's over. I
am here with you now. We are in this together. Take
some deep breaths. Take a moment to calm down.
You can do this.'

Victoria looked back into Tom's eyes. She could
feel his empathy and it was consoling. She had faced
the veiled masked dancer again without incident, she
thought. She took several deep breaths to bring her
pulse and heart rate down to a normal level. Then
she closed her eyes for a moment and said a prayer.
Holding Tom's hand gave her strength. She felt closer
to him now than she ever had before.

368

'Okay, let's go,' she said.

Tom put his arm around her shoulder and they walked slowly together into the room. As they entered the dark space, Tom slowly scanned the area with the beam of his torch. Then he gasped. There, against the far wall, was the tomb of Alexander.

'My God. It is here! We must be directly beneath the *Elephant and Obelisk*. It is literally a marker for the tomb.'

Old flambeaux lined the walls. Tom led Victoria over and lit them. They gave the room an eerie soft glow. The room, lined completely with stone, was empty except for the sarcophagus and a scallop niche above it where a portrait bust of the great king, unmistakably the work of Gianlorenzo Bernini, stood. In front of the sarcophagus was a simple stone bench, presumably where Pope Alexander VII had sat to contemplate the physical remains of his namesake.

Slowly Tom and Victoria walked up to the sarcophagus.

'Victoria, look at the top of the sarcophagus.' Tom pointed excitedly to a giant golden starburst, the symbol of the Macedonian royal family, fixed to the lid exactly above Alexander's chest.

'*That* must be how Pope Alexander VII knew about the Macedonian star. My God, *this* must be the Hellenistic sarcophagus built for Alexander in

Alexandria when they melted down his original one that was made of gold. Look – it's made of glass.'

The massive glass panels were framed in gold, probably gilt-bronze, and supported at the base by four large golden lion paws surmounted by sirens. As Tom looked more closely, he gasped again. There in the sarcophagus lay the mummified remains of Alexander the Great. As he and Victoria peered closer they saw a crown of gold upon his head. Victoria's eyes went immediately to his chest to see if the amulet was there but it was not. She heaved a sigh of relief. What was more unbelievable to Tom as he bent down over the sarcophagus was that the king's head appeared to be resting on something.

'Could it be, could it really be . . .' Tom asked himself. As soon as Tom saw it, he knew it must be the *Iliad of the Casket*. Next to it lay Alexander's dagger.

'Victoria, look! The casket and dagger are there, just as you said!' Victoria had been so preoccupied with looking for the amulet that she had not noticed the ornate casket and dagger.

Tom knelt down by Alexander's head to get a closer look with his torch. The casket under Alexander's head was exquisitely wrought in ebony, with ivory and gold inlays. On it were scenes in shallow relief. The side facing Tom depicted a bard seated on an elaborate chair. The figure held a large harp in one hand and plucked its strings with the other. In front of the bard a bird was in flight, echoing distantly the famous fresco from the Mycenaean palace at Pylos. 'That's it, of course.' Tom stood up. 'The image of bard and bird must portray the Homeric epithet "winged words" that described the heavenly performances of poets reciting the famous stories of an heroic age.'

Tom couldn't see the other sides of the casket clearly but, judging from one magnificent figure of Achilles that he could make out, his name inscribed above him, the other sides represented scenes from the *Iliad*. The casket was clearly the work of a master craftsman. It not only supported the head of the great Macedonian king but encased what was most probably Aristotle's copy of Homer's *Iliad*, the most cherished work of Greek literature ever composed – and this copy was annotated by one of the greatest thinkers of all time. Tom couldn't believe his eyes. The casket and dagger were there just as Victoria Price had described them in his office.

Victoria spoke excitedly. She had her self-assurance back. 'Tom, this bust, I would bet anything that it's the work of Bernini. It's incredible.'

Tom turned to speak to Victoria, who was examining the bust above the sarcophagus. 'Victoria, I feel like Howard Carter at the opening of King Tut's tomb. Alexander's head is resting on the *Iliad of the Casket*.

Inside, surely, must be Aristotle's copy of the *Iliad*, and given the way this sarcophagus is sealed the papyrus is probably still intact. It will be the most spectacular find of the century!'

But Victoria didn't answer. Instead, an all too familiar voice sent chills down Tom's spine. 'Good work, Mr Carr. I knew you weren't telling me everything. It *is* the most spectacular find of the century, but I'm afraid that will not go down in the history books in quite the way you imagined.'

Tom turned to see Oskar Williams standing at the entrance to the room, accompanied by three rough-looking Italian men who were brandishing handguns with long silencers screwed into their muzzles.

'What on earth are *you* doing here, Mr Williams?' Tom asked.

'Let's dispense with the formalities, shall we?' Oskar stepped a few feet closer as the three thugs looked menacingly at Tom and Victoria.

'I've been following your trail for quite some time now, Mr Carr. I, too, have long desired to find the tomb of Alexander.'

'I should've realised after our visit that you were the one behind that charade of sleuths.' Tom was still reeling in disbelief as he quickly put the pieces together in his head. 'I suppose it was you who had my laptop stolen from my home? And what about the man following me in Athens? There were reports of a nocturnal visit to the site at Dikta during the summer by some ruffians but nothing seemed to have been disturbed. Was that you, too?'

'Yes. I did see the statue and the stele after all, but they never would have led me here without your help. The statue is magnificent – or it was.' Oskar paused to let Tom register what he was saying.

'You neglected to tell me about the head . . . Too painful for you, Mr Carr? I thought about bringing it in to you on a silver platter when you were at my gallery yesterday but that would have been a little melodramatic, don't you think?' Oskar waited a moment to let the notion sink in.

'You're a madman, Williams! You'll never get away with it. Interpol already has pictures of the head. You'll never be able to sell it.'

'Not everything is about money, Mr Carr. But enough about me.' Oskar smiled. 'I suppose it's a shame that no one will ever see this chamber and know the history of Pope Alexander VII's interest in Alexander the Great. I imagine the Vatican won't mind, though, as the whole thing could easily be misconstrued as pagan idolatry. It would be unfitting for a pope, to say the least.'

'You'll never get away with this.' Victoria was both shocked and infuriated.

'On the contrary, my dear, within a matter of hours I'll have the sarcophagus and its precious contents out of here, and I know just the man who can help make that happen. Soon all of it will be safely on its way out of the country.' Oskar turned to one of the men standing next to him. In Italian, he told him to call a man named Pietro and tell him that he was needed pronto.

'But how did you get here so fast?' Tom interjected. 'We pretty much left straight for the airport after we left your gallery and came here as soon as we landed.'

'Timing is everything in my business.' Oskar indulged the question. He was in an expansive mood and it felt good to be in the driver's seat again. Mr Carr had ended their visit with him rather abruptly yesterday. That was not going to happen this time. In fact, Oskar thought, now his words would be the last that Carr would ever hear and he was going to relish the moment when the man realised it.

'I called in a favour with a friend of mine who has a private jet. I was in Rome before you even landed. My contacts were able to follow you from the time you got off the plane. You led me straight here.' Oskar paused to relish the look of horror on Tom's and Victoria's faces, then continued. 'This has been an expensive gamble for me but it's going to pay off handsomely. The gold crown, the dagger and the bust of Alexander will fetch a very fine price. But I suppose it will take a while to find a buyer for the mummy and the glass sarcophagus – though they'll bring in plenty too. Of course, I just couldn't sell the *Iliad of the Casket* in one piece. It will have to be parcelled up into sections. If it's all there – and I bet it is.' Oskar smirked. 'I'll get a lot more money for it that way. After all, people are accustomed to seeing fragmentary antiquities – a broken pot, a statue without its head or legs. I suppose that I could sell each chapter as one item – that, at least would maintain some integrity of the whole package.' Oskar paused again to make sure that Carr was listening. 'But realistically, it would make more sense to sell it one page at a time. Of course, I'll have my own time with the whole thing first. To think that Alexander the Great was probably the last person to read it.' Oskar looked Tom in the eye, an evil grin on his face.

'Some people disparage what I do. They claim that looting antiquities destroys archaeological provenance, blah, blah, blah . . . Don't give a thought to the question of provenance, Mr Carr.' Oskar always got worked up when he thought about people lecturing him on provenance. 'There are lots of people out there who don't give a damn about it. I don't have to sell my things to American museums. I can go to the Japanese, the Arabs, the Chinese, or the Russians. There are plenty of people who don't ask too many questions when they are offered something they like. And, after all, whose place is it to say who may and who may not own antiquities? All this talk about national cultural patrimony – the modern nation state of Italy was founded after the Metropolitan Museum of Art, for Christ's sake. What makes their claim on an artwork thousands of years old more just than anyone else's? It's all politics, if you ask me. Do you think they really care about the art? It's a lot of hooey. People have been plundering art since antiquity. What I do has a long and venerable tradition. Why, the ancient Romans were masters of it! They took what they wanted from the Greeks. Verrus, that governor of Sicily whom Cicero prosecuted, was a hero in my book.'

Oskar barely took a breath before continuing. He was on a roll. 'Besides, if you look over the course of history, a lot of art has been melted down or destroyed for reuse of its materials. Marble statues, even whole temples broken and demolished to make lime for cement! It was the same fate for bronzes and silver, too. If a peasant comes upon a tomb in his field and finds gold objects in it do you think he'll keep them for himself? Absolutely not, I say! He'll sell them to put food on the table for his family. What's more, if he can't get anything for them as works of art, he'll gladly melt them down and sell the gold. I save art and get it to people who appreciate it and care for it. I am a saviour, Mr Carr, not a villain.' Oskar was almost shouting now.

'Of course, I don't expect you to understand,

especially under these circumstances. To the victor belong the spoils. And today, I win.' Oskar paused for a minute to let that sink in, and then he continued more calmly. 'It's regrettable but necessary that you both will have to disappear. I simply cannot have any witnesses. Any last remarks before my associates send you to the hereafter, so to speak?'

Victoria started to cry and Tom pulled her to him.

'I'm sorry that it has to end this way for you. It's not personal, though – it's just business. Goodbye, Mr Carr.' Oskar motioned to his thugs who hand-cuffed Tom's and Victoria's hands behind their backs and forced them to the ground in preparation for their execution.

Oskar lit a cigarette and took a long drag. He walked over to the sarcophagus and peered down at the mummified remains as he waited. Oskar never enjoyed watching bloodshed, although God knew he'd seen his fair share of it over the years.

'Put your hands in the air!' a voice boomed behind Oskar. As he turned, he came face to face with four carabinieri holding Uzi sub-machine guns pointed directly at him and his companions. Between the policemen stood a tall handsome man in plain clothes, clearly another policeman, and with him a small man in tweeds, who looked surprisingly like Toad of Toad Hall in *The Wind in the Willows*. Behind them was the priest. Oskar was not happy at the sight.

'Call them off now, Williams. It's over. My name is Antonio Giussepi Moreno and I am the Captain of the Special Antiquities Division of the Italian National Police. We have been tracking you for years now. I had an e-mail report that you entered the country this morning. Finally, I have caught you in the act.'

The *carabinieri* approached Oskar and his henchmen, disarmed them, and handcuffed them. Afterwards they uncuffed Tom and Victoria.

Virgil ran up to Tom and Victoria. 'Thank the gods you are all right! We got here just in the nick of time. I acted as soon as I got your text message, Victoria, saying you were at the entrance to the tomb. It's a good thing, too. A few minutes later and we would have been too late. I happened to have interviewed Captain Moreno. We became friends, so I knew that he'd appreciate the urgency. Fortunately, he agreed to come right away. He's seen enough looted sites to know that it doesn't take long for a *tombarolo* to do his dirty work.'

Virgil turned to Oskar as the carabinieri were taking him away. 'The sword of Damakles has dropped, you scoundrel, and the swift sword of retribution is at hand.' With that, Virgil gave him the evil eye and turned back to Tom and Victoria. 'To think that I've even gotten books for that man at the Academy. Well, I have to hand it to you both. You did it. You found

Alexander's tomb. My word, I can't believe I'm standing right in front of the great king himself! This is going to make a perfect final chapter for my "secret history".'

Victoria slumped into Tom's arms for support and he held her tightly as he leaned against the wall next to the sarcophagus. Looking at Virgil in the light cast by the flambeaux, Tom could barely muster the words. 'Thank you, old friend. You're a lifesaver.'

Epilogue

TOM SAT IN the reception area outside the Director's office at the Metropolitan Museum of Art, reading the front page of the latest issue of the *Art Newspaper*. The headline read 'Tomb of Alexander Yields Priceless Art Treasures'. As he waited for his appointment, his thoughts turned to Victoria Price and the last thing she had said to him just days ago. They'd been sitting in the garden of the Villa Aurelia at the American Academy in the light of a full moon, looking out over the city. The silvery moonlight had given Victoria's silky smooth complexion a magical aura. She had literally seemed to glow and she was the most beautiful vision that Tom had ever seen. He had held her in his arms and they'd kissed once, long and passionately.

'I hope that you will remember this moment until we are together again.' Looking deep into his eyes, she got up and walked slowly away back down the Janiculum hill to her apartment in Trastevere.

Victoria had remained in Rome to paint. The adventure they had shared together had opened a well of creativity for her from which she drew deeply for inspiration. Tom could not wait to see her again. They planned a rendezvous in Rome again in a month's time.

Suddenly Tom realised that the receptionist was speaking to him.

'Mr Carr, the Director is running a bit late with another meeting. I am sorry for the delay. It should not be much longer.'

A few minutes later Tom saw the Director's door open and a tall Frenchman came out, accompanied by the Director.

Turning to his secretary, the Director said, 'Call down to Arms and Armour and have them send up someone to escort Mr Beauregard to the gallery where the sixteenth-century French armour of his ancestor is displayed. Have them open up the case and allow him to spend as much time as he desires alone with it.'

The man shook the director's hand and thanked him warmly for this courtesy. '*Au revoir, monsieur le directeur.*'

'Goodbye,' the Director said. Then he shrugged his shoulders and smiled as if to say that despite its vastness the museum was still capable of small kindnesses.

'Now, come in, Tom. I want to hear every detail of this extraordinary story. I've cleared my schedule for the rest of the afternoon. We won't be disturbed.'

Tom followed the Director into his office and sat down at the round table where he recounted the entire story from start to finish, leaving out only the details of Victoria Price's visit and her uncanny vision. He continued, 'I was with the Italian conservators in Rome earlier this week and they have already begun to work on the manuscript text of the *Iliad*. There are fourteen scrolls for the twenty-four books. Most of the scrolls have two books copied on each. Can you believe it?' Tom mused. 'Before this discovery, the earliest complete copy of Homer's *Iliad* was the one dated to the tenth century.' He paused to reflect on the importance of the find.

'The scrolls were rolled up individually. They'll need to humidify them very carefully in order to soften the papyrus and restore some of its elasticity. Hopefully, it'll be enough to allow them to lie flat. As you know, it's a time-consuming process, and they've only just begun.' Tom paused for a drink of water.

'It's remarkable. The text is annotated, presumably in Aristotle's own hand. In fact, the entire book might have been written by him. Handwriting analysis should be able to determine this. I was there when they opened the first part of the first scroll.' Tom recited the first line of the *Iliad* by heart: 'Sing, O heavenly Muse, of the wrath of Achilles . . .'

He went on: 'What is even more incredible is that the chapter begins with an exquisite little illustration. This very fact pushes back our history of illustrated manuscripts more than a thousand years.' Tom was excited and the Director was a captive audience. 'The idea might have been inspired by Egyptian sacred texts for which there was a long history of using images. The papyrus was most probably imported from Egypt. It will be absolutely fascinating to see how Aristotle's version of the *Iliad* differs from the version that's been passed down to us today. Scholars have argued for generations about the development of these epic poems.'

Tom crossed his legs and looked out the window across the green expanse of Central Park. He spotted a red-tailed hawk high in the sky, looking like one of Zeus's great portentous eagles. He continued almost to himself, as if lost in thought. 'You know, I often thought that finding the tomb would solve all our questions about Alexander the Great, that it would complete the story. In truth, though, there's an irretrievable loss of information. Standing before the corpse in its ethereal gilded glass coffin was humbling. It filled me with awe. The dead, however, do not speak. In one very tangible sense, the corpse preserves only part of the man Alexander. It is the embalmed, shrunken frame of a man, and not the remains of a god. Only myth, history and his heroic deeds in life continue to bolster the immortality of this greatest of kings.'

Tom brought his gaze back to the Director and continued soberly. 'The accounts we have of Alexander's life are all posthumous and written by others, many from the Roman period. They were composed long after Alexander's death. Each of these accounts may have elements of truth, but they also reflect the time in which they were written and the authors' own biases and backgrounds. But perhaps I'm being too cynical. Alexander's body might reveal further secrets. They've already begun examining the mummified remains. We may finally learn what was the cause of his death. Was he poisoned? Was it malaria, as some scholars have argued, or something else?'

It was finally the Director's turn to speak. 'Well, it is remarkable. I've just been on the phone with the Italian prime minister and they are thrilled about the discovery. They recognise your important contribution – it is indeed the find of the century. I am certain that they will lend us the newly discovered works from the crypt, including the gold crown and at least some parts of the *Iliad of the Casket*. If the glass sarcophagus can travel that would be a coup as well. The body will remain in Italy, as is only fitting. We are an *art* museum, after all. The loan of these objects will make a spectacular addition to your Alexander exhibition. Congratulations, Tom – it is a magnificent achievement.' The Director paused and then continued speaking to Tom in an authoritative voice. 'Still, in looking over your exhibition proposal, I think that you might want to expand your object list to include more Early Hellenistic pieces, like the Baker Dancer. I realise that it's from a later period but it would not hurt to broaden your scope. Remember, we need to appeal to the general public.'

Tom smiled. 'No, I think you're absolutely right. I'll make a revised selection – and it will certainly include the Baker Dancer.'

Acknowledgements

I am grateful to my literary representative Michael Katakis for believing in this book from the outset. For guidance and sage advice I thank my editors at Random House, Kate Elton and especially Georgina Hawtrey-Woore. I would also like to thank the following individuals for their kindness, support, and wisdom: Joseph and Patricia Czapski, Patrice Czapski, Henry P. Davis, Brian A. Gaisford, Brendan F. Hemingway, Edward B. Hemingway, my parents Gregory and Valerie Hemingway, Patrick and Carol Hemingway, Vanessa Hemingway Blumberg, Liisa Kissel, John-Michael Maas, J. Alexander MacGillivray, Stephen A. MacGillivray, Elizabeth J. Milleker, David G. Mitten, Carlos A. Picón, L. Hugh Sackett, Mason Sandell, Robin Smith, Jonathan Schaefer and Bruce Schwarz. The genesis of this book lies in the incomparable collection of Greek and Roman art at the Metropolitan Museum of Art in New York where I have been fortunate to work as a curator for many years. I am thankful for the privilege of working at that great institution with such fine colleagues and under the inspired leadership of its Director, Thomas P. Campbell, and President,

SEÁN HEMINGWAY

Emily K. Rafferty. My warmest note of thanks goes to my family, Colette, Anouk, and Chloe too, who generously shared me with this book and helped immeasurably along the way.